Death on Crimson Sails

by

Lee René

Death on Crimson Sails

Cover Art by *Abigail Owen*

The Wild Rose Press, Inc.
PO Box 708
Adams Basin, NY 14410-0708
Visit us at www.thewildrosepress.com

Publishing History
First American Rose Edition, 2020
Print ISBN 978-1-5092-3043-3
Digital ISBN 978-1-5092-3044-0

Published in the United States of America

His hand moved in the direction of eight large bales wrapped in muslin lined up on the beach next to the dead men. "The waves carried those bundles to the shore."

I crawled from the dinghy and made my way over to the strange cargo. Some of the bales were long, others short, but I noted a disquieting similarity to all. Each mimicked the shape of a human body. The now familiar iciness made another trip up my spine.

Dr. Farnsworth and Papa followed me to the odd bundles and knelt next to one, the blade of his knife glinting in the sunlight. He cut through the muslin, revealing a wan face that looked as if carved from a block of wax. The doctor sliced the fabric to the chest with great care and revealed a corpse with a line of stitches patterning the exposed flesh. Someone had sliced the body open before sewing the skin back together.

My hands shook, but not from the cold. "What is it?"

Dr. Farnsworth answered without a moment's hesitation. "One of the medical cadavers that washed up on the beach."

I heard mumblings from the onlookers at the mention of the word "cadavers." A few stragglers surrounded the muslin-covered bundles. A curious fisherman pulled back the fabric on the other corpses to look. Those in the crowd recoiled from the faces of death.

Dr. Farnsworth glanced back in Papa's direction. "The Harvard Medical School is always in need of specimens. I have no doubt the schooner was transporting them to Boston."

Dedication

This novel is dedicated to those who have passed;
my mother, Thora Pradia Miller,
my father, William Miller,
who instilled the love of reading and storytelling in me,
and Steven Lancer Whitfield, my dearest friend,
who loved New England, especially in autumn.
Tears and fondest remembrances to
writer Bridget Morrow,
who pushed me to write with every ounce of her being.

Acknowledgments

I have always loved New England and its marvelous history. Thanks to my childhood friend, Cacilda Pimental, for sharing her stories of life in Massachusetts.

Thanks also to beta-reader extraordinaire, Kristin Aragon, who was invaluable in helping me rewrite my manuscript, and to master editor, Nan Swanson, whose careful pruning transformed the work from an unwieldy manuscript to a novel.

Writer Cat Winters encouraged me and made valuable suggestions that vastly improved this work.

I received help over the years from my friends, fellow writers Dr. Caroline de Costa and New Englander Dr. Michelle Moore. Thank you for your help master quilter Sheila Erridge and the Nantucket Whaling Museum.

Hugs and kisses to dear friends and relatives—Lee Pradia Miller, Patrick and Denise Sullivan, Laurie Spacone, Flora Racely, Tim Cogshell, Wade Major, William James, Caroline Jefferson, Selma Betton, Jack and Donna Salem, Peter Taubkin, Lorrie Marlowe-Hooks, and Robert Hooks, all of whom motivated me through the years.

Chapter One

Maidenhead, Massachusetts, September 3, 1880

The forest swirled with color, for nature had already painted the woods in the vibrant hues of fall. By late August, the emerald foliage of the maple and oak trees had changed to scarlet and gold, a promise of early autumn and premature winter.

Oyster-colored clouds lined up in the sky like warriors on a battlefield. The firmament was dark with the gray smoke of silent assault.

The woods usually resonated with the music of chirping birds, but the oncoming storm caused a disquieting stillness. Some believed fairies inhabited the woodlands and enchanted the beasts of the forest with their melodies. None sang that day. The creatures living in the woods must have known a gale was brewing. Except for the distant cry of a wild goose, nothing stirred.

I stood alone and called out, my voice piercing the tranquility around me.

"Mr. Potter, are you at home?"

I approached a solitary cottage nestled in a grove of birch trees. No one walked the grounds surrounding the hut. "Mr. Potter, sir, it's Lucy Hathorne come to visit."

Caleb Potter usually sat on the makeshift veranda, enthroned in a battered rocking chair as he carved scrimshaw. His rocker sat empty that morning.

I didn't see hide nor hair of his pet bear, either. The hermit had found Pedro as a stunted cub abandoned in the forest by his mother. The runt joined Mr. Potter's menagerie of wounded foxes and broken-winged birds. He'd nurtured the ball of fur on honey and goat's milk, and the two soon became inseparable. Perhaps they had gone to the cove to scrounge for treasure.

An errant wind set a tattered remnant of Old Glory fluttering. When I turned to start the trek back to town, the cottage door creaked open, stopping me. The stench of an unwashed body assailed me when I twisted to look. Caleb Potter stood on his makeshift porch, roaring my name.

"I'm here, Miss Lucy."

He beckoned me, his feverish eyes burning cobalt blue in his red face. A stained kepi from the War of the Rebellion sat atop his thatch of dark hair. Despite the early hour, I smelled spirits on him.

"Good morning to you, sir."

Pedro, the stunted creature with a coat as black as pitch, bounded over for a head scratch.

"Hello, Pedro."

After the War of the Rebellion, Mr. Potter had returned to our village, Maidenhead, and lived a solitary existence in the birch woods. He built his hovel out of salvage purloined from the sea and had festooned the outside of his hut with shells, a broken ship's wheel, and other treasures he'd retrieved from the beach. He'd woven a pergola from old fishing nets and suspended it from his thatched roof along with a mermaid figurehead. Door chimes fashioned from old bottles tinkled in the icy wind. People said the place was enchanted.

"There's a blow coming, Miss Lucy. Can you feel it?"

"Yes, sir." I gazed up at the dark sky. "Judging from those clouds, it'll be a bad one."

I ignored his rum-scented breath and took a step toward him. "Mr. Potter, you haven't been to Sunday service in a while, and Papa wondered if you'd come. He's promised to preach a wonderful sermon."

He didn't answer and instead watched as Pedro sniffed my basket. The little bear frightened most everyone who encountered him, but not me. In God's truth, despite Papa's request, I came to visit Pedro, rather than his master. I gave Pedro's head another scratch, and he enveloped my hand with his rough tongue.

"Sorry, Miss Lucy, can't go nowhere without Pedro. Poor fellow gets lonely without me."

A blast of cold forced me to pull my cloak closer. I looked up at the heavens once again and saw that the clouds were pewter gray.

"Have to go now. I must post my father's letters before the storm. Goodbye, Mr. Potter. Goodbye, Pedro."

Caleb Potter smiled for the first time that day. "You're a grand girl, Lucy Hathorne."

I waved and off I went.

****

Instead of the usual balsam fir perfume, the air smelled of moist earth and electricity. Pocasset Square, the center of our village, rang with the shouts of fishermen bartering away the daily catch. The cacophony of voices mingled Yankee English with

Portuguese and Quebecer French. Haggling oystermen, crabmen, and greengrocers drowned out the cries of gulls foraging for scraps.

Someone shouted out my name through the din.

"Lucy Hathorne, what are you doing out when there's a squall coming?"

Zeke Newberry, a half-Nauset Indian youth, sat in the square unraveling a length of frayed cord.

"Papa sent me to post his letters. What's wrong with your rope, Zeke?"

He pushed a lock of raven hair from his eyes and scowled in frustration. "Rats got at it. I told my pa we need a new one, only he's too cheap to buy it."

Zeke's coppery skin took on an even redder glow, and he looked down at his feet. "Have you seen Cassie?"

When he mentioned Cassie, a girl I'd known since birth, I had to bite my lip to stifle a giggle. "Sorry, Zeke, haven't laid eyes on her today."

The poor fellow couldn't hide his disappointment. "Well, if you do, will you give her my regards?"

"Of course I will. So long, Zeke."

I waved my farewell and continued my trek through the square down Maidenhead's cobbled streets. As I passed, the congregants filled my basket with offerings. A slab of bacon, some beach plums, and a few potatoes found their way into my old hamper, along with fresh eggs and half a wheel of cheddar.

Mr. Tateshall, the town chandler, smiled at my approach, his white teeth contrasting with his black skin. He plopped a giant fish on top of the rest of the booty.

"One of my sons caught the cod this morning. It

should cook up good for dinner tonight." He looked up at the sky. "When you get home, tell the Reverend to put up your shutters. There'll be a dinger of a nor'easter."

"Yes, the sky looks fearsome. Thanks for the cod, Mr. Tateshall. I must be off."

A steep plank sidewalk led to the dock. All manner of vessels—trawlers, clippers, windjammers, and yawls—fought for space, and sails of every size and color crowded the horizon. The wind tore at my bonnet, almost ripping it from my head. As I passed shopkeepers scrambling to shutter their windows, the zephyr teased and twisted my cloak.

A heavy gale pushed me backward, yet I fought the wind and shoved forward. I finally reached my destination, a two-story brick building covered by a shingled roof, Brigham's Dry Goods, Telegraph and Post Office. The clicking of a spanking new Morse Telegraph register welcomed me when I crossed the doorstep. Familiar scents—Baker's Chocolate, coffee, wood chips, and dried Sweet Annie—greeted me like old friends.

Two elderly men sat at the chessboard next to the potbelly stove, concentrating on the same game they'd played since Moses parted the Red Sea. The ancient chess pieces sat in place as if glued to the board while the geezers stared at them.

My boots made a terrible racket as they clomped across the plank floor, but the old fellows were deaf to it. Pyrtle Brigham, my best friend in the world, looked up from the telegraph machine. The green celluloid eyeshade that held her flame-red hair obscured her hazel eyes.

"Hello, Lucy. Whatever brings you to town on such a nasty day?"

Zeke's ladylove, Cassie Silva, a handsome Cape Verdean girl with ebony orbs and tawny skin, sat next to her. Despite being short of stature, Cassie had a boy's muscular shoulders and forearms. She could out-row most of the lads in town and arm-wrestle them under the table.

Pyrtle waved me over, a pout marring her pretty face. "Lucy, I'm stuck on the telegraph waiting on Lincoln to return from fishing, the lazy dolt." She'd complained about her brother's lack of interest in telegraphy for so long that her grumbling fell on deaf ears.

"If Cassie hadn't stopped in to buy tobacco for her father, I'd be bored silly." Pyrtle placed on the counter the engravings of wedding veils they'd been poring over. "She's helping me pick the perfect one."

The fashion plates were beautiful, but Pyrtle's nuptials weren't until the summer. "Isn't it a bit early for veils? You haven't even chosen your gown yet."

My friend appeared taken aback by my words. "Lucy, a girl can't start planning the most important day of her life too soon." She pointed to an empty chair. "Why don't you sit a spell?"

I tossed down a coin and swooped up a newspaper. "Sorry, I'm needed at home and don't have time to jabber, especially with a storm coming."

Cassie remained silent, and I couldn't stop myself from teasing. "By the way, Miss Cacilda Silva, Zeke Newberry sends his regards."

She flushed red, her black eyes flashing like chunks of polished jet.

Pyrtle glanced at her sideways and smirked. "Somebody's got an admirer. If truth be told, Cassie's as sweet on Zeke as he is on her, but it would take wild horses to drag the truth out of her."

Cassie dismissed Pyrtle with a shrug. "I can't stop him from liking me, can I?"

Before I could reply, the telegraph machine came alive with a series of clicks. Pyrtle clapped her hands together. "Lucy, Cassie, Mr. Goodbody is on the wire."

At sixteen, all of Massachusetts celebrated Pyrtle's skill at the telegraph machine. Her celebrity had won her a boon, betrothal to Mr. Joshua Goodbody, a fellow tapper who lived in the village of Rachel's Pride. He'd set his cap for her even before they met in the flesh and declared his undying affection over the wire each day.

Pencil in hand, she translated the clicks in cursive. "You'll both be happy to know that Mr. Goodbody won't rest until we're married. He says, 'Dearest Pyrtle, I adore you, you transfix my soul. Please take the word 'obey' out of our wedding vows. You are my helpmate, not my slave, the woman who has captured my heart.'"

Cassie looked down at the missive. "Well, if that don't beat all. You 'transfix his soul,' do you? Mr. Goodbody is a regular Longfellow."

In summer, I'd seen the two of them courting. Pyrtle and her beau had promenaded through the square with her mother, Mrs. Brigham, following as chaperone. Mr. Goodbody seemed a pleasant sort, nineteen years old, freckle-faced, and besotted with Pyrtle. Of course, once she'd decided to wed him, he never stood a chance.

The corners of Pyrtle's mouth curved into a wicked smile. "I'll telegraph him saying I'm still thinking over his proposal."

Cassie didn't bother to conceal her annoyance. "Shame on you, Pyrtle Brigham, tormenting poor Mr. Goodbody. He's all you've been talking about day and night, and you've already said you'll have a summer wedding. You've sworn to everyone he's the only fellow you'll marry."

Pyrtle arched an eyebrow. "But he doesn't have to know, does he? I'll keep him guessing for another week, and then I'll accept. Old Modesty said I'll be Mrs. Joshua Goodbody before I'm seventeen." Like many in Maidenhead, Pyrtle swore by predictions of the town seer, an ancient blind woman named Modesty Chafee. "If Modesty says it's so, it's so."

Although I considered her as close as a sister, Pyrtle could be vexing at times. "You didn't need one of Modesty's visions. Once you decided you'd be the first from our circle to wed, you trapped the poor fellow like a lobster."

Cassie nodded in agreement. "I swear, Pyrtle, you came out of your mother's womb with a wedding bouquet in hand."

Pyrtle ignored both of us. "I'll soon wed a sterling fellow who adores me, and that's all that matters."

Cassie and I exchanged a look, since neither of us shared Pyrtle's obsession with marriage. I placed several letters on the counter along with the coins for postage. "I've lollygagged for too long. Time to go home. Papa's correspondence has to go out on the next sailing packet heading to Boston."

Pyrtle examined the envelopes. "If there's no storm, the packet will be off to Boston by noon."

I turned to leave, but her voice stopped me. "Wait,

Lucy. I almost forgot—I have a telegram for your father."

"A telegram for Papa? Whatever does it say?"

She slid a sealed envelope over the counter. Her eyes narrowed into hazel slits, and she winked at Cassie. "Well, since it's addressed to the Reverend Braddock Hathorne and not to you, it's for me to know and you to find out."

Cassie stifled a titter, and Pyrtle sniggered in the most annoying way.

I wasn't having her nonsense. "Pyrtle Brigham, you can be exasperating. If you'd been born in Salem two hundred years ago, they'd have burned you for a witch."

She cackled like an old crone, and I stormed off as fast as I could. I had half a mind to turn back and give her a tongue-lashing but thought the better of it. I'd learn the telegram's contents soon enough.

Chapter Two
The Telegram

When I returned to the square, the clouds were the color of gunmetal. A nor'easter was on the way, but sailors continued haggling with the Boston fishmongers who packed the dock.

A voice called out, "Lucy."

Kimball Prince stood on the plank sidewalk, a grin waltzing across his lips, his blond curls peeking from beneath a black tuque. He smelled of Florida Water, a spicy fragrance that gentlemen sometimes used to perfume themselves. Since Kimball mingled with the wealthiest men in Maidenhead, he often imitated their dress and manner.

He smirked in my direction, but I refused to be the object of one of his silly jests and walked on at a clipped pace, ignoring the weight of my basket. "Sorry, Kimball, I can't dawdle. Papa received a telegram, and there's a blow coming, so I have to run along."

"Well, I'll run along with you." He grabbed the hamper, his green eyes sparkling with mischief. "Better take it before your arms fall off."

My arms ached from the weight of the basket. Still, the only pleasantry I could manage when he relieved me of my burden was a half-hearted, "Thank you."

Kimball bowed like a cavalier of old. "You're

welcome, Miss Hathorne."

As Kimball chattered away, we trod the wooden sidewalk, clomped past Madame St. Pierre's Elegant Gowns, Crackbone's Apothecary, Winston's Photography Studio, and Stowe's Tonsorial Emporium, all shuttered against the storm. "I came from the parsonage. Your mother gave me tea and gingerbread for helping Reverend Hathorne put up the shutters in the rectory. Can't be too careful with a blow coming, can we, Miss Lucy Stone Hathorne?"

By the time we reached the square, the bustling from merchants had come to an abrupt stop.

I found him more exasperating than usual. "No, I guess we can't, but with the weather being so bad, why aren't you helping your mother at the inn?"

He groaned as if I'd annoyed him, but I knew I hadn't. "Because we'd already put up our shutters, you ninny."

Many girls in town thought him good-looking, but I wasn't one of them. He had a decent enough face if one overlooked his abominable manners and penchant for silly jokes. Although I found him tiresome, I tried to sound pleasant. "I said thank you, didn't I?"

Kimball's brows furrowed with disapproval, yet his eyes gleamed with merriment. "Yes, but you were awfully snippy about it." He glanced down at the heavy basket and spied the envelope. "Aren't you going to tell me what that telegram says?"

I shrugged my shoulders. "I would if Pyrtle had told me instead of crowing on about Mr. Goodbody. Hasn't even said 'yes' to the poor man but insists she'll be a married woman by the summer. Of course, sixteen is young for marriage, but once Pyrtle has made up her mind, you can't change it. Mr. Goodbody is courting her by telegraph machine. Doesn't sound romantic to me."

He snorted at my words. "It's not so bad. At least they love each other." He brushed his shoulder against mine. "You know, there could be another wedding, even before Pyrtle's."

Kimball and I had been fast friends since childhood, but in the last two years, everything had changed. He towered over me, his voice had deepened, and he even shaved. Still, Kimball had transformed in more than height and whiskers. Sometimes he'd stop tormenting me with his jokes and he'd stare in the most ungentlemanly way. His constant harping about being my sweetheart annoyed me even more than his dreadful metamorphosis.

"Mr. Prince, I've made it clear on numerous occasions I plan to travel the road of life as a spinster and work for the betterment of women. My parents named me after the great champion of women's rights, Miss Lucy Stone, for a reason. I'll never marry."

Kimball rolled his eyes. "Oh, so it's Mr. Prince, is it? Let me remind you, Lucy Stone did wed."

"But she didn't take her husband's name."

Kimball snorted at my words. "And that's fine by my way of thinking. You can stay Lucy Hathorne if you wish, but we'll wed one day, and that's the end of it. I'll be studying the law soon, so you'll have four years to get used to the idea of marrying me. Besides, you'll need a Harvard lawyer around to keep you out of jail."

Thank the Lord we reached the rectory before the downpour. And talk of our marriage would soon be at an end. He opened the gate just as a roar of thunder announced the oncoming rain.

"Let me carry your hamper inside. Don't want your arms yanked from the sockets."

I shook my head. "That won't be necessary, Mr. Prince. I'm quite strong."

He placed the basket on the ground. When he took my face in his calloused hands, I didn't pull away. Kimball could be irksome, yet I found his gentleness pleasing. I'd known the direction of my life since childhood, so why did my pulse race whenever he was near? He kept interrupting my thoughts, and lately, he'd even intruded into my dreams.

I felt the heat of a blush warm my face. Despite his incessant joshing, I had a slight fondness for him. Perhaps I'd even erred about his looks. Upon closer inspection, I found him quite handsome, with fine features, a strong chin, and the most glorious smile in Massachusetts. For a moment, looking into his green eyes, I almost forgot how much he vexed me.

"You're a heartbreaker, Lucy Hathorne."

He turned and strolled away.

Heartbreaker? Me?

I looked up at the sky. My skin turned to gooseflesh as a blast of freezing air went up my spine. The heavens were black.

****

The rectory had the distinction of being the newest home in Maidenhead. A rogue spark from a fireplace had burned the old rectory to the ground shortly after my fourth birthday. Instead of a sloping saltbox, Grandfather had built our new home in the style favored in Boston, a fine two-storied frame house with an attic and a circular piazza.

Our door was usually open to anyone, but not on that stormy day. The wind raged against me as I labored to secure the front door against the storm. I thanked the Lord when I finally locked it. Once inside, a gust of warmth welcomed me with a toasty hello. Papa's cape hung from the cloak rack. He'd left the door to his study ajar, and I gave a peek. Rumpled sheets of paper covered his desk. Letters from abolitionists, including the great Frederick Douglass, plastered the scarlet walls. They took their place next to the framed missives from those valiant souls who continued the fight for women's suffrage, including my namesake, Lucy Stone.

I heard grumbling, and pipe smoke wafted into the alcove, a sign my father had locked himself in a battle with Sunday's sermon. His hair was as rumpled as the sheets of paper that covered his desk.

I trod lightly as I made my way to the kitchen, the heart of our home.

The scent of cinnamon, rum, and allspice embraced me, and the earthen walls half-covered in wainscoting comforted me. Mama looked up from the wood-burning stove where she'd been laboring most of the morning. Dark curls framed a face shaped like a perfect heart, her eyes accented by heavy brows and lashes. My own countenance, round, with cheeks as full as a chipmunk, must have come from elsewhere in the family.

"Kimball helped your father put up the shutters against the storm." Her accent, though slight, revealed her Quebecois roots. "Gingerbread and hot tea were scant payment for his labors, but he seemed pleased. He's a wonderful boy."

Since she adored Kimball, I thought it best to agree

with her. "Yes, Mama, Kimball is wonderful. Annoying, but wonderful."

How I managed to lift the basket onto the kitchen table I'll never know. "Mr. Tateshall gave me a fish as big as a whale. We'll have cod cakes for a week."

Mama wiped her hands on her apron and sorted through the gifts, marveling at our bounty. "My, our congregants were especially generous, weren't they?"

A sigh escaped my lips. "I stopped by Caleb Potter's hut just as Papa had asked. Mr. Potter was drunk, as usual."

Mama's mouth tightened, and I read the disapproval on her face. "Caleb Potter is our friend, Lucy. The poor man suffered greatly in the past. He might still have his arms and legs, but the war broke his spirit. We must pity him."

Perhaps she was right. Maybe I should have been more understanding, but I'd simply repeated what everyone knew. Caleb Potter, the poor sot, lived on rum and walked around Maidenhead talking to himself like a madman. I only offered him friendship because Papa insisted on it. Besides, I loved Pedro.

"Mama, you must admit Mr. Potter is the devil when he's liquored up. He's not coming to church this Sunday, either."

I handed her the telegram.

"Pyrtle gave this to me for Papa but wouldn't tell me what it said. Really, she can be so annoying, and snappish, too, so I left the dry goods store. I met Kimball on the way home, and of course he was obnoxious, as usual, although not as horrible as Pyrtle. She made me so angry I—"

Mama fingered the envelope. "I'll hold this for

your father. Now it's time to stop your chatter. We've cooking, mending, letter writing, and your music lesson. I've made gingerbread, enough for the girls in your quilting bee. They'll want it with their tea on Sunday."

I had more on my mind than spicy indulgences. "Mama, aren't you the least bit curious about Papa's telegram? Pyrtle sealed the envelope so no one could read it, but you're his wife, after all, and I'm sure Papa wouldn't mind if you open it."

A male voice interrupted. "Papa wouldn't mind what?"

Papa entered in shirtsleeves, his brown hair still tousled, his fingers stained with ink. I knew tomorrow's sermon would be a fierce one. "What's this I hear about a telegram, Lucy?"

I passed him the envelope. "It came in today, but Pyrtle wouldn't tell me what it says. Papa, read it, please."

He winked at Mama. "Dear Madeleine, have I ever told you what a demanding creature our daughter is?"

His eyebrows knotted as he scrutinized the envelope. My father opened it and unfolded the telegram. "It's from Bangor. Who do we know in Bangor?"

What did I care about Bangor? "What does it say, Papa? Please."

Without warning, his demeanor changed from jovial to serious. "It says we'll soon have a visitor."

Before he could finish his sentence, the front door swung open and a huge gust of wind transformed the toasty kitchen into a frozen box. The gale turned into a vicious fist that pummeled our home. The icy blow ripped the telegram from Papa's hands and it sailed around the room. I managed to pluck it from the air and read it aloud:

"September 2, 1880

Reverend Braddock Hathorne

First Congregational Church of Maidenhead

Maidenhead, Massachusetts

Dear Uncle Braddock,

I shall arrive in Maidenhead soon and visit for a day. I shall not bring my affianced and will be alone.

We have much to talk about.

Your devoted nephew,

Sebastian Hathorne"

Chapter Three
Crimson Sails

My father rushed from the kitchen, racing down the hall to the front door. I followed. "Papa, I swear I locked it shut." Metal scraped against wood as he battled the wind and an old iron latch to secure the heavy oak portal. I heard a loud thump when he finally bolted it shut.

Mama rushed to him, telegram in hand. "Braddock, we must send a reply. Please, ask him to delay his arrival, because we're unprepared for visitors."

He brushed an errant curl from his forehead. "It's too late, my love. I'm surprised Sebastian hasn't arrived by now. Perhaps he can stay at the inn."

Her eyes widened at his words. "He's your dead brother's son. My own dear sister, Veronique, was his mother. He'll be our guest. Lucy and I will ready the spare room. It's the least we can do."

Papa took the telegram from Mama and stuffed it into his pocket. "Very well. I don't understand why he's traveling in the first place. Shouldn't he be in Boston courting his lovely fiancée?"

My father pointed to a carte de visite affixed to the wall, a nuptial photograph sent to us by Sebastian's intended, Miss Ida Stoker, daughter of the acclaimed physician, Dr. Quinton Stoker. A flawless beauty of eighteen, she'd posed in a lace gown with a small bustle and long train, a rose bouquet clasped in her hands. Sebastian, clad in a natty waistcoat and striped trousers, stood next her, as straight and tall as a Grecian pillar. He looked as handsome as any thespian who had trod the boards.

Papa pulled Ida's image from the wall. "Why would he leave such a lovely girl?"

A streak of electricity attacked the lightning rod atop our roof and silenced my father. The bolt lit the house with a blinding flash. A roar of thunder followed, followed by rhythmic thudding, a deluge.

Papa looked up at the ceiling.

"Dear Lord, the squall is here."

Muted rumbling from a cannon overwhelmed the howling rain. Our beacon, Virgin's Light, had stood on her high perch overlooking the bay ever since the first Englishman set foot in Maidenhead. Cassie's father toiled there as the lightkeeper and fired the ancient relic to warn vessels from plowing into the rocks during a gale or dense fog.

Another flash of electricity, paired with a roar of thunder, sent Mama fleeing into Papa's embrace. He looked up at the ceiling. "Sounds like a humdinger. Don't be afraid, my darling. We have a new lightning rod and a shuttered rectory."

We hovered around the warmth of the stove and waited out the storm in the kitchen. For a moment, silence enveloped the room, and we hoped the storm had ended, but no. The most ominous sound of all, the metallic clang of the old cast-iron bell from the clock tower, announced the worst.

I saw the panic in Papa's face when he looked

down at me. "Dear Father in Heaven, a ship's in trouble. Lucy, we must help them."

From the angry glint in my mother's eyes, I knew she'd argue, but the wind intruded before she could say a word. A furious gust blew the front door open once again. Papa and I rushed to rebolt the portal together, but an arctic gust of preternatural strength slammed us into each other.

Through the churning gale, I made out a figure driving two draft horses down the cobbled road. The horses whinnied and snapped, yet the fellow flicked a whip over their heads and urged them forward. Kimball sat behind the reins. He called out to us, but the squall obliterated his words.

I ran from the rectory, battling the force of the storm and air as frigid as an icebox. The wind swirled about me, almost pushing me to the ground, loosening the braid holding my locks in place. "Kimball."

He opened his mackintosh and pulled me to him. "There's a schooner heading toward Chastity Cove. It was listing even before the storm, but in this fury it'll surely capsize."

I clasped him, comforted by the heat of his body and the scent of Florida Water.

"Kimball, we can take one of the dinghies moored at the dock and help them, can't we?"

He shook his head. "No, my Lucy, you and I won't take a dinghy. You stay in the rectory, and I'll go out with Cassie. She's already saved five lives, six if you count the drunken sailor she fished out of the dock last week."

Before I could answer, Papa made his way to us. "Lucy!"

I tore away from Kimball and raced to my father. "Kimball says a schooner is in trouble. He and Cassie are rowing out to the bay."

My father waved to Kimball to follow us and turned back to the rectory. If Papa hadn't yelled at the top of his lungs, his words would have been lost. "Lucy, change into your roughest clothes. We must help those poor fellows."

"Yes, Papa."

My mother barred the door, her face white with dread. "Lucy, you won't leave this house."

I couldn't believe my ears. "But you heard Papa. I'm needed."

Kimball looked down at me, his eyes searching my face. "Do you think you can do it, Lucy?"

"Yes, of course. Papa trained me to row so I could help during a storm."

Kimball walked up the piazza steps. "I understand your reluctance, Mrs. Hathorne. I'd prefer she stay here too, but Lucy is good at the oars. Those fellows on that schooner need all the aid they can get."

The downpour had drenched my gown. Hair fell onto my face, my teeth chattered, and I must have looked like a drowned cat. I darted off to the scullery to change into the patched cotton dress I wore on laundry day.

Mama's voice followed me as it reverberated throughout the rectory. "Kimball, you're as foolish as my husband. Braddock, tell that silly girl to stay."

Papa spoke through gritted teeth. "Madeleine, Lucy can be of help."

I changed from my sodden frock and donned my mackintosh. When I raced down the corridor, I found

Mama still standing at the front door. She ignored Kimball and turned her face to my father, tears rolling down her cheeks. "Braddock, are you insane? You almost drowned in the last squall."

I'd never seen my mother so angry or heard her speak to Papa in such a manner. He addressed her in gentle tones. "Madeleine, my love, there are men in peril. It's our duty to help in the rescue. I'm a strong rower, and I wouldn't bring Lucy with me if I thought she'd be in danger."

Instead of calming her, Papa's words only fueled my mother's rage. "Rescue them? They're strangers. Let the villagers save them."

Kimball's voice quivered when he spoke. "Mrs. Hathorne, we all must do our best for them. It's our duty to be of aid. Suppose someone died because we were too frightened to help them?"

I took Mama's hand in mine, but she yanked it away in anger.

"Papa and I are both skilled at the oars."

My mother folded her arms over her bosom. "Maybe in calm waters, but not in a storm, especially a horror like today. If Kimball wants to risk his life and break his poor mother's heart, so be it. You'll both stay here with me."

I couldn't give in to my mother's fears despite her anger. "Papa taught me to row as soon as I learned to walk. Mama, it's our duty."

My mother stood steadfast at the door. My father lifted her away from the entrance. She glared at him, but didn't move. Kimball and I rushed out, Papa at our heels.

As we made our way down the rectory steps, my

mother called out, "You're all determined to kill yourselves."

My father turned back to her. "The Lord will protect us, Madeleine."

Papa walked into the squall with me following, and Mama yelled out to him, "Braddock, if something happens to my girl, I'll never forgive you, or you either, Kimball Prince."

We didn't look back, even when we heard her sobbing.

****

Kimball managed to drive the skittish horses into the barn next to the town fishery. The three of us battled the wind as we trudged to the dock, the walk so steep we fought to remain vertical. Cassie had already taken her place between the oars in a large rowboat.

Zeke sat in the bow and waved us over. "Come, Kimball, there's no time to dawdle."

Cassie pointed to a smaller dinghy bobbing up and down in the turbulent water. "Kimball and I will go with Zeke, and Reverend, you and Lucy can take Pa's boat. She may not look like much, but she's a sturdy craft."

A slap of thunder sent Kimball scrambling into Zeke's dinghy.

Before we shoved off, three figures in rough clothing made their way to us. The trio pushed against the angry gusts—Mrs. Brigham, a plump, handsome woman, trudging to the dock, her children following. One would never guess she'd given birth to either Pyrtle or Lincoln. Instead of her children's vibrant red hair and hazel eyes, she had the coloring of a gypsy, a gift from her Portuguese mother. Pyrtle and Lincoln limped behind her, struggling with two large bundles covered in oilcloth.

"Children, put everything in the boat." She handed Papa a kerosene lantern and a bottle of whiskey. "Reverend Hathorne, there's dry clothing belonging to my late husband, a lantern, and strong liquor. I know some disapprove of spirits, but the survivors will thank you. Bring whomever you rescue to the stable. Dr. Farnsworth will tend to them there."

A flash of lightning arced through the sky, followed by a thunderous boom. Pyrtle looked up to the heavens before shooting a fierce look in my direction. "Lucy Hathorne, you'd better come back in an hour, or I'll go out looking for you myself."

"With the help of the Lord, I will, Pyrtle."

Papa sat at the bow of the bobbing dinghy. I took my place at the stern after I'd freed the little boat from the dock. We strapped our feet into the footplates and shoved off.

The evil wind whipped the waters into a devilish fury. The gale knocked the fishing vessels about the bay like paper boats. Icy seawater attacked our boat as if Satan himself was beating the sea with sticks of thunder. A flash of lightning filled the air with the scent of ozone.

Despite the furious waves, Papa steered us forward. We made headway, rowing in tandem as my father sang out, "Row girl, row, and put your shoulders into it."

I'd never rowed in turbulent waters before. A part of me wished I'd remained in the safety of the rectory, yet I knew where my Christian duty lay. My shoulders ached, my skin stung, and water soaked through my mackintosh.

Papa rowed on like a lunatic. I heard a slap just as a huge wave engulfed our little craft. The power of the squall had taken us both by surprise, but we'd come too far to turn back.

We managed to keep the dinghy upright and moved on through the satanic flurry. Salt water smacked our faces and stung our eyes. My body throbbed from battling the storm. The pounding of the waves almost obliterated the faint screams of male voices. My father pointed to something in the distance.

"Lucy, we've almost reached the schooner. Row harder, girl."

I followed his arm, my jaw nearly dropping to the bottom boards. The schooner loomed against the dark horizon, a ship at least a hundred feet in length, an elegant creation built by master hands. The three masts pronounced her a Canadian rig, and her sleek lines and red sails declared her a pleasure boat. On another day, the schooner would have cut through calm waters like a knife through butter, but from her tilt, she was in a heap of trouble. She'd either be crushed on the rocks or end up at the bottom of the bay. When we rowed closer, my head thumped like a bass drum.

"Papa, no one's at the helm."

A sailor jumped ship and swam toward Zeke's boat. He cried out for help in Quebecois French, "Aidez-moi! Aidez-moi!" The poor fellow gave one more shriek before the sea sucked him under.

"We've lost him, Lucy."

Yes, we'd lost him, but another seaman fought the waves and swam toward Zeke's dinghy.

The waves crashed around us as the schooner tilted even more.

I looked into a nightmare—a crewman imprisoned by the rigging. Papa and I watched as he fought to free himself. His cries chilled us, but if the schooner tipped over, trying to save him would put us in peril. My father stretched his arm to Zeke's dinghy as it made its way toward the ship.

"Praise the Lord." Unfortunately, my father's joy was short lived. "There's another man in the distance." He pointed to a head bobbing up from the water.

I heard a faint voice crying in the darkness, his words in English. "Help me, help me, please!"

My arms and shoulders throbbed in agony. Papa and I were both at the point of exhaustion, and I wondered how much longer we could battle the churning sea. Undaunted by nature's fury, my father pushed us on. "Row, my girl, row."

The man's head vanished beneath the choppy water. Nature had thrown down her gauntlet, and Papa and I accepted her challenge. We fought on, assaulting the sea, our oars our only weapons. Wave after wave shoved us backward, away from him. It took three brutal attempts before we reached the spot where the fellow had been. I looked into my father's face. "I think the poor man has drowned."

My father looked crestfallen. "Yes, we lost him."

Suddenly, a dark head popped up from the waves.

"Papa, look, he's over there."

We summoned the last of our strength and paddled forward before the swirling vortex sucked him under one more time. The man's outstretched arms entreated us. Papa pulled off his mackintosh and tied a rope around his waist. "I'll jump in and find him."

The wind almost obscured my voice as I grabbed

his arm. "No, Papa, you can't. If you dive into the water, it's certain death for you, and it will be for me too, because I swear, I'll jump in after you!"

The man's head bounced up once again, and my father pushed a paddle in his direction. The fellow grabbed it and held on for dear life.

My father and I dragged the man toward us, until, without warning, the sea devoured him once more. The fellow's determination matched ours, and his head bobbed up once again. My father pulled the rope from his body, tied one of the ends into a noose, and tossed it into the sea like a lasso. The man seized it and held fast, managing to tread water as we towed him toward the boat. A white hand grabbed onto the side, the fingers long, tapered, and un-calloused, those of a gentleman rather than a fisherman.

It took both of us at the rope to drag him toward the boat. Without gloves, my palms burned as if someone had held a torch to them, yet I labored on.

A final tug and an arm, followed by a leg, made it over the side.

I wanted to cheer, but the ordeal had robbed me of strength.

My father grabbed the fellow by the shoulders and tugged. "Help me, Lucy." He yelled out, "Heave ho!"

Somehow, we found the strength to pull the man into the dinghy. It seemed as if iron ingots weighed him down. Pain shot through my arms and back, and my palms ached from rope burns, but the Lord rewarded our efforts.

The fellow tumbled into the boat and collapsed onto the blankets, his skin blue from the cold, his teeth chattering. He stretched out at the bottom of the boat, his body fully as tall as father's, well over six feet.

Miracle of miracles, the sun broke through, and I made out his features. Although we hadn't seen each other since his twelfth birthday, I knew him immediately.

Papa and I had rescued Cousin Sebastian.

Chapter Four
Death in the Sand

My cousin's dark lashes fluttered against his pale cheeks. His gray eyes opened, and he stared up at my father. "Uncle Braddock, is it you?"

Papa looked down at him, concern etched on his face. "Yes, but don't speak, my boy. Save your strength."

Despite his ordeal, Sebastian looked even more angelic than the little boy I remembered from my childhood. His face resembled a work from a master sculptor chiseled from the finest marble.

"Sebastian, it's me, Cousin Lucy."

His gaze met mine and never left my face. When he gasped and spit out water, I feared his heart might give out. "Oh, Lucy—it seems like a million years since we last saw each other—I'd have known you anywhere—you're the image of my mother."

I had only vague memories of Aunt Veronique, Mama's beautiful sister. She'd died in a horrible fire when I was four. I'd heard how much we resembled one another from the time I could fathom it. Sebastian's eyes remained on me even as Papa rifled through the provisions.

"Sebastian, my boy, don't speak. You must save your breath."

My father scrounged through the pile of blankets, searching for Mr. Brigham's moth-eaten pea coat. He pulled it from the bottom of the craft. "We'll take off that drenched topper. This might be threadbare, but it's clean and dry."

I continued rowing while Papa helped Sebastian out of his sodden jacket.

He draped a blanket over my cousin's shoulders and handed him the whiskey.

"Drink this, Sebastian."

"Thank you, Uncle Braddock. I don't normally indulge in spirits, but I'm sure the Lord will forgive me this one time."

Sebastian took a healthy swig and his skin flushed with color. He attempted a smile, but even that small effort appeared too much for him. His eyes closed and his head fell back onto a makeshift pillow.

Papa grabbed the other oars. "Row with all your might, Lucy. We must get him to the rectory."

A bolt of lightning illuminated the sky, followed by thunder and, thank the Lord, a miracle. The water stilled, the wind died, and the squall ended as quickly as it had begun. The battling clouds parted and abandoned the sky even as the wind vanished, leaving the air as muggy as a summer day. The sun's rays warmed us, and beams of light fell from the sky. The beach beckoned from the distance.

Despite the blankets, dry clothes, and whiskey, Sebastian shivered. Exhaustion claimed Papa and me, but we rowed like two people possessed.

By the time we reached the shore, it appeared Dr. Farnsworth had rounded up every fellow in Maidenhead and half the women. Papa yelled out, "We found a survivor."

A rousing cheer arose from the shore. Dr. Farnsworth waded into the water and sloshed over to the dinghy. He called out to a gang of hip-booted fellows. "Take him to the stable with the others."

Papa halted the men in their tracks. "No, not to the stables. He's my nephew. He'll go to the rectory."

When Dr. Farnsworth prodded Sebastian's arms and shoulders, my cousin let out a low moan. "He's bruised, but I don't think any bones are broken. The lad needs a doctor, but I can't attend to him separately. He'd be looked after if he were with the other survivors."

My father grabbed at Dr. Farnsworth's sleeve. "Atticus, he's my dead brother's son."

Dr. Farnsworth murmured into Papa's ear, "Others are dead or dying, Braddock. Sorry, I can't leave them for one boy." He signaled to the waiting men. "You heard Reverend Hathorne. Take the lad to the rectory."

The good doctor pointed to a young girl dawdling on the shore. "You, find Bathsheba, the midwife, and tell her to go to the rectory." When the lass dashed off, the good doctor turned to my father. "Bathsheba can attend to him until I'm able to look in on the boy."

The fellows pulled Sebastian from the skiff and placed him into Kimball's wagon. Papa started to follow them as they moved my cousin, but he turned back to Dr. Farnsworth. "How many from the crew were you able to save?"

"Cassie Silva and the boys, Zeke and Kimball, rescued three, along with the corpse of a fourth who'd died in the rigging." He pointed to the beach. "His body is over there with the others."

I felt the hair at the nape of my neck stand on end, and I'm sure the color deserted my face. A chill snaked up my backbone, and my skin turned to gooseflesh. The men had laid out five blanket-covered bodies on the sand. I strained to hear Dr. Farnsworth's voice above those of the other men on the beach.

"One young fellow gave his last gasp after swimming to shore, three more washed up on the waterside. We've bedded the five men in the stable, but the rocks crushed three. I couldn't save them. One has a broken back and another is delirious. I fear none will survive."

Dr. Farnsworth paused as if searching for the right words. His mouth pursed into a straight line, and his eyes misted. Finally, he sighed in resignation.

"Tragic, isn't it? The lads died in a blink. The men will bring the bodies to my practice for embalming, but there's another matter."

His hand moved in the direction of eight large bales wrapped in muslin lined up on the beach next to the dead men. "The waves carried those bundles to the shore."

I crawled from the dinghy and made my way over to the strange cargo. Some of the bales were long, others short, but I noted a disquieting similarity to all. Each mimicked the shape of a human body. The now familiar iciness made another trip up my spine.

Dr. Farnsworth and Papa followed me to the odd bundles and knelt next to one, the blade of his knife glinting in the sunlight. He cut through the muslin, revealing a wan face that looked as if carved from a block of wax. The doctor sliced the fabric to the chest with great care and revealed a corpse with a line of stitches patterning the exposed flesh. Someone had sliced the body open before sewing the skin back together.

My hands shook, but not from the cold. "What is it?"

Dr. Farnsworth answered without a moment's hesitation. "One of the medical cadavers that washed up on the beach."

I heard mumblings from the onlookers at the mention of the word "cadavers." A few stragglers surrounded the muslin-covered bundles. A curious fisherman pulled back the fabric on the other corpses to look. Those in the crowd recoiled from the faces of death.

Dr. Farnsworth glanced back in Papa's direction. "The Harvard Medical School is always in need of specimens. I have no doubt the schooner was transporting them to Boston." He took my father's arm. "Sebastian would know about them, wouldn't he?"

Papa nodded in agreement. "Yes, but the boy's been through a horrible ordeal. For now, let him rest. I'll ask Pyrtle to telegraph Harvard. They must be informed about the squall, the schooner, and those cadavers."

The doctor called out to the men, "Carry the specimens to the icehouse until I figure out what's to be done with them." He turned to my father and spoke in a whisper, "Pardon me, Braddock, but I must care for the young men in the stable."

Papa and I trudged away from the beach, walked down Pocasset Square, and surveyed Maidenhead by the light of day. A dead horse and two dogs lay in the middle of the square. Bodies of gulls embedded in sea refuse covered the streets, and the stench of effluvia permeated the town.

The sun's warmth couldn't erase the memories of the day. I thought about the drowned bodies and cadavers spread on the beach like bales of cotton. No matter how I tried, I couldn't stop emotions from getting the better of me. I halted our march and burst into tears. How I wished Kimball had come with us. Where was he when I needed him?

"Everything is horrible, Papa."

My father wrapped his arms around me. "My poor Lucy, this has been a nightmare of a day. You saw things no child should. I know your mother's ire is up, but perhaps she understood the wisdom of our actions after poor Sebastian arrived at the rectory."

My father dug into his pockets. Miracle of miracles, he found a dry kerchief and mopped the tears from my face.

"We have to be careful, my dear. Please do as I ask. Don't tell your mother about the horror of the storm, the medical specimens, and seeing that sailor trapped in the rigging. She'd worked herself up to a dreadful state when we left, and I don't want to make it worse. Swear to me you won't dwell on any of it. She'll learn soon enough."

"I swear, Papa."

He seemed relieved and forged ahead at a rapid pace with me at his heels. "Let's speak of it no more, my darling."

Chapter Five
Cousin Sebastian

When we returned to the warmth of the rectory, Mama awaited us, her blue eyes brilliant in a face scarlet with rage. She sprang at Papa like an angry hound. "Braddock, were you mad? You both could have drowned. What would I have done?"

My mother stormed off to the kitchen. Papa seemed reluctant to deal with her, but I nipped at her heels. "Mama, please, you mustn't be cross with Papa. We did what any good Christian would."

She turned, reared back, and slapped me hard across the face. "You foolish, foolish girl! I knew Sebastian's telegram signaled no good."

Sheer anger propelled her hand. My cheek burned, my ears rang, and the force of the blow filled my eyes with tears. She raised her hand once more, but Papa caught her arm and held fast. "No, Madeleine, you won't hit Lucy again."

The dam suddenly broke and a deluge of bitter tears rolled down her cheeks. Papa enfolded her in his arms. "There, there, my darling. Lucy and I are home safe and sound."

From the power of her blow, I knew my cheek would be red for the rest of the day. Her palm must have stung as much as my face. I'd been unprepared for her fury. In all my sixteen years, I couldn't remember a cross word or an angry slap until that day.

Voices drifted from the spare bedchamber on the second floor. Before I could mount the stairs, I heard the whistling of the kettle. It wasn't like Mama, no matter how upset she might be, to leave the stove unattended.

I raced to the kitchen and discovered a visitor.

Kimball's mother, Mrs. Prince, a handsome widow with the same lively green eyes and golden curls as her son, fussed over a pot of tea. A pot of beans bubbled on the stove along with a cauldron of chicken and dumplings. She'd sliced a loaf of fresh-baked bread and placed it on the kitchen table next to a small crock of butter and a jar of huckleberry preserves.

Mrs. Prince wiped her hand on her apron and hurried over to me, her arms open in embrace. "Lucy, my love. Velda and I dropped in the moment I heard about your cousin." She held me for a moment. When she pulled back, she noted my injured cheek. "What's wrong with your face, my darling?"

She stroked my injured cheek, and I winced at her touch. Thankfully, she hadn't witnessed my humiliation at my mother's hand. I hated telling a falsehood, but did so anyway. "I had a fall."

She took my chin in her hand, turning my face from side to side as she perused it. "Hmmm, if we were at the inn, I'd put ice chips on your cheek. You're a brave creature, Lucy, but I'm afraid you've taken years off your mother's life. The poor lady was quite distraught when I arrived. Whatever possessed you to go out in that storm?"

"Papa and I had to help those poor men. Sebastian would have died if we hadn't. How is he?"

She looked up at the ceiling. "He's a bit bruised, but fit as fiddle. If I didn't know of your valiant rescue, I'd never suspect anything that horrible had happened to your cousin. Bathsheba is clucking over the boy like an old hen, and my empty-headed twit of a daughter has already thrown herself at his feet. Go upstairs and say hello."

I shook my head. "But Mrs. Prince, I don't wish to bother Sebastian. Surely he needs his rest."

She pulled off my mackintosh and placed it in the scullery next to Sebastian's drenched clothing. "Pooh, go upstairs and cheer up your cousin. Give him some of these vittles when he's up to it." Mrs. Prince looked around as if guarding her words and spoke in a whisper. "I knew Sebastian as a tiny lad, and he's as charming as ever. He's already mesmerized my Velda, foolish child."

"Velda?" At sixteen, my friend had already earned a reputation as the biggest flirt in Maidenhead. "I'm afraid I'd better remind her that my cousin is engaged to be married."

Her mother chuckled as if resigned to her daughter's romantic notions. "Yes, and tell the silly creature she's needed at the inn."

When I bounded up the narrow staircase, a girlish titter alerted me that my old friend was playing the coquette, as usual.

"I'm sure Lucy won't mind if you have her molasses cake, Sebastian. How brave you are. I pale at the thought of your ordeal."

An older voice harrumphed. "Velda, we need to leave the boy alone so he can get some rest."

I entered the room unbidden and found Bathsheba

Ferris, the town midwife, looking down at the narrow bed, her brows furrowed in concern.

Bathsheba always garbed herself in a black gown of perpetual widowhood. The darkness of the gown set off her fair skin, and she'd braided her silver hair into a regal coronet.

My dear friend Velda stood across from Bathsheba, golden tendrils curling about her face. I smelled her fragrance before I saw her—the lilac scent perfumed the room. She gazed at Sebastian through green eyes sparkling like twin emeralds. Her attention remained fixed on my beautiful cousin, and I noted she licked her lips as if she planned to devour him whole.

Sebastian sat up in bed, a pillow buttressing his back, a bright quilt covering his legs, an empty bowl of Mrs. Prince's pepper pot and a plate of Mama's molasses cake on a battered bedside table. He wore one of Papa's nightshirts, his handsome face serene in the face of the evils of the day. Sebastian's eyes fell on me. He sat up and the sound of his laughter filled the room. He flung back the coverlet.

"My savior! My Lucy, my darling Lucy. Ladies, this lovely creature is the reason I'm alive!"

Bathsheba pushed him back onto the pillow. "You must rest, my boy."

I moved toward the bed. "Thank you for the kind words, Sebastian, but Papa found you, not me."

He shook his head. "Oh, no, my Lucy, you were the angel who lifted me from the sea. You saved me from certain death." The thought of his brush with a horrible demise appeared to overtake him and, in an instant, his laughter turned to sobs. "Dear Lord, I almost died."

A hush filled the room. I whispered to Velda, "Your mother needs you. It's time to return to the inn. Besides, Sebastian has a fiancée and doesn't need you fluttering around him like a besotted bat."

Velda gazed into Sebastian's face, her green eyes gleaming, a pout on her beautiful lips. "Very well, but I'll be back." She shrugged her dainty shoulders and stomped from the room.

Bathsheba's mouth spread into a wide grin. "Thank the Lord, that lovesick puppy is gone. She's mesmerized half of Massachusetts and besotted every man in town. Doesn't she have enough suitors without trying to ensnare your cousin?" The old midwife whispered into Sebastian's ear, "Take no notice of that silly girl."

She poured some amber-colored liquid into a mug and handed it to him. "I mixed some laudanum with ginger and honey to disguise the taste." Bathsheba became quite grave when she handed the cup to my cousin. "Drink it, boy. You need your sleep. Do as I ask."

Sebastian gulped a generous dose of the concoction before settling his head on the pillow. His gaze remained on me. "We have much to talk about, Cousin Lucy, but I'm too fatigued to chat."

With that, he shut his eyes.

Bathsheba dimmed the lamp, and we tiptoed from the chamber.

My parents stood in the corridor, wrapped in each other's arms. I'd grown up around their frequent shows of affection, but Bathsheba hadn't. The older woman cleared her throat in warning, and they pulled apart. Mama rushed off to the kitchen.

Bathsheba sauntered toward Papa, her tread so light the only sound was the swish of her petticoat.

"I examined Sebastian, Reverend Hathorne. His bruises will fade soon enough. However, I'm afraid the memory of what he's endured won't. The boy asked if someone would salvage his things from the schooner and bring them to him. He's most concerned about his Saratoga trunk with his papers and his books. He had his initials engraved on the lock. Can you see to it, Reverend?"

Papa nodded. "Yes, of course, the boy has his studies. He's already astounded those Harvard fellows with his brilliance. Despite his youth, he's well on his way to becoming a physician. I am grateful to our Father in Heaven for saving him. The men reached the vessel before it crashed against the rocks. I'll ask them to find his luggage if they can."

When Bathsheba spoke again, her voice was low, her words halting. "I hesitate to bring this up now, Reverend Hathorne. My great-grandmother began having visions over a fortnight ago. She saw a ship with crimson sails, one that brought death to Maidenhead."

Although Papa was a man of the cloth, he had great faith in Modesty's skills as a seer. He stepped away from Bathsheba, his face devoid of all color. I shivered involuntarily.

"You heard her say it?"

She nodded. "Yes, Reverend, as did others. Her prophesy has come to fruition. We must make the best of it."

Papa stood in silence as Bathsheba scurried down the corridor and left the rectory.

****

Our evening meal turned out to be a subdued affair. We joined hands and Papa led us in prayer. "Thank you, Our Father in Heaven, for sparing Sebastian, my dead brother's child." His face became somber when he turned his head and glanced at Mama. "Thank you also for giving us a brave and obedient daughter."

Papa and I exchanged a smile that warmed me to my core. I ignored my sore cheek and aching shoulders and looked forward to our Saturday baths the next day, to soak away the pain. Our dining table groaned with food from well-wishers, but the strain of the day dampened the joy of our evening repast.

Hours later, I ascended the staircase and entered my bedroom, a plain chamber except for the red and gold fleurs de lis stenciled on the walls. My old bisque doll stared at me through glass eyes. A cupboard housed my books, shells, and scrimshaw, and the few frocks I owned hung in a small wardrobe. A weathered nautical window salvaged from a beached schooner gave a clear view of the birch grove at the rear of the house.

Despite being bone tired and aching from the rowing in the middle of the storm, I found sleep eluded me. I hadn't seen Sebastian in the flesh since the day I turned twelve. Why had he come back to Maidenhead? What had he wanted to say to me? I found it most confusing. Exhausted, I rolled over and finally drifted into the arms of Morpheus.

Chapter Six
Aftermath

The loud whack of an axe against wood awakened me the next morning. I jumped from my bed and peered out my bedroom window. The nautical glass gave me a view of the arbor at the rear of the rectory. Sebastian labored away, clad in one of Papa's old shirts and a pair of his ragged trousers. My cousin threw himself into the task, putting his back into the rhythmical wallops as he chopped blocks of cedar and pine for kindling, as Bullet, our old chestnut, watched him from the barn door.

"Sebastian, what are you doing?" Mama rushed from the kitchen, her voice loud enough to carry into the house. "Are you mad? You need your rest."

An errant lock of dark hair fell into my cousin's pale face, and his inky eyebrows knotted together as he split another block of wood in two.

"Aunt Madeleine, what kind of guest takes advantage of his host's hospitality without pitching in? I fed Bullet, took the old boy for an early morning trot, and I assure you, I know how to chop wood too. You were low on kindling, and with everyone taking their baths tonight, I had to remedy it."

I grabbed my robe, dashed down the stairs, and rushed through the fragrant warmth of the kitchen toward the arbor. Pine scented the chilly air, and a blast of cold slapped my face.

"Sebastian, Mama is right, you should be resting. I'll finish the kindling."

Sebastian rolled his eyes in my direction and went back to his work. "Lucy, I'm twice as big as you and strong as an ox. Let me finish. After breakfast, perhaps we can visit my mother's grave—that is, if Aunt Madeleine gives us permission."

Mama barked out her words as she walked back to the kitchen. "Very well, you pig-headed boy, chop all the wood you wish. Lucy can take you to the cemetery, but I insist you take to your bed upon your return."

She'd left a pitcher of hot water for my morning ablutions. After I washed, I slipped into a simple calico dress and raced downstairs. By the time I reached the kitchen, Papa had already poured himself a mug of steaming coffee. "Where's Sebastian?"

The ax clomped once again. I pointed to the arbor. "He's chopping wood and refused to heed Mama when she told him to stop."

Papa stepped into the summer kitchen and watched Sebastian. "He seems all right. Hard work won't hurt him."

Mama wiped her hands on her apron and brushed a curl from her forehead. "He wants to visit the cemetery."

Silence overwhelmed the room, and it was as if time stopped. No one moved, and my father pondered her words for a long moment. "Very well. I trust our Lucy will bring him back to us in one piece."

He turned to me. "Watch out for him, and please, don't tarry in the woods, my love."

I couldn't fathom Papa's words but nodded in

agreement. "Yes, I'll make sure we don't linger in the forest."

By midmorning, Sebastian had chopped enough kindling to last a week; by late morning, the sun showed her glorious face. The storm had ravaged our bower, but a few flowers had escaped its wrath. I spied purple blooms, beaten down yet resilient, and picked enough white and gold-capped flowers also to make a bouquet.

"Look, Sebastian, the last of the Shasta daisies. I'll pick them while you cut some butterfly bush."

Bouquets in hand, Sebastian and I trekked through the woods, clomping across a stone bridge and past the old gristmill as we made our way to the village cemetery. The rain had brought the woods to life, and the forest teemed with the music of the woodland critters. It smelled like a perfumed garden, the air spicy with pine and damp earth, the grounds slippery with sodden leaves. We marched on until we reached the birch grove where Caleb Potter's cottage sat undisturbed.

The tiny dwelling had a serenity about it, and except for pools of water on the forest floor, neither the grove nor his hovel had suffered from the violent storm.

"Mr. Potter? Pedro?"

Sebastian grabbed my hand. "Don't tell me you're calling for Caleb Potter, that drunk? I remember him from childhood, walking through Maidenhead, talking to himself about all manner of things."

I laughed at my cousin's words. "Oh, he's harmless enough. His bear, Pedro, might frighten some, but not me."

"A bear? He keeps a bear?"

"Yes, but he's a gentle one and quite small. Mr. Potter used to have a little red vixen, but she ran off into the forest one day, probably searching for a mate."

No voice boomed in a rum-fueled greeting, no friendly growl welcomed us. "He and Pedro must be scavenging the beach for bounty. Sometimes he searches for old whale bones and such."

We moved on through the rain-soaked forest, past the freshwater pools on the verdant floor. I clasped Sebastian's hand. "I've heard giant eels sometimes crawl to the woods from the sea. Some swear they make their way to the forest to slumber in the fresh water, but I've never seen one."

"Nor will you ever, dear Lucy. It's superstition, my darling."

"Well, superstition or not, it's a great yarn to tell children."

We heard the rustle of leaves brushed by the wind. If one listened carefully, the sounds of the forest merged into a symphony of tweeting birds and rustling pines.

Sebastian and I continued our journey through the sodden woods. By the time we reached the cemetery's wrought-iron gate, the sun's early morning warmth had disappeared. A fierce, wintry chill enveloped me and rendered my cloak worthless. The oak trees had retained their foliage, and the only sound we heard was the rustling of the wind among their leaves. We passed weathered grave markers etched with curious markings. Two centuries before, villagers had carved the granite with symbols from a past no one remembered.

The storm had soaked the grounds, and the place lay deserted except for us. Sebastian looked about the graveyard. "Why is the cemetery empty?"

"Maidenhead hasn't had a passing since a babe toddled away from his farm during a snowstorm two years ago. The searchers found him frozen to death in the forest. The tyke lay in the icehouse until the spring thaw allowed us to bury him. I suppose those poor seamen from the schooner will be buried in the Catholic cemetery soon enough."

Sebastian's face darkened, but he didn't say a word.

We walked through the hush, past stone gravestones etched with strange symbols obscured by moss. After a short climb, we reached the Hathorne family plot, nestled among the weathered granite gravestones that dated from Pilgrim times, gravestones etched with symbols from a past no living person remembered. The Hathornes had ministered to Maidenhead for almost two centuries.

I pulled Sebastian over to a headstone, its granite polished to a dark sheen by twelve winters.

"Your mother rests here. See, 'Veronique Charbonneau Hathorne, Constant Wife, Devoted Mother, 1842-1868.'"

I replaced the old flowers with a sodden bouquet.

Sebastian fell to his knees and ran his hands over the stone. "It's as if someone scoured it."

I knelt next to him, thankful the granite protected my gown from the wet earth. "I tend our family's graves, Sebastian. It's my duty and honor."

I took his hand in mine, the hand of scholar, the palms uncalloused, his tapered fingers long and pale. "Sebastian, I have memories of your mother singing to me."

My cousin gazed into my face, his eyes brimming with tears, his mouth quivering. He broke into sobs and began rocking back and forth. Bitter tears rolled down his face. "She was so beautiful, Lucy. I only had her. She loved me when others didn't."

I'm sure my jaw dropped. "What are you saying, Sebastian? Everyone adored you."

Tears ran down his face as he placed the bouquet on his mother's grave. He pulled out his kerchief and mopped his eyes. "No, Grandfather didn't love me, and neither did Father. They hated me, and I never knew the reason. I only had my mother, but she died and I had nothing." He gazed into my face. "I detested Father."

The ferocity of his words shocked me. "You shouldn't say such things, Sebastian."

"But it's true, Lucy. Father paraded me around to his colleagues, proclaimed me a prodigy. He hauled me off to Europe because they thought me a genius, yet he never loved me, only Mama did. When I think of the way she perished, I wished I'd died with her."

"You were only six when the fire occurred in the rectory. You couldn't have saved her, and neither could I."

Sebastian gazed intently into my eyes, his brow furrowed. Without warning, his face lit up as if a portal to the sun had opened.

"You are so much like her, Lucy. Do you remember when I told you we'd be married one day?"

I couldn't stop myself from tittering at the memory of his childish proposal. "Of course I do. How could one forget a six-year-old boy with black curls who proclaimed his love for his four-year-old cousin? Two tykes as close as brother and sister. I remember when that little lad played his pennywhistle for her."

He clasped my hand so tightly I nearly winced from the pain. "I kept my pennywhistle, and I've often thought about that lovely four-year-old I wished to wed." Sebastian stared into my face for the longest time. "I still want to marry her. She's the reason I'm here."

A chill crawled up my backbone, for he seemed quite serious. At that moment, I remembered his fondness for jesting and laughed off his words. "Oh, Sebastian, stop joking, you silly boy. You have a fiancée, and besides, we're double first cousins. We could never wed."

He released me without speaking, his eyes on my face. Suddenly, I had the most unpleasant feeling that he hadn't said his words in jest. We rose from the grave and headed toward the cemetery gate.

I'd learned what he wanted to tell me and found it frightening. The two of us were as close in blood as brother and sister, yet he wanted marriage. When I looked into his face, the intensity of his expression frightened me. We raced home, serenaded by the lament of a whippoorwill.

I wondered if I should mention Sebastian's words to my parents, but I thought the better of it. It might cause them distress, and besides, the more I thought of what he'd said, it seemed surely spoken in jest.

The scent of tobacco met us at the rectory door. Dr. Farnsworth paced the corridor in front of my father's study, while he and my father engaged in conversation. They parted when we approached.

The doctor fixed his eyes on Sebastian, examining him like a prize bull for sale. "Considering his ordeal, the boy radiates health." He gave Sebastian a fatherly pat on the back. "You must have the constitution of old Bullet, my son. I need to examine you, but before I do, what can you tell me about those cadavers?"

Sebastian's joyous expression suddenly disappeared. His face paled, and his gray eyes sparked like flares.

"You attended Harvard, didn't you? The medical school is always in need, but Boston's city fathers stand in the way of progress. They're a bunch of superstitious fools who know nothing. Those cadavers are essential. I brought them from Canada." He grabbed Dr. Farnsworth by the arm, his eyes burning. "Where are they? I must know! I was charged with bringing them to the medical school."

Papa placed a restraining hand on Sebastian's shoulder, but my cousin shook it off. "Sebastian, remember where you are. The doctor is our guest."

My cousin appeared deaf to Papa's words. "I asked you, where are they? Those specimens are very important to our work."

Dr. Farnsworth paused before speaking, his face unreadable. "We placed them in the icehouse. They'll be safe there."

"And the bodies of the crew?"

"My dear wife and I have embalmed all those who've died. They're in the icehouse too. We'll send them back to their families."

Sebastian's eyes widened. The doctor's words appeared to inflame him, and his body quaked with rage.

"No, that won't do, you'll do no such thing! Those sailors were ruffians of the worse kind, drunken trash from the docks, all without kin, worthless to everyone but the medical school. They would have killed me with their rum-fueled shenanigans. Harvard needs their bodies, sir. Specimens are hard to come by. Don't you understand? We can't waste them to molder in the grave." He grabbed Dr. Farnsworth by the lapels. "We can't, we can't, we just can't!"

Mama heard the kerfuffle and raced from the drawing room. "What's happened?"

Sebastian's violent explosion appeared to take the wind out of him. His shoulders drooped, his head bowed. For the second time that day, he broke into tears. "I'm sorry, so very sorry."

Dr. Farnsworth took him by the arm and led him up the stairs. "There, there, my boy. Come with me." He looked down at Mama. "Mrs. Hathorne, could I trouble you to bring up a spot of chamomile tea for the lad?"

My mother stood as still as a post until they had ascended the stairs. Then she shook her head and returned to the kitchen.

I looked at my father.

His face betrayed nothing, but for some reason, his eyes misted.

"What could be gone wrong? Sebastian's spirits were fine when we visited the graveyard," I said.

Papa glanced up at the stairs once before turning back to me, an absentminded smile on his lips. "I'm sure they were." He turned his gaze to me, so deep and penetrating I wondered if he saw into my soul. "In the woods this morning, did Sebastian say anything untoward?"

I'd decided against mentioning his silly proposal. "No, not really, but he did cry at Aunt Veronique's grave, but that's to be expected, isn't it?"

My father took a puff from his pipe, his face betraying nothing. "Sebastian has the mercurial disposition of some of the Hathorne men. My own uncle possessed the same explosive temper, as did your late Uncle Frederick. The doctor will look after Sebastian. Now, you must excuse me, my dear. I've a sermon to write."

He turned away and soon closeted himself in his study. When I reached the kitchen, I heard my mother's sobs. "Mama, what's wrong?"

When I entered, she turned away and wiped her face on her apron. "Nothing, my love. It just pains me to see my sister's child in such a state. I remember what a merry little tyke he once was. Come, let's serve supper, and get the water ready for the bathing."

An hour later, Dr. Farnsworth descended the stairs, his dark thoughts etched on his face. My parents surrounded him, their whispers out of earshot.

The rectory took on a disturbing calm. The kitchen became my sanctuary, and I busied myself with dinner. It was a solitary task and reminded me how much I wished the Lord had blessed my parents with other children. As a little girl, I'd begged each year for a sibling, but it was not to be. It pained me not to have a sister or brother with whom to share my concerns.

Chicken and potatoes boiled on the stove. I retrieved pickled fiddleheads and beets from the pantry, and buttered the bread Mrs. Prince had left. Perhaps Sebastian wouldn't be joining us, but I still set the table for four.

After I'd finished preparing supper, I ascended the stairs and knocked on his door. "Sebastian, supper is ready."

He didn't answer. "Sebastian, please, we want you to join us."

When he responded with a resounding silence, I knew we'd lost what had begun as a promising day.

I peeked into Papa's study through a crack in the doorjamb. There he sat, motionless, staring at the grandfather clock, transfixed.

"Papa, come to supper."

My words roused him from his stupor. "Yes, my dear."

He rose from his great desk and followed me into the dining room. We sat for grace, and I prepared myself to endure a silent dinner.

Papa began the blessing. "Heavenly Father, we thank you for this bounty—"

Before my father could finish, I heard a foot tread followed by my cousin's gentle voice. "Excuse me, Lucy, Uncle Braddock, and Aunt Madeleine."

Sebastian entered the dining room, a hangdog expression on his angelic face. "Please, I must apologize for my behavior this afternoon. I'm so sorry for acting like some varlet from the street, but sometimes a fury overcomes me. I don't know where it comes from, but I'll try to control it. I swear it won't happen again."

Papa jumped up from his chair and placed his arms around Sebastian's shoulders. He walked him over to the table. "My boy, you are welcome. We'll forget this afternoon. Please, sit and eat."

After grace, I put a question to my father. "Tell us, Papa, what will you preach about tomorrow?"

My father struggled to answer. "Well, uh, it is—"

He stopped mid sentence and took a long look at Sebastian. "Acceptance. My sermon will be about acceptance."

No one said a word as we reflected on my father's utterance. The silence disappeared when Sebastian tossed his head back and laughed. Papa's words had worked a miracle. The day's tension disappeared, and we enjoyed a hearty supper.

Later that evening, every pot in the kitchen boiled over in preparation for our weekly baths. We entered the scullery one after another and took our place in the cast-iron tub filled with hot water. Papa usually sang to us from the kitchen as we scrubbed away, but not that Saturday. The bittersweet tranquility returned and enveloped the rectory. I heard the muffled whispers of my parents through the quietness.

I learned back in the cast-iron tub, soaking away the aches from the previous day, serenaded by the plaintive tones of a pennywhistle.

Chapter Seven
Sabbath

That Sunday morning would be a special one. I decided to wear my best dress, a red-and-blue plaid with a narrow skirt and small bustle. Mama had refashioned one of her old bonnets with crimson ribbons for me, and the bright hue set off my dark coloring to perfection. I wore my best dimity corset and coiffed my hair into curls that trailed down my back. Kimball had always admired me in red, and I could hardly wait to see his reaction.

I descended the stairs and found Sebastian begging to join us for Sunday services. "Please Uncle Braddock, I want to be part of Maidenhead again. Aunt Madeleine loaned me one of your frockcoats. Please, Uncle."

He gazed into Papa's face with the earnestness of a puppy, his face a portrait of cherubic innocence, like a painting by Botticelli. His cheeks glowed with the rosy smoothness of an infant, and his eyes sparkled with enthusiasm. Papa couldn't deny him.

"Very well, Sebastian. You're welcome to join us, but remember you are convalescing."

Sebastian cut quite a dashing figure in Papa's frockcoat, and I knew Velda would use her wiles on him. I prayed he'd dismiss her for the silly goose she was.

The ladies of our congregation had erased all

evidence of the storm, swept the courtyard free of refuse, and draped the pillars at the entrance to the church with the brightly colored bunting left from summer festivities. The sun peeked out from the clouds, and the apples and fall flowers in the bower scented the morning air. Papa welcomed one and all, with Sebastian taking a place next to him.

"My friends, this is my nephew, Sebastian. Please welcome him into your hearts."

And so they did. Sebastian shook every hand, patted every back, and kissed the head of every baby placed before him. It warmed me to see my cousin mingling with the congregants.

Velda sauntered past, giggling all the while. Every eye was upon her as she simpered and posed in her newest frock. She wore a lovely gown of polished cotton in a deep claret hue, with a ruffled bodice and satin bustle. My friend glanced at Sebastian and flashed a dazzling smile in his direction before she sashayed into the church.

I heard a whisper puncture the hubbub. "Great-grandmother, come this way."

Bathsheba clasped the arm of her great-grandmother, Modesty Chafee. Old Modesty, a stunted creature, so ancient not a soul alive knew her real age, had been born sightless. Tinted spectacles covered her deformed eyes. Everyone in Maidenhead held her in great regard, for she'd achieved renown throughout our village for her gifts as a seer. I knew her to be a woman of great virtue, but her presence had frightened me since childhood.

She turned her blind eyes in my direction. I felt an unspoken secret sat entrapped on her lips. A chill crawled down my spine when I looked at her, yet she never uttered a word.

The congregants parted when the two walked into the court. Bathsheba wore her usual black bombazine, her silver hair covered by an ebony bonnet with purple plumes. Modesty had garbed herself in a once-stylish traveling gown of green velvet, most probably acquired in payment for reading a villager's future. She'd grown deaf in her old age and held a silver ear trumpet with ivory earpiece.

The tiny unsighted woman took a step forward, but stopped dead in her tracks. Her head darted around as if she looked for something, but of course she couldn't see. She hesitated before calling out, "I feel a presence."

For some reason, Sebastian appeared shaken and pale at the sight of old Modesty. When he regained his composure, he shared a brotherly embrace with a sailor who'd taken part in his rescue. "It's time for me to go inside." He excused himself with a sunny smile, and I followed him.

The storm and Sebastian's rages forgotten, Papa's good temper had returned. I ascended the steps to the choir loft and propped myself behind the organ. Most of Maidenhead, at least the Congregationalists who weren't at sea, packed our little church that morning. The good people appeared eager to thank the Lord because the storm had ended.

Mama gave a nod in my direction, and the music began. She led the choir in Amazing Grace, her face radiant as if illuminated by an inner candle. I played with all the passion I could muster. I'd survived the storm when others hadn't and gave thanks. The sopranos sang out, and their voices filled the rafters with celestial enchantment. Papa stood behind the pulpit, overflowing with the spirit, igniting the congregation with his fervor, infusing me with the spirit of the Lord.

"My good people, although we lost five young visitors in that horrible storm, Fortune has smiled on Maidenhead."

Those in the congregation broke out in joyful gasps and some even applauded. Papa looked down at Sebastian.

"I am thankful the Lord spared my nephew, who has returned home after so many years. In these modern times, kerosene and gaslight illuminate, there is no need to plunder the seas for the great beasts. The end of whaling sucked asunder villages throughout Massachusetts, but not Maidenhead. Our fishermen drag their nets for cod and lobster, our glassworks transform sand into objects of beauty, our looms weave cotton into cloth, and our cobblers make the finest shoes in the world. However, Fortune has ignored some and others have not prospered. What of them? What of them, my friends?"

His words made me remember poor, friendless Caleb Potter. How shamefully I'd treated him. I resolved to engage him in conversation the next time I brought Pedro a treat. Papa continued his sermon, his enthusiasm mounting with every word.

"What about the poor among us? Look around, my friends. What of the afflicted?" All eyes turned to Modesty. "What of the lonely widow? What of the poor farmer whose crops have failed or the fisherman who returns from the sea with an empty net? Who among our neighbors remains alone and friendless? Whom do we shun, whom do we ignore?"

At that moment, I vowed to become Mr. Potter's friend and confidant; I'd share Bible verses and speak to him about his drinking, I'd— Plop. Someone blew a spitball in my direction, and I knew the culprit's identity, the lead baritone, Kimball Prince.

When I glared in his direction, the villain had the nerve to cross his eyes at me. His spitball assault continued through the rest of the service, despite my obvious displeasure. How could I think of him with affection when he wouldn't stop his incessant teasing? How could I have thought of him fondly or found him attractive? I ignored the rotter, refusing to let him get the better of me.

Services ended on a resounding note, and I joined my parents as they mingled with the congregation. Sebastian stood with us, a joyful expression on his face, until I felt him stiffen. The ancient blind woman emerged from the church arm in arm with Bathsheba.

His face turned starch white and he whispered to Papa, "Uncle Braddock, I feel a bit faint. Perhaps I should lie down for a moment."

He darted off, abandoning my father to the village tykes who swarmed over him like ants to honey. When a golden-haired child rushed into Papa's arms, my father threw the giggling child into the air. "Up you go, my boy."

Papa doted on children, yet only had me. Why had the Lord in his infinite wisdom only given my parents a single child? I'd been four when, in my innocence, I asked Mama for a little brother. Her face darkened and she walked away. I never asked again.

Another tyke tugged at my father's trouser leg. Papa scooped the other boy up and walked around the courtyard, a giggling lad under each arm.

I couldn't avoid Mr. Kimball Prince and walked past the grinning lout, arm in arm with Pyrtle. We followed the little ones into our garden, where Velda, another member of our quilting circle, awaited us.

"Velda, your brother is horrible. He flicked wads of paper at me throughout the sermon. I insist that you speak to him immediately."

She snickered at me. "What do you expect from a youth of eighteen, Lucy Hathorne? You know very well that nothing I say will stop him. He loves you, you goose."

Drat, that odious word "love" again. "Kimball loves me? He certainly has a strange way of showing it."

Instead of supporting her friend, Velda had the gall to chortle in my face. "He acts like those churls at school, with their childish pranks. Don't worry, though. He'll be off to Harvard soon and won't be around to tease you, at least for a while."

"Well, it won't be soon enough."

She looked into my face and broke into giggles. "Lucy, why do you get so vexed at Kimball when you know you adore him?"

"What? Adore, why I—"

Before I could correct her, Cassie joined us. She'd come from attending Mass at St. John the Baptist, the Portuguese church on the other side of town. It didn't matter if Cassie followed the Roman church, since we all loved her as a sister. Cassie's strong arms encircled my waist and Velda's.

"C'mon, girls, it's quilting time."

I turned up my nose at Mr. Prince and the four of us walked to the parsonage. The rascal guffawed like a hyena.

Chapter Eight
The Quilting Girls

Girlish titters reverberated through the rectory as we began our Sunday ritual of poetry, tea, and sweets as a prelude to sewing.

The four of us sat in our parlor, a large room with plank floors waxed to a brilliant shine and bottle-green walls covered with somber portraits of generations of Hathornes. The rococo flourishes carved on Mama's harp warmed the chamber with a bit of European ostentation.

We usually began our quilting sessions with a poem, but I decided to discuss the prickliest topic of the day. The Presidential election loomed over us, yet no woman I knew could cast a ballot. A discourse about universal suffrage was in order.

"As you all know, Mr. Garfield and General Hancock are fighting each other for the presidency. I'd love to vote for Mr. Garfield, but once again, men have shut out those of us who are mothers, wives, daughters. I think it's dreadful that a common seaman can vote, yet women of accomplishment can't."

A loud sigh escaped Velda's lips. "Oh, Lucy, please, can we have one Sunday morning without you prattling on about women's suffrage? I was so looking forward to tea and a poem...perhaps 'Rose' by Miss Dickinson."

I couldn't stifle a sigh of my own. "Velda, your mother owns the town inn, yet she can't vote, and you don't give a fig about women's rights. Very well, Velda Rose Prince, we'll have a poem, but one Cassie has requested."

Velda's lips twisted into a pout, and she had the unmitigated gall to sneer at me. "Poo, Lucy, you are such a bluestocking."

I ignored her and began "Success is Counted Sweetest" by Miss Emily Dickinson, Massachusetts born and bred. Although Miss Dickinson didn't have the fame of other poets, we adored the Amherst bard.

"Success is counted sweetest
By those who ne'er succeed.
To comprehend a nectar…"

Before I spoke another line, the door from the corridor opened.

Sebastian, still resplendent in Papa's frockcoat, stood at the threshold. He finished the poem in his resonant voice, his impassioned declaiming keeping us spellbound until the end.

"Requires sorest need.
Not one of all the purple host
Who took the flag today
Can tell the definition,
So clear, of victory!
As he, defeated, dying,
On whose forbidden ear
The distant strains of triumph
Burst agonized and clear!"

When we applauded, Sebastian's cheeks colored bright pink as he bowed with a flourish. Velda rose from her chair.

"Ladies, allow me to introduce you to Mr. Sebastian Hathorne, Lucy's cousin, survivor of the horrible catastrophe that occurred on Friday." She placed her hand in the crook of his arm and led him to my flame-haired friend. "Sebastian, may I present Miss Pyrtle Brigham, town telegrapher, the fastest Western Union wire tapper in all Massachusetts?"

She extended her hand like a true lady. "I'll gladly send any telegraphs you need, Mr. Hathorne."

Sebastian bowed once again before kissing her hand. We were simple girls, not used to city ostentation. Pyrtle's face flared as red as her hair.

When I pulled Sebastian away from Velda's clutches, my silly friend appeared much chagrined. I ignored her sulking and marched Cassie over to him. "Sebastian, this young lady is Cassie Silva. Cassie is a wondrous rower and searched for you too."

His lips spread into a wide grin. "What a brave girl you are, Cassie Silva, like Miss Ida Lewis, the lighthouse keeper who risked life and limb to save those in danger. I'm afraid we don't have young ladies of your mettle in Boston." He gazed into her face. "Are you Cape Verdean? I imagine the Queen of Sheba looked much like you when she conquered King Solomon with the bat of an eyelash."

His words rendered Cassie speechless, and Velda inserted herself between the two of them before Cassie could respond.

"After all the sadness of the past days, I decided to cheer up everyone by wearing my newest frock. Madame St. Pierre created it for me. Do you like it, Sebastian?"

Sebastian bowed like a knight of old for a third

time, and spun Velda in one graceful turn. He stepped back from her and bowed once again. "I'm afraid I know nothing of ladies' gowns, but your frock is truly one of the most beautiful I've ever seen."

As the daughter of a prosperous innkeeper, Velda had more dresses than the rest of us combined. Like all young women of style, she devoured the repository of Fashion, Pleasure and Instruction, Harper's Bazaar.

Velda beamed, her face bright pink, her green eyes flashing like emerald sconces. My beautiful friend had begun enslaving the men of Maidenhead at the age of thirteen. She generally favored making older men her conquests and had caught the eye of an oily sot of a fellow of thirty-five, Mr. Hiram Endicott, a distant cousin of the famed Boston Endicotts. For the first time, however, she appeared enthralled by a young man close to her own age.

She twirled once again. "I wager no other girl in town has such a fashionable frock. Madame St. Pierre calls it a toilette de promenade, the kind of gown ladies of fashion wear on their afternoon strolls. Since she comes from Paris, she is an expert."

Madame St. Pierre's claims of being a Parisian may have fooled Velda and the matrons who summered in our village, but she'd never taken in Mama. Despite the woman's attempts to conceal it, my mother recognized her Quebecois accent.

Velda popped open her matching parasol and posed so prettily even Cassie applauded.

"It's stunning."

As she twirled the parasol, I knew her show was for only one person: Sebastian. "Yes, it is stunning, isn't it? Tell me, dear Sebastian, would you mistake me for a Boston Blue Blood?"

Sebastian's grin brightened the room. "Yes, with the bluest blood in all of Massachusetts. Except for my dear Ida, no girl in the city can hold a candle to you." He bowed once again before turning to Pyrtle and Cassie. "I'm afraid I'll have to be on my way, ladies."

Velda rushed over to him, her face marred by a petulant frown. "So soon? We want to hear about the grand balls."

He laughed. "I don't know much about dancing, although my darling Ida adores the Boston waltz. I promise to visit later, but there are important matters I must attend to. Goodbye, ladies."

Sebastian left the room. Velda followed his retreat. Her shoulders slumped. "I wish he'd stayed."

We usually perused copies of Harper's Bazaar and Ridley's Fashion Magazine before quilting, but I brought out Sebastian and Ida's portraits instead. Pyrtle mimicked Ida's imperious stance. "She's a true lady of fashion, haughty and magnificent."

Cassie nodded in agreement. "She's lovely." Cassie looked up from the photos with a smirk. "Lucy, your cousin is what the factory girls call a 'ripper.'"

Velda ignored Ida's photograph, concentrating on Sebastian's instead. "Yes, Sebastian is quite the handsome fellow, and charming too. He's been awfully chipper despite his horrible ordeal. He said Miss Stoker lives in a fine house with gaslights, indoor plumbing, and servants."

She picked up Ida's portrait and sneered at it. "Can you imagine? She's only two years older than we are, yet she's affianced to the most dashing boy in Boston. Of course, she probably has money to burn. I'll wager she wears elegant gowns and bonnets every day, and jaunts through the streets of Boston in a grand brougham with a liveried driver and a team of white stallions. In the future, I'll have one of my own."

Velda placed Ida's photograph down with a snort and swooped up Sebastian's again, almost swooning as she caressed it. "Lucy, your cousin is the most dashing gentleman I've ever seen. It's as if he leapt from the pages of Wuthering Heights." She rolled back her shoulders, a defiant sneer on her lips. "Perhaps you girls are content to live in Maidenhead, but when I meet my own Heathcliff, I'll leave this place forever."

Pyrtle thumbed through the worn copy of Wuthering Heights that Velda always carried.

"Oh, you will, will you? Listen to this. 'A ray fell on his features; the cheeks were sallow, and half covered with black whiskers; the brows lowering, the eyes deep-set and singular.'" Pyrtle looked for another passage regarding Heathcliff's image. "Ha! 'A half-civilized ferocity lurked yet in the depressed brows and eyes full of black fire…' " She stopped reading and narrowed her eyes. "Velda, this Heathcliff fellow sounds as ugly as sin."

Cassie chimed in. "I agree. Give me a handsome sailor any day."

Velda glowered at her tormentors. "Cassie Silva, you'll get your wish when you marry Zeke Newberry and end up smelling of codfish—or worse, whale blubber. As for you, Pyrtle Brigham, I wouldn't expect you to understand or appreciate a great work of literature. Perhaps Louisa May Alcott is more to your taste."

Velda held Sebastian's photograph up to the light.

"This is how my Heathcliff looks, not that you would know the difference."

Cassie hooted at their squabbling. "Hush up, Velda. I'm here to quilt, not to listen to your caterwauling."

Her words had no effect on my warring friends. Providence had cursed Pyrtle with a peppery temper, and once she got her dander up, nothing could silence her.

"I know one thing, Miss Velda Prince. You'll probably marry some old buzzard with a pot of money and no teeth, like Hiram Endicott. You'll spend your days wiping gruel off his chin."

Velda turned up her pert nose. "Pyrtle Brigham, you'll end up an old maid because you're so sour no man will have you." She gave a dainty snort. "I'll have you know that Hiram does have teeth!"

Cassie called out once again. "Enough! You both need a good switching."

While Pyrtle and Velda glared at each other, I took the opportunity to rescue Cousin Sebastian's photograph. "Honestly, you two might as well engage in fisticuffs. We'll never finish Pyrtle's quilt at this rate. I have a suggestion. Let's send Ida the crazy quilt we just finished, in honor of her engagement. Sebastian is far too busy to be concerned about such a trifle."

Velda's rancor returned. "Why would such an elegant lady, a girl who has everything, want one of our little quilts?"

Pyrtle nodded in my direction. "I think it's a capital idea, Lucy. I'm sure she'll appreciate it. I'll mail it off right away." She scowled at Velda before she cried out, "Let the quilting commence!"

We positioned the wooden quilt frame in the middle of the parlor and pulled out our needles, thimbles, and thread. Mrs. Brigham had even provided tailor's pins, a great extravagance.

I stroked the beautiful quilt, a Rose of Sharon in a sea of white cotton. "Girls, be proud we didn't use some old-fogey pattern but drew our own."

Pyrtle pretended to mope like a sulky child. "It is beautiful, but maybe I won't marry. Perhaps I'll pursue the maiden lady life of a suffragist like our dear Lucy."

Velda smirked just like her scoundrel of a brother. "Pyrtle, our dear Lucy will never lead the life of a spinster. When Kimball becomes a Harvard lawyer, Lucy will wed him, and they'll have babies crawling all over their parlor."

My so-called friends kept laughing until Mama's loud harrumph of displeasure rolled through the corridor from the kitchen. The sewing began, and we worked at a frantic pace until late afternoon.

Cassie rose from her chair and gave her arms a stretch. "Girls, the hour's getting late, and I must be off. Let's meet tomorrow, shall we say at five o'clock?" She glanced my way. "Lucy, would your mother and father allow it?"

I knew my parents wouldn't mind. Papa swore the rectory came alive with the sound of girlish laughter.

"Of course. Tomorrow it is."

The quilting bee ended, and I spent the rest of the evening practicing my harp, making heavenly music on the heavy strings.

At dusk, the sun deserted the sky and slumber beckoned. After the events of the week, I looked forward to a good night's sleep. I took to my bed, reveling in its warmth, and soon dozed off. I dreamed of walking the forest path and stopping in front of the ancient gristmill. The twittering of birds mingled with the voices of the fairies who danced in the woods. Someone whispered my name in tones as dulcet as dark honey. "Lucy."

I recognized the voice and swiveled to face Kimball. For once, he wasn't smiling. I'm sure he could hear the pounding of my heart. He took my hand in his and kissed it. We gazed at each other for an eternity, and then he bent over as if to kiss me. My heart nearly burst. I felt the warmth of his skin, smelled the spice of his cologne. He moved closer, his breath warm and scented by peppermint—but before he kissed me, a noise from outside awakened me.

A trespasser roamed around the arbor. I left the warmth of my bed and looked out my bedroom window. Sebastian paced about the arbor grounds, mumbling to himself. Despite the chill of the night, he wore only Papa's nightshirt. I jumped from my bed to rescue him. My dreams would have to wait for another night.

Chapter Nine
The Good Friend

The next morning I awoke to stillness, a hollow quiet as if everyone had abandoned my home. My face warmed at the thought of my delicious, aborted dream. I crept out of bed and knocked on Sebastian's door. No one answered. I swung the portal open to an empty room, books and papers askew. I called out, "Mama, Papa, Sebastian."

Mama responded, "I'm in the parlor."

I bounded downstairs. The perfume of molasses, cloves, and ginger enveloped me. I strolled into the parlor, where I found my mother arranging chairs. "Mama, why didn't you wake me? It's already seven in the morning."

She continued her task without looking at me. "I thought a bit of extra sleep wouldn't hurt you. I left out oatmeal and fruit compote for breakfast. There's plenty of hot water in the scullery, but leave the molasses cookies alone. They're for the children after Bible study this afternoon."

My eyes searched the corridor. "Where's Sebastian?"

When Mama turned in my direction, I noted her mouth tightened at the mention of his name. "That restless boy kept us up all night with his ranting in the arbor. Thank the Lord you rescued us. Sebastian calmed down and insisted on accompanying your father on his rounds, so they took the carriage. He wanted to see the schooner, too, although why, I'll never know. I suppose the chandler will make a pretty penny getting her sea shape again."

She acted like Mama of old—that is, until her face darkened and she abruptly pointed her forefinger toward the kitchen. "Go eat your breakfast, Lucy."

I heard the frostiness in her voice, but spoke despite it. "When I finish, may I visit Pyrtle? She promised to send off that crazy quilt to Boston, but she's so preoccupied with wedding veils she might forget."

Mama appeared exasperated and threw down her cleaning rag. "Go to her, but I expect you back in time for your French lesson."

Considering her coolness, perhaps I took a chance in asking, "May I visit Caleb Potter, too? I haven't seen him in days. Would it be all right if I took one of your Jamaica black cakes? I could give a piece to Mr. Potter and divide the rest with those poor men in the stables."

From her coldness, I knew she was still angry about me rushing off during the storm. It would take time for her anger to subside.

"Please, Mama? Please let me bring some leftover cake to those unfortunate sailors."

She'd occupied herself removing ashes from the fireplace, turned away from me. "Why do you ask my permission, Lucy? You seem determined to do whatever you wish. Eat your breakfast and get dressed or you'll never leave."

I dashed off before she changed her mind. After I completed my morning ablutions and wolfed down breakfast, I bounced up the stairs to my room. In the event I ran into Kimball, I donned a simple red-and-white gingham frock and my Sunday bonnet trimmed with scarlet ribbons. Although Mr. Kimball Prince annoyed me no end, I loved the way his eyes sparkled whenever I wore the gown.

I finished dressing and braced myself for another encounter with Mama. I found her removing the ashes from the stove. Her head whipped around at my approach, and she took in my appearance. "Lucy, aren't you a bit formal for a jaunt to Brigham's and the stables?"

"Well, I thought if it's all right with you, I'd inquire about Velda and Kimball, too."

She arched an eyebrow. "Oh, yes, Velda and, of course, Kimball. Well, out with you."

I picked up my basket and put in the cake. Before I set off for my trek into the white woods, I added some treats for Pedro.

Once inside the forest, tranquility greeted me. Nothing rustled. I found the silence as disturbing as the day of the storm. "Mr. Potter, it's Lucy Hathorne here for a visit. Where are you?"

A chickadee sang out, breaking the uneasy quiet. I called out to the bear. "Here, Pedro, here, Pedro. I have something for you. Come to me."

I heard no drunken rants, no bearish grunts, only the hush of the forest. Mr. Potter had deserted his rocking chair once again, and his shack stood empty. I turned and trudged back to town.

****

"Take your hands off this one. It belongs to me. I seen it first, and I'm gonna cook it up for supper."

Except for two women quibbling over the remains of the morning catch, villagers had deserted Pocasset Square. I heard voices in the distance and followed them up the steep incline to the dock. As I moved closer, a faint hubbub became a roar. When I finally reached the harbor, I found most of Maidenhead there.

A bear's growl tore through the cacophony. Pedro bounced over, almost knocking me to the ground. I tossed him the piece of cod and a bit of salt pork, both of which I'd brought for him. He devoured the treat in a wink and licked my hand in thanks before lumbering away toward the beach. Caleb must have been near, prowling for salvage.

The object of the town's curiosity, the giant schooner, loomed before us all, naked in her ruined splendor. The sea had soaked her crimson sails, left them intact, but split the main mast in two. I made out the name, Bon Ami, emblazoned on the mahogany bow. Such irony. Bon Ami meant Good Friend. She hadn't been a good friend to those who drowned.

A mob of admirers hemmed Cassie in, but she managed to make her way to the vessel. Zeke gazed at her from afar, his coppery skin glowing redder with her every step. Mr. Tateshaw strode up to my brave friend. He'd whaled with her father years before, and slapped her on the back like an old salt. "You did good, Cassie, cutting that fellow from the mast rigging like you did. Too bad he was already dead."

She turned away from him, her face blank, her demeanor grim. "Yes, sir, too bad."

Before I could reach Cassie, I felt a hand on my arm.

"Lucy, wait a moment. I must talk to you."

I turned to face Dr. Farnsworth, his eyes red-rimmed, his fair hair uncombed. He'd abandoned his hat and stood before me in shirtsleeves. "Thank goodness, I've found you."

I held up my basket. "I was on my way to the stable, sir. Mama baked a Jamaica black cake, and I thought the young men might enjoy it."

His mouth twisted into a grim line, and he shook his head. "I'm afraid there'll be no cake for those fellows. Both are at death's door. Follow me." He marched away with a determined stride. "They're Quebecers who don't speak English, and I don't speak French. Lucy, I need your help."

Although I tried to match his steps with my own, I could barely keep up. "You said two men? Weren't there five? That would make six with Sebastian, wouldn't it? Don't tell me four have died?"

"We've lost three." Dr. Farnsworth stopped in his tracks. "Sebastian visited the stables this morning. I remember him as a child, such a bright tyke, curious about everything. Now, he's a gentleman. He stopped by to see the sailors with your father, but being near them upset him. After all, he'd almost died himself. The lad ran out of the stables and didn't come back. Your father is searching for him."

He pointed toward an old barn next to the glassworks. His brow furrowed. "I hate the thought of those boys dying in a stable, Lucy. I'd bring them to my practice, but neither would survive the move. We found the ship's manifest, but it tells us little, just lists names of the crew, but not where they came from."

"Couldn't Sebastian supply that information?"

He shook his head as if trying to clear it. "I'm

afraid he didn't know them. They were a rough and tumble group, and he stayed away. Considering the cargo, I'm sure the captain took what dregs he could get." A quizzical smile crossed his lips. "Years ago, when I was in medical school, in less enlightened times, the authorities got wind of an illegal shipment of medical specimens. The crew abandoned the cargo of cadavers on the docks. The embalmers had packed them in piano crates so no one would know the truth. The bodies weren't found until they began to decompose. The stench led the constables to them."

Dr. Farnsworth didn't notice that I quaked and nearly lost my breakfast at the thought of corpses rotting on a dock.

The good doctor snorted out a bitter laugh. "Well, at least your cousin survived. He may be just a youth, but Sebastian has the constitution of a bull." He headed toward the stable. "Those young men won't last much longer. One has a broken neck and the other crashed against the rocks."

He stopped walking and took me by the arm. "Can you speak to the boy with the broken neck? We've given him morphine, but you might be able to find out who those poor lads were."

It seemed a small request. "Of course, Dr. Farnsworth, I'll do what I can."

When we entered the stable, the scent of human filth and vomit wafted up to the rafters and obliterated the sweet smell of hay and manure. Horses' nickering and the ragged breaths of one of the remaining sailors broke the silence. A beam of sunlight slanted down from the high windows, adding a glint to the stable's only illumination, a single lantern. The two survivors lay on their backs on cots in a corner of the stable.

Mrs. Farnsworth stood over one of the stricken men, with Bathsheba at her side. A gasp and then the heavy breathing stopped abruptly. She turned at our approach, pince-nez spectacles obscuring her lively brown eyes. The specter of death had banished her usual sunny disposition.

"Bathsheba and I did our best for him, but the Lord had other ideas. I fear whatever he could have told us died with him."

Bathsheba stared down at the dead fellow. "The morphine we gave him caused the lad to see things. He had a hard death."

A hard death indeed. His eyes and mouth lolled open as if he'd seen something horrible.

Dr. Farnsworth shook his head. He'd splinted and bandaged every inch of the boy, who looked no more than eighteen. "Now the storm has cut the boy down before he even tasted life."

A gasp in the corner brought the four of us to the side of the other man. The sole survivor amongst the sailors now, his face battered and bruised, he gasped for air. Dr. Farnsworth motioned to me. "Ask him his name."

"Comment vous appelez-vous?"

The young man responded in a weak whisper. "Remy, Remy Bouchard."

More French tumbled from his lips. "Je te prie, j'ai besoin d'un prêtre! Je serai condamné sans confession. Amene-moi un prêtre!"

"He wants a priest, Dr. Farnsworth. He's begging for a priest, so he can confess." A tear rolled down the sailor's cheek.

I took Dr. Farnsworth's arm. "There's a Portuguese priest at the Catholic church, sir. I'll bring him to you."

The doctor stared down at the young man. "We've already sent for the priest. He's away in New Bedford and won't return until tomorrow. It'll be too late."

"Mama speaks French. Perhaps she could comfort him."

Dr. Farnsworth stroked the young sailor's forehead. "I doubt the lad will last another five minutes. Remy, my poor boy."

A horse whinnied, and the young man's eyes popped open. He turned to Dr. Farnsworth, his cracked lips spread in a beatific smile.

"Bénissez-moi, mon père, car j'ai péché."

I took a step back from the fellow. "Dr. Farnsworth, he thinks you're a priest. He said, 'Bless me, Father, for I have sinned.'"

The young man murmured more words. "La mort est proche et je prie pour pardon. Cette affreux maladie et l'orage étaient la juste punition de Dieu pour le mal on a fait. Maintenant, on va tous mourir."

"He says his death is near and that he prays for forgiveness. The storm was God's just punishment for the evil they did. Now they'll all die."

The young man gasped again and whispered, "Cadavers."

I murmured into Remy's ear. The youth closed his eyes, gave a final gasp, and his breathing stopped.

Bathsheba pulled the blanket up to his face and had almost covered it when we heard a whimper. Remy's eyes fluttered open. "Dieu, pardonne-moi! Pardonne-moi!"

"He says, 'God, forgive me. Forgive me.'"

Dr. Farnsworth took my arm. "Tell Remy God forgives him."

I did as he asked. "Dieu vous pardonne." The words appeared to comfort the young man. His eyes rolled back in his head, and he took one final gasp. Dr. Farnsworth placed his fingers on the deceased boy's wrist.

"There's no pulse." Dr. Farnsworth closed the young man's eyes, but they fluttered open again. He held the lids down longer, finally shutting the fellow's eyes. The youth looked at peace. "He's gone." Dr. Farnsworth looked up at the two women. "You made a valiant effort, but we lost. Wash up, go home, and rest. I'll have the men bring the bodies to my practice."

The doctor stomped through the straw-laden floor to a small wooden table where a bar of disinfectant soap, a basin of water, and clean towels awaited him. He scoured his hands with the soap and hot water, scrubbing them until they turned red.

"I couldn't save them."

He chuckled, his laughter mirthless and cynical. The good doctor turned from me and donned his waistcoat. "Now, if you'll excuse me, Lucy, I have to prepare for the embalming."

The doctor noticed I shivered at the last word. "My dear girl, I learned embalming during the war. It may seem barbaric to some, but how else could we send the bodies of those slain on the battlefield back to their loved ones?"

My nerves got the best of me, and I began to shake. Dr. Farnsworth took my arm and spoke in a whisper as faint as the hiss of a teakettle. "Those boys who perished were all stout sailors. They should have survived even in so fierce a storm, but they'd all ingested something that weakened or even killed them."

I found his words incredulous. "Are you saying someone murdered them?"

He considered my question for a moment. "I don't know, but poison doesn't crawl into food or drink without help. I've stored the cadavers in the icehouse until I can arrange a transport to Harvard. In the event we can't find their relations, and I'm sure we won't, we'll include these boys with the rest."

He turned to leave but swiveled back to me, his brow furrowed. "Perhaps I shouldn't mention it. Harvard is the home of an anatomical society, a most secretive one whose name I can't utter. As a medical student, I belonged, and now so does Sebastian. They are in need of fresh bodies to dissect." Dr. Farnsworth looked down at Remy's corpse. "They'll all end up on Harvard's dissection tables. I'm afraid we can't waste a body. Goodbye, Lucy."

He opened the stable doors and walked away into the sunlight, leaving me alone with the horses and the two corpses.

Chapter Ten
The Good Hope Inn

Whaling gold had once brought vast wealth to Massachusetts. The Prince family built the Good Hope Inn during those heady times when hunting the great beasts of the sea had been a way of life in Maidenhead. Everyone who saw it declared the Good Hope Inn the handsomest edifice in Maidenhead, even finer than the mayor's residence and the great mansions in the tonier part of town. In the eighteenth century, Ethan Prince had shipped the enormous front portal from England along with the supporting pillars and hand-carved lintel. He'd filled the inn with fine English furniture, bone china, and silver. It even boasted an indoor privy and gaslights.

I walked into a rumble of male voices. The lobby smelled of mulberry, pine, and cigars. Ancient harpoons, toggles, and hooks, remnants from Maidenhead's whaling past, covered the walls. A wizened fiddler sat near the vast stone fireplace, pouring his heart into a plaintive rendition of "Oh, Shenandoah."

The gents who governed Maidenhead huddled together in the main room, guzzling rum punch. Mayor Stoddard, a corpulent man with a brusque manner, paced in front of the fireplace, puffing on a stogie.

"What a storm it was. We found Jonas Peck's prize

stallion dead in the street, and a tree through old Mother Clarke's roof. It's a miracle the poor woman wasn't killed."

The mayor let a blob of tobacco-tinged spit fly into a copper spittoon and then continued his pacing and puffing. "Those cadavers on the beach were a nasty business, too."

Constable Heath pulled out a leather pouch. His chubby fingers packed a large wad of tobacco into the bowl of his pipe before lighting it. The fragrant smoke curled up to the coffered ceiling.

A thin and wiry fellow, his looks in great contrast to the portly mayor, questioned, "What will happen to them?"

The mayor answered with a droll chuckle. "I wanted to throw them down a hole and be done with it, but we'll store them in the ice house until we find where to send them." He pulled the pipe from his mouth and let out another bubble of spit. "Tateshall's the only fellow who stands to make money from the storm. Fixing the schooner should make him a pretty penny."

The gentlemen grumbled in agreement. I passed through the lobby unnoticed, since Mrs. Prince held every eye in the place. All the village fathers, including those who were married, coveted the affections of the prosperous and comely widow, but she flounced past the ogling men and ignored their admiring glances.

Mrs. Prince drove a red-hot poker into a pewter tankard filled with buttered rum. She kept a smirk on her handsome face as she sauntered among the town fathers, ladling the warm spirits into their mugs. "Enjoy your drinks, sirs."

The mayor appraised Mrs. Prince's voluptuous form and took another puff on his cigar. His gaze strayed and turned to me.

"There she is, one of our Valkyries!"

The men applauded when the mayor ambled over to bestow a fatherly embrace. He attempted to kiss me, but I averted my face, and extricated myself from his tobacco-scented breath. I made a polite curtsy before crossing over to Mrs. Prince. "Mrs. Prince, can you please direct me to Kimball?"

She brushed an errant curl from her forehead and gave me a knowing smile. "He's out back, chopping wood."

Mrs. Prince went on with her duties. I pinched my cheeks to redden them, and bit into a clove I always carried in my pocket to freshen my breath. Then I moved past the hubbub of drunken laughter and into the smelly chaos of the kitchen. Chickens, geese, and piglets hung from the ceiling or roasted on spits in the inn's stone fireplace. A stout, red-faced cook ordered around the scullery crew. "Get on with it, you lazy good-for-nothings!"

Once outside, I heard the rhythmical thump of an axe. The stench of coops filled with squabbling hens, ducks, and geese, along with the stink of penned-up swine, caused my gorge to rise. One of the cooks had plucked a brood of chickens and bloodied feathers lay everywhere.

Unlike Sebastian, Kimball stood naked to the waist as he chopped the cords of wood. His shoulders had broadened over the years. His arms rippled with muscles, his body as brawny and robust as a Greek god. I needn't have pinched my cheeks, for a surge of warmth heated my face.

I coughed to announce my presence, along with, "Excuse me, Kimball," and then turned my back while he dressed.

I heard him snicker at my discomfort. "Wait a moment." After what seemed an eternity, he called out to me, "Lucy, I'm decent. You can look."

When I turned, he greeted me with his usual jaunty smile, but for some reason his flippant attitude didn't annoy me as it once had.

"Hello, Miss Hathorne." His gaze swept over me, which brought even more warmth to my face. "May I say you look quite fetching, Lucy. What brings you here?"

I surveyed the yard, searching at every nook and cranny. "Kimball, are you sure we're alone?"

He chuckled. "Of course we are. Since there's wood to chop, no one else is around."

I lowered my voice in the event a scullion might interrupt us. "I brought you a piece of Mama's Jamaican black cake. I'd hope to share it with those poor sailors, but unfortunately, they have all died."

Kimball searched my face. His grin revealed the most handsome dimples I'd ever seen. "Even if you meant the cake for dead men, I appreciate the gesture."

His nearness disoriented me for a moment, but I remembered the purpose of my visit. "What I have to say is of a most disturbing nature. No one knows about it except for Dr. Farnsworth and, possibly, Sebastian."

At the mention of my cousin's name, the chickens began squawking and fluttering. What set them off? We looked around and saw no one.

He turned back to me. "What do you have to tell

me, Lucy?"

"Dr. Farnsworth thinks someone poisoned the crew. Who would do such a thing?"

His brow furrowed slightly. "Your cousin seems to be in fine health."

I took a step back from him. "Kimball, you can't possibly think Sebastian had anything to do with it. Poisoning the crew would have meant his certain death. No, someone else must have adulterated their food or drink." I took a deep breath. Before he could reply, the pigs squealed, their shrieks frightening enough to set my teeth on edge. I stepped away, my eyes searching the grounds. We were still alone.

Kimball led me away. "Nature seems to be rebelling today. Let's go up to the widow's walk."

I followed him up the winding steps past the attic. He opened a trap door, and we climbed a wooden stairway until we reached the roof. All the great mansions built from whaling wealth had their own widow's walks, but the walk at the Good Hope Inn outdid them all in magnificence. An aquamarine sky, the glorious sun, and all of Maidenhead greeted us when we reached our destination. Elaborate finials enclosed a gazebo with a shining copper cupola.

New England legends told of women gazing out to the horizon as they searched for a glimpse of their lover's ship. It didn't matter if the stories were untrue; the romantic lie won out.

The bay lay before us in all its magnificence. Even from such a distance I could taste the salt of the sea, smell its perfume, and hear the gulls cawing as they circled the dock.

"Kimball, if I lived here, it would be hard to leave

this place."

He stood behind me, his arms encircling my waist. I fought to keep my composure.

"You could live here, Lucy, if you wanted to."

At that moment, I felt a powerful stirring and wished to stay with him forever, but when I looked out into the horizon, the schooner's sails flared red in the sun.

I felt his sweet breath on my neck, his arms around my waist. He whispered, his voice soft and sweet, "All this could be yours, my Lucy."

We stood together, alternately taking in the beauty surrounding us and staring at each other, unable to move. What was this strange and wonderful feeling?

Chapter Eleven
Home

Laughter greeted us when we moved through the lobby. The city leaders had consumed copious amounts of rum and jousted with each other like rowdy schoolboys. Their raucous behavior didn't infect us. Kimball scowled at the boisterous men. I longed for the quiet of the rectory, for I needed to think.

"Kimball, I should go home. Mama still hasn't forgiven me for rowing out with Papa in the middle of a storm."

He placed a calloused hand on my cheek. "May I visit you after dinner?"

My heart fluttered just as it had on the widow's walk. "Oh, yes, please."

A loud belch followed by hearty guffaws from the older men caused Kimball's lips to curl in disgust.

I stumbled down the stone pathway to the parsonage, as narcotized as an opium eater in one of Velda's pulp romances. I have no idea how I managed to find my way back home after the day's events and encountering Kimball. Dr. Farnsworth's words frightened me, while my feelings for Kimball had left me confused and exhausted.

When I opened the rectory door, the smell of a tasty stew said hello. I hadn't eaten since early morning, and my stomach growled. An unbaked piecrust sat on the counter. I set to work coring apples, gobbling up half the fruit as I labored. Mama sauntered into the kitchen from the orchard. She carried a load of apples in her apron and plopped them on the kitchen table.

"They delivered Sebastian's trunk this morning. He'll be glad to know it's none the worse for wear. One of the fellows who brought it said old Modesty is ailing. I don't know when I can go visit her. Oh, well, here are more apples for you to core."

She looked up at me, her face unreadable. I braced myself for another slap. "I'm sorry I'm late, Mama."

I broke down, perhaps from the strain of the day or the past week. Instead of striking me, she took me in her arms and stroked my hair.

"I'm so proud of you, my brave, brave girl."

She sat, pulled me onto her lap, and rocked me as she did when I was a tyke. "I never should have slapped you, but I feared I'd lose you."

The rancor of the previous days melted away, and we were mother and child once again.

The warmth of her body engulfed me, wrapping me in a robe of maternal love.

Before I said another word, I heard footsteps. Papa entered the kitchen, and I leapt up. She rose from the chair and rushed over to him. Mama buried her head in my father's chest.

Papa gazed at me, his face in a grim line. "Did you speak to Dr. Farnsworth?"

I dropped my head. "Yes, sir. He told me the crew had been poisoned."

Mama looked up and gasped. "How could something so dreadful have happened?"

Papa shook his head in disbelief. "Those poor young men. Well, we can at least pray for them in the cemetery tomorrow."

Before anyone could answer, the rectory door opened. I heard a bouncy tread and then a raucous laugh. Sebastian barreled into the room. He'd garbed his lanky body in one of Papa's old shirts and patched trousers, and a fisherman's cap set at a jaunty angle covered his dark locks. Still, something appeared amiss. His eyes glinted like a maniac's, and a feverish smile lit his face.

"Uncle Braddock and I went on churchly rounds before we visited the schooner this morning. You'll be glad to know Old Bullet is safely ensconced in the barn, and I gave him extra oats." He threw his head back and his mad laughter filled the rectory. "I'm afraid the ordeal of nearly sinking wore the old girl out, but your chandler, a very pleasant fellow by the way, says he can have her shipshape in no time. My Harvard chums have already wired money for her rehabilitation."

He pulled off his cap. "Uncle Braddock introduced me to Mr. Crackbone, the chemist. Luckily, the trunk with my books and medicines survived. I asked the men to bring it to the rectory rather than the apothecary. Crackbone's methods are as moldy as he is, but I might as well help the old fellow out while I'm here in Maidenhead."

Sebastian chortled, loud and hard. His laughter stopped the moment he looked into Papa's face. His heavy brows knotted in concern. "Is something wrong, Uncle Braddock?"

Papa turned to me, his face somber and pale. "Lucy, please set the table for supper while your mother and I have a word with Sebastian."

He clasped Sebastian's hand in his. "Come to the study, my boy."

Mama followed them and whispered to me before closing the door, "Lucy, prepare supper."

My parents had banished me from their conversation with Sebastian, so I busied myself with preparations for the evening meal. As I set the plates out on the dinner table, my cousin's keening punctured the rectory's tranquility. He bellowed as if a beloved child had passed, as if the woes of the world had collapsed on his shoulders. Perhaps I shouldn't have, but I crept into the corridor toward the study and found myself in front of the heavy portal. Closed doors both fascinated and frightened me. Who knew what one would find on the other side? I pressed my ear against the polished oak.

Mama's voice soared over his cries. "Sebastian, calm yourself."

Papa's words came out in measured tones. "The crew were all God's children, dear boy. Could they have ingested some sort of poison?"

Sebastian's voice quaked with emotion. "Are you accusing me of poisoning them?" Despite the closed door, his sobs filled the rectory. "Uncle, don't look at me with that pompous face of accusation."

My father whispered softly, "Dr. Farnsworth said someone poisoned the crew with arsenic."

Without warning, Sebastian began screaming at the top of his voice. "Uncle, why do you torture me with such a question? They were a bunch of drunken louts, the only seamen willing to transport cadavers. If they were poisoned, it wasn't by my hand. I'm a healer.

Dear God, I'd rather die than displease you, but I take my directives from the Lord."

Stillness filled the room until another scream shattered the tranquility. "Please, Aunt Madeleine, don't look at me like that."

Mama spoke in hushed tones. "Calm down, my darling. We're not accusing you of anything."

I heard Sebastian sobbing once again.

After a moment, Papa finally spoke. "We'll sort this out later, my boy. Let's have dinner now."

The moment I heard my father's words, I made a mad rush to the dining room. I finished the table in an instant, taking special pains with the china Mama's Huguenot mother had brought from France.

Sebastian had been adamant during his confusing diatribe. He swore he hadn't poisoned the sailors. Of course, killing them would have brought about his own death. I wondered how my parents could be so calm in the face of his insane outburst. I vowed to find the answer, but first, I had to serve up boiled ham and cabbage for supper.

****

Later that evening, Velda and Pyrtle sat in the parlor, battling as usual.

Pyrtle gave an angry toss of her flame-colored locks and held up two crimson rose petals cut from an old silk dress. "Velda, this shade of red doesn't match the other pieces. I wanted a silk rose, surrounded by buds, in the center so it'll look as if the flower is bursting through the fabric."

Velda wrinkled her nose at my flame-haired friend. "Pyrtle, you can't match red cotton with red silk, but it looks close enough. Let's outline the rose with white stitches, and then it will be time to add the batting and sew it together."

My quilting friends normally used old towels and rags to add heft to a quilt, but Mrs. Brigham had provided us with fine cotton batting, along with new thimbles and needles. We sewed at a feverish pace, chatting all the while about death, telegrams, and a schooner with crimson sails. Brigham's Dry Goods had been the town hub for years, and Pyrtle shared the latest news.

"Lucy, your cousin must have charmed all of Massachusetts. He's been receiving telegraphs for days."

I resolved to ask her about the content of those telegrams when we were alone.

Velda stitched the last winding stem before she looked up from her labors. "Truer words were never spoken. Sebastian stopped by the inn for a visit. He's turned Mother's head and he's all she talks about."

Pyrtle held her needle up to the lamp's bright glow and threaded it. "He's bewitched half the town, at least the ladies. He came into the store today to telegraph his betrothed, Ida." She moved her head closer into the circle. "She's sent him many telegrams begging him to return home. How she must adore him."

Velda scowled at the mention of Sebastian's fiancée, but Pyrtle ignored her pouts. "He insisted I call him Sebastian instead of Mr. Hathorne." She paused, an impish smile on her lips. "Since I'm an engaged woman, I did. I must say, Sebastian is a jolly fellow." My red-haired chum looked around the room. "Where is he? I thought he might visit with us."

How could I tell my friends that Mama had dosed

Sebastian with laudanum to stop his rants? "He took to his bed after supper."

Cassie occupied herself with the quilt's backing. "I saw him nosing around the schooner this afternoon, checking on Mr. Tateshall. He was quite amiable and even spoke a bit of Portuguese to me."

I decided to change the conversation. "Tomorrow my family will visit the True Believers' Burial Ground. We'll pray for those who died in the storm at the Tomb of the Unknown Seamen. Those young men might join those who've washed up on our shores over the years."

The chatting stopped. My friends looked from one to the other without a word until Pyrtle spoke out. "What time, Lucy?"

"Papa said at one in the afternoon."

Velda looked up from her stitching. "Will Sebastian be there?"

Her words confused me. "Yes, but why—"

She went back to her stitching with a cackle. "I'll do my part and make a wreath for the poor things."

Pyrtle spoke in a rush. "I'll be there. Lincoln can take over the telegraph machine this one time."

Her devotion to her Catholic faith had prevented Cassie from ever setting foot in the True Believers' Burial Ground. She looked at her bosom friends. "I'll come too."

I had no doubt that my friends would be true to their word. We didn't know those sailors, but we'd mourn them all the same.

Chapter Twelve
Mr. Prince

I crept into my bedchamber, praying I wouldn't disturb Sebastian. His sobs had vibrated through the rectory most of the evening, but finally, he was silent. I prepared for bed, but before I could change into my nightgown, a pebble hit my window. I thought I imagined it, but I heard another ping, followed by one more. I peered down into the arbor. Kimball stood alone in the cold, lantern in hand.

A minute later, I tiptoed downstairs, my cloak cocooning me against the chilly air. I knew my parents would disapprove, but I must admit I enjoyed playing the saucy wench tiptoeing down the dark staircase for a tryst with a young man.

Despite the cold, the arbor smelled of lilac and jasmine. Kimball knelt before me on one knee. "Fair lady, it is I, your knight errant."

I placed my finger to my lip before I spoke. "Thank you for the flowery words, but we have to take care not wake my parents or Sebastian."

I looked into Kimball's smiling face. Where had my childhood friend gone? The young man before me stood tall and strapping. His manly beauty astounded me.

We moved farther into the bower and away from the rectory, whispering as we walked. "We're praying for the sailors tomorrow. Mayor Stoddard won't let us bury them, but we can honor them in death. Please, don't mention what I told you about their being poisoned. I'm afraid Sebastian will be there."

My words caused our stroll to come to an abrupt stop. Even in the dim lantern light, I could see Kimball's anger rise. For a moment, I couldn't speak, but then words flew from my mouth in a rush. "My parents won't talk about it, but I think Sebastian is insane."

His eyes revealed his confusion. "Insane? The only thing wrong with Sebastian is his arrogance."

I shook my head. "No, he appears calm, thoughtful and yes, arrogant, but you've never seen his outbursts of anger. Dr. Farnsworth says someone gave arsenic to the crew."

Kimball pressed his arms around me. "You don't think Sebastian poisoned them, do you?"

His proximity warmed me. "I don't know what to think." I pulled away and took his hand in mine. "He had no sympathy for the young men who died in the storm and insisted their bodies must go to Harvard for dissection."

We moved farther again into the arbor, away from earshot. "He'll stay here in Maidenhead."

He took a step toward me. "But I won't. Lucy, I'll be moving to Cambridge."

Cambridge? "You're going to Harvard so soon? I thought you weren't leaving until next year."

His lips stretched in a broad grin. "Yes, I thought so too, but thanks to your father, my knowledge of Latin impressed them. One must be well versed in Latin to study law."

What marvelous news for him, but not for me. "How wonderful, Kimball."

I threw myself in his arms, then remembered myself and quickly pulled away. "I'm happy for you. Imagine, you a Harvard man. I'm sure you'll be too grand to associate with the rustics of Maidenhead."

His grin disappeared. "Never, my darling Lucy. I've told you I love you. I've always loved you, and I'll never stop proclaiming it. When I'm in Cambridge, I'll dream of you every night."

I placed my hand over his mouth. "Please, you mustn't say such words."

Kimball turned my hand palm up and kissed it. He moved so close that I smelled the sea on him. "But I must. Promise you'll write. Promise you won't forget me. Promise one day we'll be wed."

I couldn't pull away from the comfort of his arms, and yet, I couldn't tell him I loved him too. "I'll promise the first two. I'll write daily if you wish. How can I forget a rascal like you? The last is impossible. I've told you, I plan to devote myself to the fight for women's suffrage, and I won't slave over a stove or scrub dirty britches for anyone."

He chuckled, his breath warm against my neck. "Well, Elizabeth Cady Stanton had seven children, and they didn't stop her from fighting for votes for women. Besides, if you married me, you wouldn't have to cook or clean. I grew up in an inn. I know my way around a stove. I'm the fastest chicken plucker in Massachusetts, and I can scrub my own britches. Don't forget, if you're a suffragist, you may need a lawyer in the future to keep you out of jail. If you don't marry me, I'll become a hermit like Caleb Potter, unwashed and unkempt, tripping over my long white beard, and it'll be your fault."

My face burned. I prayed he couldn't see my blush in the darkness of the garden. "Well, since you put it that way, Kimball, if I must marry, I suppose you'd be as good as any other man."

His teeth gleamed in the light, and his laughter filled the air. I feared he'd wake my parents, and I put my finger to my lips.

He took a step toward me and whispered into my ear, "I'll hold you to it, Lucy Stone Hathorne."

With that, he walked away, whistling.

I returned to my chamber, elated because I had a sweetheart, a Harvard man, and he loved me. The thought of Kimball's words made me swirl around the room, to dance in the dim light. Elated, I changed into my nightclothes and climbed into bed. I lay back on my pillow, giggling to myself. Of course, I wouldn't tell anyone about Kimball for a while, but nothing would ever be the same.

Then, in the stillness of the night, I heard a fierce howling from the bower. Agony filled every scream. The darkness of the keening took me aback. I looked down and saw Sebastian baying at the moon like a madman. Papa entered the garden, took him by the hand, and led him upstairs.

Chapter Thirteen
The Farewell

Sebastian awakened late the next morning, subdued and restrained. The hysteria of the previous day had disappeared. His lips trembled as he looked into the somber faces at the breakfast table, and the words tumbled from his mouth. "I'm so sorry for my behavior. Please forgive me."

Papa's lips tightened. "We forgive you, Sebastian. Now, have some breakfast."

My cousin sat and ate in silence.

The morning passed without incident. The four of us dressed in our Sunday togs in preparation for the funeral, Mama in a lovely wine-colored gown, Papa and Sebastian in matching frock coats. I wore a dark teal dress, the matching bonnet covering my head.

Papa checked his timepiece. "It's12:45. We should be on our way."

When we marched into the woods, we found Mr. Potter awaiting us in front of his hut. He stood at attention in his blue Union uniform, with Pedro crouched at his side.

"The gravediggers said you're praying for those lost boys today, Reverend Hathorne. Can me and Pedro walk with your family, sir?"

My father nodded to him. "Yes, Caleb, of course you're most welcome to join us. Those sailors will have few mourners. I pray they will look down at you from Heaven and bless you for your kindness."

We moved on to the True Believers' Burial Ground. Sebastian looked ahead and never uttered a word. When we reached the gate, Papa stopped the bear from following us into the graveyard. "Pedro, wait here."

Pedro plopped down on his haunches like a giant dog and didn't move.

Mama and I each carried bouquets made from the last of the flowers in our arbor. The weather had warmed, and the sky shone bright azure. Between the birds chirping and the whispering of the wind, the forest had come alive again. God had tasked us with praying for strangers on a magnificent day.

Doctor and Mrs. Farnsworth stood in wait near a moss-covered slab that a stoneworker had carved into the shape of a ship decades before. Cassie, Pyrtle, and Velda stood with Zeke and Kimball. Caleb took his place next to Sebastian, while Pedro remained near the weathered gate. Papa withdrew his pocket watch, noting the time. He opened his Bible and read from Corinthians:

"Now this I say, brethren, that flesh and blood cannot inherit the kingdom of God; neither doth corruption inherit incorruption. Behold, I shew you a mystery; We shall not all sleep, but we shall all be changed, In a moment, in the twinkling of an eye, at the last trump: for the trumpet shall sound, and the dead shall be raised incorruptible, and we shall be changed. For this corruptible must put on incorruption, and this mortal must put on immortality. So when this corruptible shall have put on incorruption, and this mortal shall have put on immortality, then shall be brought to pass the saying that is written, Death is swallowed up in victory. O death, where is thy sting? O grave, where is thy victory? The sting of death is sin; and the strength of sin is the law. But thanks be to God, which giveth us the victory through our Lord Jesus Christ.

"Therefore, my beloved brethren, be ye steadfast, unmovable, always abounding in the work of the Lord, forasmuch as ye know that your labor is not in vain in the Lord."

He closed his Bible and looked out at the mourners. "We didn't know the lost boys. They came to us from the water like Moses in the rushes. Just as the Egyptians of old took in the infant Moses, we embraced them as our own. Why did the Lord take young men so early? It is one of the mysteries only He can explain. Now their souls rest in the comfort of His bosom."

Without warning, Sebastian pulled his battered pennywhistle from his pocket and played a plaintive melody. Everything appeared tranquil until Caleb Potter started mumbling in soft whispers. "Goodbye, boys. Death is everywhere, all around us. The Lord always takes the best to Heaven, leaving us alone. Now these young fellows have joined my lost love."

He looked up to the heavens, tears rolling down his face. "They're dead like all those boys who shed their blood on the field of battle—dead!"

Everyone, including the gravediggers averted their heads in embarrassment. Mr. Potter called out, "Lord, why didn't you take me too? Why did you leave me in this living hell?"

The outburst ended. The embarrassed mourners

shifted in place. Mr. Potter suddenly stormed from the cemetery with Pedro plodding after him. Sebastian broke down into tears. "Oh, that poor, tormented man."

Velda rushed up to him, her arms open in embrace. "My darling Sebastian, you mustn't cry."

Except for her romantic fantasies, silly flirtations, and little vanities, Velda had once been a sensible girl who was devoted to her faith. Now Fate had turned the tables. Now the most flirtatious girl in the village was trapped in her own seductive web.

Kimball left Cassie's side and inched over to me. He spoke in whispers, his face as red as a tomato, his rage barely contained.

"Sebastian has bewitched my sister."

I averted my head. "Yes, I'm afraid he has. And she knows he's engaged to be married."

"It doesn't matter to Velda. He's all she talks about. I beg you, Lucy, speak to her."

His voice calmed. My gaze wandered back to his face. "I'll go to the inn and have a word with her. Let's hope she'll listen."

His teasing smile returned. "I'll never understand the ways of young girls, especially one young girl in particular."

I tossed my shoulders back. "Mr. Prince, I find young ladies to be much more sensible than young men."

****

That evening Mama and I began the most tedious part of quilting, attaching the quilt, the batting, and the backing together. The process took strong hands and a great deal of time. She caressed the cotton batting against her face. "I've always used rags and old blankets for batting, but I'm told this is the best made. Look at how full it is, so beautiful."

"It will make a splendid quilt." I'd thought about Caleb Potter's impassioned tirade all day and finally asked, "Mama, what happened to poor Mr. Potter to turn him into a lunatic?"

She looked up from her sewing. "It's a sad story, my love. The war ended fifteen years ago, but the horror of it left Caleb with a soldier's heart. When the madness comes on him, no one can reason with the poor man. The war broke him, as it did so many. We must—"

A rap at the door interrupted her words. She glanced up at the grandfather clock. "Eight o'clock? Who could be calling on us at this late hour?"

"I'll see, Mama."

I ambled down the hallway and opened the front portal. Sebastian stood at the threshold, grinning like a madman.

"Hello, my darling girl."

"Sebastian, why aren't you upstairs? Why did you knock, when you live here? Where have you been?"

Sebastian strode into the corridor, a silly smirk on his face. He couldn't seem to stop tittering. Where was the sensitive young man who had been devastated over poor Caleb?

"I've been a naughty boy, dear Lucy. I snuck out when no one was watching and went to the inn to sample its hospitality. Perhaps it's wrong to imbibe, but the mayor insisted on buying me a drink. Please, don't think I've turned into Caleb Potter. I only had two glasses of port, and now I must talk to my uncle."

Without warning, he swept me into his arms. "My

darling girl, I've thought of nothing but you all day." Sebastian spun me around before plunking me down and pulling away with a mad giggle. He walked toward the study, beaming all the while, reached his destination, and knocked on the closed door. "Uncle Braddock, I must talk to you."

Papa opened the door and stuck his head out. "What is it, Sebastian?"

"Uncle Braddock, after great thought, I've decided to move to the inn. My mentor at Harvard has wired funds, and I won't be a burden to you or Aunt Madeleine any longer."

My unsmiling father welcomed him into the room. "Come in, my boy. We must discuss it."

Before he strolled inside, Cousin Sebastian turned back to me with a broad grin on his angelic face. Papa closed the door.

When I rejoined my mother, she sat frozen on the settee.

"Mama, you were talking about the batting."

It took her a moment to focus on the task. "What? Oh, yes. We'll attach the quilt together with the rocking stitch. It needs a strong hand, a sharp needle, and a good thimble."

Before we could make a stitch, the shouting began. Papa's voice boomed through the closed door. Mama's head bounced up from where it was bent over the quilt.

"Sebastian, if you tell people about your voices, they'll think you're mad. Please, my boy, stay here in the rectory. Your aunt and I will take care of you."

My cousin chortled, but there was no mirth in it. "I'm not a child, Uncle Braddock. I'm eighteen, and I can take care of myself. Besides, the Lord in Heaven is watching over me. He speaks to me, you know."

I heard the urgency in Papa's voice. "You need us to protect you. You need sleep, Sebastian, rest, fresh air, and the love of your family. Please, stay here with those who want to protect you. Later, when you're stronger, we'll talk about moving elsewhere, but while you're in Maidenhead, you'll stay with us."

Sebastian snarled at my father, his dark voice filled with menace. "No, Uncle, you want to put me away in chains just as my father did. You hate me just because you know what an accomplished fellow Sebastian Hathorne is. I've surpassed every young man in my class at Harvard. You don't understand. The Lord has revealed to me that my brilliance will save the world."

Mama gasped at my cousin's words. Before she could speak, we heard scuffling at the study door. Had they come to blows?

Papa shouted out, "Sebastian, you can't leave! You must stay with us."

"Never!"

A loud boom told me the atlas had fallen or been thrown from its perch. Mama jumped up from her chair and rushed to the door, with me at her heels.

Papa continued reasoning with my cousin.

"Where does this rancor come from, Sebastian? My brother adored you—you were his pride and joy. Your aunt and I have always loved you. Your father wrote me when you turned fourteen. The change in you frightened him. When your father died, we opened our home to you, but you chose to stay in Boston with Dr. Stoker. We didn't argue because we knew life in a fishing village would stifle a boy of your brilliance, but now, we want you here. You are our blood, after all."

Another noise, as if someone threw a chair across the room.

"I knew it. Father betrayed me. Well, he's dead now and doesn't matter. He's just another blockhead who was jealous of my ability. Now I have to deal with Farnsworth, that pompous ass of a country doctor. I'm leaving here, Uncle, and I am overjoyed. I can't stand another day of the stench of boiled cabbage and the outdoor privy. I'll move to the inn, where I can bathe daily and use a flush toilet."

The room went silent until Papa spoke in gentle tones. "Very well, if you've already decided to go, then go, but know one thing. I'll be watching your every move."

The door opened, and Sebastian rushed out without glancing our way as he stormed from the house. Mama closed her eyes in relief. "Thank the Lord it's over."

The two of us looked into the study. Letters from abolitionists, including the great Frederick Douglass, had plastered the scarlet walls for years. They lay on the floor along with framed missives from those valiant souls who continued the fight for women's suffrage, including those of my namesake, Lucy Stone.

The room looked like the scene of an epic battle, furniture overturned, the pictures and letters still on the walls hanging askew. My father's papers from his desk were strewn across the room along with the broken frames and their contents.

Papa stared down at the destruction around him, his face solemn.

He turned toward me. "Poor Sebastian. I fear I've lost my nephew forever."

Chapter Fourteen
The Seer

The next morning, I found my father pacing up and down the length of the kitchen. He took a sip of coffee, placed the mug on the kitchen table, and continued moving from one side of the room to the other. From the set of his jaw and the look of determination etched on his face, I knew Sebastian's bizarre behavior consumed him.

Mama glared at Papa, crossed her arms, and pointed to the table.

"Braddock, sit down and finish your coffee."

He did as she asked, mumbling all the while. "That boy can't walk the streets of Maidenhead spewing his mad rants. I'll bring him back if I have to hogtie him."

"Promise me you won't let your temper get the worst of you and hurt him."

He softened for a moment. "Of course I won't. He may be a lunatic, but I love him like a son."

Papa brushed his lips against her forehead before racing off in search of my errant cousin.

Her shoulders slumped as she watched him depart. She turned to me after a long moment.

"Lucy, I need wood for the stove."

Sebastian had chopped enough wood to last throughout the winter, but I knew enough not to argue with her. I hacked a block of oak into kindling, dusted and swept the parlor, and made my way to the piazza. Broom in hand, my shoulders steeled, I battled the dirt from the street.

A pair of heavy boots clomped my way. I heard their thud against the cobblestones and turned in that direction. Papa made his way up the steps, his shoulders drooping. "I visited the apothecary, but Mr. Crackbone didn't know what mischief he was up to. I went to the inn to talk to Sebastian, but he refused to open the door to me."

I remembered Sebastian's outburst the night before. "Papa, let me find him. I'll talk some sense into him. Kimball asked me to speak to Velda, too. He's afraid she's falling under Sebastian's thrall."

Papa's face flushed scarlet, and he looked away. "With his charm and handsome looks, Sebastian will turn Velda's foolish head. Perhaps I should go with you."

I took his arm. "No, please. It would be better if Velda and I met alone. It's a delicate matter, and we both know she's prone to romantic notions."

Papa gave a shrug of resignation. "Yes, perhaps it would be a good idea, since you are her age."

"While I'm in town, I'll visit old Modesty, too. I've heard she's ailing. Scripture might be a comfort to her."

My father took the broom from my hands and began sweeping. "Your mother made gingerbread, Sebastian's favorite when he was a child. Maybe gingerbread will be your siren's call to the boy. It might do Modesty some good, too."

I remembered his love of gingerbread. "Mama's baking would cheer up anyone, and maybe I can convince Sebastian to return home. If he won't come, I'll ask Kimball to keep an eye on him."

When I turned toward the kitchen, Papa called out to me. "Before you go to town, stop by Caleb Potter's place. No one has seen hide nor hair of the poor fellow."

****

It sounded as if a thousand birds, revived by the warm air, twittered in the birch grooves. Although I wasn't looking forward to searching out Sebastian or conversing with Velda, I found myself cheered by the beauty surrounding me. "Mr. Potter, it's Lucy Hathorne."

Silence. I was sure his friend, demon rum, kept him company, and he slept away in his cottage, comforted by the bottle.

"Pedro. Pedro!"

I heard no growls or whimpers but left stew meat and a loaf of stale bread for the little bear anyway.

By the time I reached town, the square bustled with activity. Although few in Maidenhead hunted the giant beasts anymore, a whaler had docked the night before. When I moved past the Red Dog, the place rocked with the roar of hell-raising and ribald singing.

A group of sailors smoked their pipes and cigars in front of the Good Hope's entrance. They tipped their caps as I entered, but catcalled like vulgar hooligans when I passed. Kimball served rum punch to a group of rowdy fellows who elbowed each other when I entered. I ignored their rude stares and lewd whispers.

Kimball walked among the men, filling their mugs with hot rum. Warmth radiated throughout my body at his approach. How I loved him. He surely heard the drumming of my heart. It took all my strength not to break into nervous giggles. Instead, I kept my face averted so he couldn't see the flush crawling up my face

"Hello, Kimball, I've come to speak to Velda as you asked."

He gave a shake of his head. "I'm afraid you won't be able to. She, Fatima, and Cassie are upstairs with Sebastian. He's mesmerized my foolish sister, along with half the young girls in Maidenhead. Mayor Stoddard and Constable Heath came earlier and had a jolly time with him."

"Where is he?"

Kimball pointed to the staircase with a sneer. "Holding court in the big room on the second floor. He's bought out the haberdashery and is prancing around in his fine duds."

We gazed at each other for a moment. My pulse quickened and I saw a blush come to his face. "Kimball, Papa asked that you watch out for Sebastian. He seems out of sorts lately."

Kimball's lips twisted into another sneer. "I'll watch him, all right. I don't trust him a whit."

I ascended the staircase and made my way down the dimly lit corridor, the hiss of gas jets the only sound.

As I moved closer to my cousin's room, girlish tittering drifted down the corridor. The oak door stood ajar. I peeked into the anteroom, its amber walls covered with engravings of whaling ships. Empty boxes, twine, and torn shop paper lay scattered about the floor.

Sebastian, clean-shaven and impeccably groomed,

preened before a full-length mirror. From all the parcels littering the place, it appeared he'd emptied the haberdashery. He swiveled and posed, showing off his new attire. "Ladies, what do you think?"

I moved closer into the doorway. Fatima, a little Portuguese serving girl, stood next to Cassie, their hands clasped. Velda lay across the four-poster bed and simpered like a child. "Dear Sebastian, forgive my forwardness, but I must say you cut a fine figure."

He raised an eyebrow in her direction. "You vixen, are you trying to turn my head?"

Velda tossed back a curl. "Yes!"

The chamber rocked with girlish laughter. I entered unbidden. A blast of warm air greeted me when I crossed the threshold. "Sebastian, how are you?"

Sebastian raced over to me, his laughter almost musical. He took me by the waist and lifted me high in the air. "My savior, my darling cousin."

Cassie and Fatima applauded as he spun me around. "Oh, my dear girl, I owe you my life and will be in your debt forever." He turned his neck toward my face. "Tell me, Lucy, do I smell like a gentleman? I've scented myself with Marlborough, a British fragrance favored by gentlemen."

"Yes, it's quite wonderful." I found the fragrance cloying, but lied. He placed me back onto the floor but kept his eyes on my face.

I whipped the cake and a jar of hard sauce from my basket. The smell of ginger and molasses permeated the room and vanquished the Marlborough. "Sebastian, I brought a treat for you, some of Mama's gingerbread. You'll never taste better, except for Velda's wild strawberry tart."

When he turned his eyes to Velda, her skin colored bright pink. "You bake wild strawberry tarts? Why haven't you mentioned it? I'd climb up to the bluffs here with my mother when I was child and pick them. I haven't tasted their like since I moved to the city."

Cassie's attention remained on the gingerbread. "I'd love some, Lucy. I'm starving, and it smells heavenly."

Sebastian turned his gray eyes to me. Although he seemed in good spirits, they were dark and unfathomable. I giggled whenever I felt ill at ease and couldn't stop tittering like a ninny from the intensity of his gaze. "There's more than enough for everyone, and—please, keep this under your hats—I poured extra rum in the hard sauce, so be careful with your portions."

Velda dug a teapot from beneath a mound of brown paper. "I can attest to Mrs. Hathorne's skill at baking. Her cakes are marvels. We'll have a splendid tea."

Perhaps it was due to the events of the previous days combined with the overheated room and my cousin's cologne, but my head pounded like a bass drum. "Thank you for the invitation, Sebastian, but you have guests. Let's plan on a visit at another time."

He barred my way, took my wrist, and held it in his firm grip. "No, darling girl, you must stay and have tea."

Velda seconded his words. "Yes, Lucy, you must stay and make merry with us."

He continued holding on to me as I inched toward the door. "I'd love to, but I promised to stop by and see old Modesty. She's in poor health, so if you don't mind, I must say goodbye."

Sebastian relaxed his hold of my wrist. He turned to the girls, his lips spread in a warm smile. "Young ladies, please excuse me for a moment. I'll just accompany my cousin to the corridor. I'll return soon. I can't stay parted from such enchanting creatures."

He winked. Velda and Fatima tee-heed in unison, obviously smitten. Cassie didn't have a flirtatious bone in her body, and was consumed with the gingerbread.

Sebastian closed the door behind us. His jolly demeanor deserted him. "Lucy, we've much to discuss."

"Yes, we do. My parents want you home with them. We don't have an indoor privy, but Papa plans to build one. Until then, you can bathe every day if you wish. I'll prepare the water myself. Please, come back to the rectory with me."

He shook his head, determination etched on his face. "No, I must remain here. I've work to do before the schooner sails. The Lord spared me for a purpose. As much as I'd love to stay here in Maidenhead, my Lucy, I have to fulfill my destiny."

Manly chortling rolled up the stairwell from the lobby. Sebastian looked downstairs and his lip curled. "What rowdy fellows they are." He kissed my hand and bowed. "Will you ask your parents to forgive my horrible comments last night? I'm afraid I wasn't myself."

He smiled at me like a lost child, and my heart broke. I wanted to cup his beautiful face in my hands and spirit him away to the rectory. Instead, I turned and raced down the stairs to more loud guffaws. My unease increased at the proximity of the leering young men.

Kimball brushed past me with a tray full of mugs.

Before he dashed off, he managed to murmur in my ear, "Those hooligans came from Boston in an ice ship. They're taking the medical cadavers and those dead sailors with them."

Dear God in Heaven. I rushed outside.

****

A shiver went up my back the instant I saw the white sails of the ice ship moored at the dock. I marched in the direction of the oldest section of Maidenhead, toward the thatch-roofed cottages built when Pilgrims walked through streets rutted with mud. When I turned a corner, I smelled old lavender and heard the whisper of an ancient voice. "Bathsheba, I'm fatigued, take me home. There is death in the air."

Bathsheba held onto the arm of the blind seer and steered her down a cobbled street. Modesty had clad herself in emerald velvet and steadied herself with a crystal-headed walking stick. A sudden chill in the warm air circled me, but I approached them in spite of it and spoke into Modesty's right ear.

"Hello, Bathsheba. Modesty, it's Lucy Hathorne, Reverend Hathorne's daughter. Pyrtle Brigham said you were ailing. I'd planned to visit you, but you seem in fine fettle today."

Her blind eyes moved in the direction of my voice. "I am a very old woman, I shall never be fine, my dear. Still, my great-granddaughter, Bathsheba, nurses me and I am alive, but not for long. The Lord will call me to him soon." She sniffed the air. "I smell ginger through the scent of the dead."

"The scent of the dead?" My heart began racing. "It's the gingerbread I brought for you."

The ancient woman smiled, revealing a set of white

teeth as perfect as those of a young girl. "We will have tea, and I shall answer the questions you have."

What questions? I followed them toward the edge of town.

****

Bathsheba Ferris lived in a stone cottage built two centuries ago when the Indians had named the village Massasoit after a Wampanoag prince. English settlers christened it Maidenhead in tribute to a virgin who leapt to her death rather than surrender her virtue. The vine-covered hut had medicinal herbs and flowers planted in the surrounding earth, and the place smelled of purple Echinacea, day lily, and lavender.

I walked into the little dwelling, its walls painted dark crimson, the plank floors wide, from the last century. They'd replaced the thatched roof with white pine shingles and cooked on a wood-burning stove, but otherwise the cottage was much the same as when it had been built. Rusted lanterns barely illuminated the darkness.

We sat across from each other at a table hewn out of oak by Modesty's Pilgrim forbearers. "Sit here, Lucy, so I may hear you better." She positioned me next to her ear trumpet.

Some said Modesty had been a young girl during the Revolution and had met George Washington. Perhaps the story wasn't true, but many in Maidenhead swore the old seer was over a century in age. She wore tinted spectacles over her useless eyes and sat in a worn but richly upholstered parlor chair.

We sipped our tea from ancient china cups while Bathsheba slathered the gingerbread with hard sauce. Modesty placed her cup on the table and turned her blind eyes in my direction. The temperature inside the overheated cottage suddenly chilled.

"Dear child, in their wish to protect you, your parents have done you a grave disservice. Now the evil of the past has come to fruition, and you must be warned."

Bathsheba placed a restraining hand on the old seer's shoulder and spoke into her silver horn. "Great-Grandmother, perhaps we can discuss this at a different time."

The old woman ignored Bathsheba and signaled in my direction. "Move your chair closer, Lucy."

I shifted in my seat, straining to hear her tiny voice. The ancient one took my hand in her wrinkled paw. "Did you know you are related to the great writer Nathaniel?"

"Yes, Papa said a branch of the Hathorne clan changed the family name after the witch trials of Salem by adding a 'w' to their surname. The Hathornes of Maidenhead kept the original spelling."

Old Modesty furrowed her brow. "Yes, but did he tell you why they changed the name? Guilt. It was because of guilt. Did he tell you there were witch trials here in Maidenhead as well as in Salem?"

Everyone in Maidenhead had heard the stories, but few believed them. "But that's just an old tale, isn't it?"

The ancient gave her head a shake. "No. The Hathornes hanged my own great-grandmother as a witch. I do not blame you or your father. Reverend Hathorne is a virtuous man, but his ancestors were mad as hatters. They brought their English malady to Maidenhead."

At that moment, the grandfather clock chimed, and

I almost jumped from my chair. "But you're wrong, Modesty. There is no madness in my family, except for—" I thought of Sebastian and suddenly couldn't utter a word.

Modesty chuckled without mirth, her teeth white in the dim light. "Another lunatic has come to tear our little village asunder. You know I speak the truth. Ask your father why you have no siblings. Insist he tell you everything. The boy, Sebastian, cannot help bringing ruination with him." She moved closer. "My girl, his desire for you is unnatural and dangerous."

Without warning, the old woman's head sank to her chest and nodded to the side as if she'd fallen asleep. Except for the crackling of logs in the fire, the hut was still.

Bathsheba took my hand. "It's time you leave, my dear."

Chapter Fifteen
A Truth Revealed

I stumbled from Bathsheba's cottage, so stunned by Modesty's words I could barely make my way to the street. Instead of returning home, I walked through the woods to the burial ground. After the old woman's comments about my family, I longed for quiet. I made my way to the family plot, past the old proper names, Everlasting, Forbearance, Sanctity, all my ancestors, all Hathornes. Tea with Modesty had ripped the scales from my eyes. For some reason, most Hathorne women remained spinsters, but those who hadn't done so and hadn't died in childbirth managed to live well into middle age. It was not the same with the males, however. Few Hathorne men reached thirty.

A sudden wind gust caused me to drop my basket. I stooped to retrieve it. A powerful sensation overwhelmed me, as if a pair of eyes bore into my back. I spun around and saw no one. My skin turned to gooseflesh. Someone or something watched me. I rushed through the woods and passed Caleb Potter's hut.

"Mr. Potter? Pedro?"

I found the quiet deafening and thought about entering his little hovel unannounced. Instead, I trudged back to the rectory.

****

I crawled up the piazza steps and fumbled the front door open. A glissando from my mother's harp led me into the parlor. Mama sat behind the instrument, turning the tuning-key with one hand, plucking the strings with the other. "The harp sounded a bit sharp, but she's fine now." She gazed into my face. "What's wrong?"

I felt my lip trembling. "I've come from Bathsheba's cottage. Old Modesty told me things, horrible things. She said the Hathornes have madness in their bloodline. Please, tell me it's not true, please."

Mama's eyes opened wide. She jumped up from the harp and wrung her hands as she often did when her nerves got the better of her. She twisted the blood from them, and her fingers looked as if a sculptor had carved them from alabaster. "How I wish I could say it's not true, but I can't." My mother gazed into my face. "Yes, there's insanity in your father's family, and no cure. I'd hoped to spare you the truth for a bit longer."

Tears rolled down my cheeks like rivers. "Will I go mad too?"

She rose and took my hand. "No, my darling, not you, never you. Come with me to the arbor. We must talk to your father."

Papa always sat on the ancient wooden bench in our little orchard among the McIntosh and peach trees when he reflected on life. Mama perched herself in a weathered Adirondack chair, and I plunked down next to my father without a word. My head throbbed, my pulse raced, and I turned into a mass of jangled nerves the moment I sat. I couldn't stop my giggles, but thankfully, Papa calmed the titters away by stroking my hand.

Black-capped chickadees serenaded us as we drank

hot cider. Cinnamon and apples spiced the air. Although I found the homey fragrance comforting, my words came out in halting phrases.

"I visited Old Modesty today. Oh, Papa—" I found it almost impossible to continue. "She spoke of madness in our family." I found myself fighting back my tears. "You have to tell me. Is it true? Will I go insane like Sebastian?"

I threw myself into his arms. He rocked me the same way he did when I suffered nightmares as a child.

"Shush, my darling, not you. Insanity has plagued the Hathorne family for centuries, even before we came to Maidenhead. The malady ravages the most gifted, often before they see their twenty-fifth birthday." A sob erupted from his chest, and the tears rolled down his face.

"You never knew my older brother Carlyle. A brilliant Harvard jurist, adored by the gods and the fairer sex, yet he died by his own hand at twenty-six."

Papa allowed the words to sink in before he spoke. "It's always the same, my dear. First, deep sadness, followed by grandiose behavior, bold words, voices from beyond, and extreme carnal desire. My father spoke to an alienist but couldn't help him. He planned to place Carlyle in an asylum, but his suicide thwarted his hand."

He slid closer, and I felt the weight of his arm around my shoulder. "I'm sorry, Lucy. We should have told you."

The sound of honking flooded the sky. Papa stopped speaking and looked up at the heavens as a flock of wild geese flew past. How I wished I could have flown away with them.

I looked to Mama. "Does this mean I'll go mad, turn into a criminal or a wanton woman, or end up on the gallows?"

She'd been silent all the while. "No, not you. It only afflicts the Hathorne boys."

My tears continued to fall, but they were tears of relief. Mama knelt in front of my chair. "When we wed, your father and I decided against having children. It pained both of us, more than I can say. We both love children so much." Tears rolled down her cheeks. "I only had my sister, and your father had lost Carlyle. I wanted a baby so badly." She glanced back at Papa. "We swore we'd be careful, but we loved each other with such passion. When I became enceinte, I didn't tell your father until it was too late."

I knew that midwives had teas that brought on a woman's monthly courses, but never did I think my mother would have used them. "You tricked Papa? Papa, you didn't want me?"

My father rose from the bench and tipped my face toward his.

"Of course we wanted you! When you came to us, it was the most joyful day of our lives. When you were born, I carried you around Maidenhead because I wanted everyone to see my beautiful daughter. You gave us so much happiness." He sat down next to me. "We wanted a house full of girlish laughter, but we dared not chance another baby because it might be a boy. Bathsheba used her skill at midwifery to help us. I've often wished we'd tried one more time, but after seeing Sebastian, I can only give thanks we didn't."

I blurted another secret. "Sebastian claims he wants to marry me."

Papa's face darkened. "Yes, I know, my darling. He has already asked for your hand. When I told him it was impossible, he howled like a lunatic."

As I sat in the quiet, pondering my father's words, my thoughts turned to Kimball. He adored babies and would want a family. I looked from my father to my mother.

"Does this mean I should never have children?"

Neither answered. The three of us sat together in silence until my parents left me alone in the arbor.

****

The next afternoon, after I completed my chores, I left for the inn once more to speak to Velda. I couldn't break my promise to Kimball.

When I arrived, I found him at the entrance, clipping the hedges. How could I tell him we'd never wed? I'd thought long and hard about it. I'd planned to devote my life to women's suffrage, but in my heart of hearts, I'd harbored a secret hope for marriage and children too. Now I knew it would never happen.

I curtsied, and attempted a smile.

"Good day, Kimball. I'm here to speak to Velda."

When Kimball's face broke into a glorious grin, I felt my eyes filling with tears and looked away. We could never be more to each other than friends.

"Be firm with her, my Lucy."

His gaze stayed on me, and I could barely look at him. I saw concern in his face. "Is something the matter?"

How could I tell him that my world had been ripped apart? "Oh, I'm quite well, Kimball. I'll be firm with Velda. Where is she?"

He pointed upstairs. "You'll find her preparing

rooms for our guests."

I ascended the stairway, unsure of what I'd say to my friend, and paused at the head of the stairs before I shambled down the corridor. When I reached Sebastian's room, I tiptoed past, hoping he wouldn't hear my footsteps. Velda's voice pulled me back.

"Please, Sebastian, we shouldn't."

"But why not, my love? I promise you, I'll be gentle. You mustn't worry, my sweet. I'm practically a doctor. My body aches at the thought that you are mine. Let me look at you, my darling."

He spoke in honeyed tones. "I sometimes have a queer feeling with regard to you, especially when you are near me, as now. It is as if I had a string somewhere under my left ribs, tightly and inextricably knotted to a similar string situated in the corresponding quarter of your little frame."

The rotter had quoted from Jane Eyre, and seduced my friend with Bronte's words.

Velda's moans punctured the silence. She groaned the same sounds I'd heard through my bedroom wall, ones Mama often made in the dark of night with Papa, whispers of pleasure.

Sebastian spoke in a lewd whisper. "I have for the first time found what I can truly love. I have found you. You are my sympathy, my better self, my good angel. Ah, yes, my darling girl."

At that point, I called out in the corridor, "Velda, Velda, where are you? Your mother is looking for you."

The chamber door opened, and Velda rushed out, her hair trailing to her waist, her bodice askew. I looked into the room. Her split drawers lay on the floor.

I stormed into the chamber as bold as brass and

grabbed Velda's underwear from the floor. Sebastian had a massive bulge bursting from his trousers, and I looked away. Yes, I'd grown up in a rectory, but I knew about male arousal.

Sebastian called out to me, his voice urgent. "Lucy, you don't understand. Please, my darling."

I understood all right, but instead of confronting him, I slammed the door in his face.

Velda stood in the hallway, her head leaning against the wall, her body wracked with sobs. I placed a hand on her shoulder, and she turned to me, tears rolling down her cheeks.

"Please, Lucy, don't tell Mother. She'll put me out, and I'll be disgraced. This was the first time I let Sebastian touch me, I swear. He's begged me from the beginning, just as Hiram Endicott did. I still have my virtue, Lucy. I swear I do."

I smelled his cologne on her, and prayed she didn't lie. "Velda, you must stay away from him. Sebastian can't help himself. He'll be your ruin. Promise me you'll stay away from him."

When I handed her the underwear, Velda's face turned scarlet. "Lucy, I can't promise. I love him, and he loves me too."

I wanted to share Sebastian's mad fantasies about me, but I decided against it. "Sebastian has a fiancée, a beautiful, wealthy young woman whom he professes to adore. I'm sure despite his youth he's romanced others."

She shook her head. "How can you or Cassie or Pyrtle understand? You haven't known passion as I have."

When I took her arm, she shook me off. "Sebastian

said someone might try to say horrible things about him, but he thought it would be your father. Your father hates him."

I threw my shoulders back. "Papa loves him like a son and wants him to return home, to the rectory, where he can be protected."

Velda turned to me, and I saw the determination in her green eyes. Nothing I could say would dissuade her. She straightened her bodice and then looked me dead in the eye.

"Lucy, I'm not brave like Cassie, or a scholar like you, or clever like Pyrtle. I'm pretty, men like me, but none of it mattered until I met Sebastian."

At that moment, I wanted to thrash her. Instead, I took her by the shoulders and shook her with as much force as I could muster. "You've heard his rants. You must realize he's insane."

Velda wrenched away and spat her words at me. "Sebastian told me people would say he's a madman, but I didn't think you would be one of them. He's a genius, too brilliant for this world."

She attempted to pass, but I stepped in front of her. "Maidenhead is a small town, Velda. If anyone finds out about your dalliance with Sebastian, the consequences will be dire. Kimball might kill him if he discovers what you've done."

At the mention of her brother, I glimpsed a modicum of her fear mingled with reason.

"Wash your face, braid your hair, and please, put on your underclothes."

The tears continued rolling down her cheeks. I took her face in my hands. "I'm your friend, Velda. I don't judge you."

Before she raced off, she gave my cheek a sisterly kiss and left me alone to ponder my lie.

I did judge her. Velda knew Sebastian had a fiancée even before she met him. She'd heard the insanity in his words, yet chose to ignore it. Perhaps he hadn't taken her virginity yet, but she possessed a volatile nature. She imagined herself a combination of Jane Eyre and Catherine Earnshaw, with Sebastian as both her Heathcliff and her Mr. Rochester. She dreamed of a Thornfield Hall somewhere in Boston. Unfortunately, instead of a mad wife chained in the attic, the maniac was her hero.

The lobby still vibrated with male laughter when I returned downstairs. Kimball poured rum for the rowdy crowd. He glanced up at my approach. The ruffians were too involved in drunken antics to notice when he took me aside.

"What happened with my sister?"

I censored the salacious details of our meeting. "We spoke. I think Velda will walk the straight and narrow, but please watch her, and keep her away from my cousin. I'm afraid Sebastian can't control his baser nature."

Kimball's face reddened, and his smile vanished in an instant. "Are you saying he's had his way with her?"

He lurched toward the stairs, but I grabbed his arm. "No, there's nothing between them, just a flirtation, but you know her romantic fantasies. Please, Kimball, keep her away from him."

A roar went up from the men. "More rum, barkeep."

Kimball looked from them to me and then marched toward the hooligans without a word.

****

The heat from the potbelly stove enveloped me the moment I entered Brigham's Dry Goods. The place bustled with patrons spending their precious coin on lanterns, candles, and wooly blankets in the event of another squall. Mrs. Brigham unfolded a union suit and held it up to the light. Mrs. Tateshall, the chandler's wife, scrutinized the underwear and ran her finger up and down each seam.

"My son wears his long underwear for weeks on end when he's out fishing. I have to boil them clean, so they better be strong."

Mrs. Brigham turned the garment over. "Look at this stitching and the two flaps, one in the back, one in the front. You'd have to search far and wide, Mrs. Tateshall, to find better than this."

The chess-playing old salts kept to their game, ignoring the droning hubbub about the dead sailors. They remained deaf to the conversation about the cadavers washed up on the shoreline that buzzed throughout the place.

Zeke inspected a cord of hemp rope with Lincoln, Pyrtle's younger brother. Lincoln may not have been the best speller in Maidenhead, but everyone in town marveled at his skill at selling.

"It's the strongest made, stronger than what they sell in the chandlery."

Pyrtle sat at her counter, giving a telegram the final flourish in her beautiful cursive. She looked up and waved me over.

My friend sniggered when I approached. From her mischievous expression, I knew she had a quip ready. "Good to see you, Lucy Hathorne. Tell me, have you

125

gone searching for another body?"

I didn't care for her jocular manner, but remained polite. "No." I looked around the store and murmured my question. "Pyrtle, I have a question, and please, be honest with me. Has my cousin been acting, well, peculiar?"

She scrutinized me, her head turning from one side to the other. "Sebastian? No, he's the jolliest of fellows, although, I must admit, he gets a bit saucy at times. I had to remind him more than once I'm an engaged woman."

I couldn't stop a sigh of relief from escaping my lips. She turned her head from side to side, obviously confused, and I decided to change the subject.

"You'll be happy to hear Mama and I have made great headway on your quilt. We might finish it ourselves."

Her hazel eyes narrowed. "You won't. It's my quilt, for my wedding, and I want it to look the way I wish. Perhaps Cassie and I can stop by the parsonage tonight after supper."

Having the girls over would be a respite from the intensity of the past day. "Fine. You might want to ask Velda, too."

She gave a toss of her red hair. "Velda? I don't think so. She's been quite strange lately. All she talks about is Sebastian. I told her it's unseemly, but she doesn't care."

I looked away. "Ask her. I have the feeling she might want to join us."

Pyrtle pursed her lips in a pout. "Well, if you want the silly goose to quilt with us, I'll invite her." She looked at me, a saucy grin on her face. "But enough of

Velda. A certain somebody got a parcel all the way from Boston."

I'd seen my cousin's stacks of letters and telegrams. "Sebastian gets his share of correspondence, doesn't he?"

Her grin turned peevish. "It's not for your cousin, it's for you, you blockhead, a parcel from Miss Ida Stoker. I'm expecting that you'll open it tonight."

I decided to give Pyrtle a dose of her own medicine. "Maybe I will and maybe I won't."

She rolled her eyes as she handed me an oblong box wrapped in brown shop paper.

I walked out of the store with my nose in the air.

Chapter Sixteen
Gifts

After supper, my parents and I huddled over the package. Mama took great care not to tear the brown shop paper covering the Spanish cedar box embossed with golden fleurs de lis. "Have you ever seen anything so beautiful before? I'll save it for Christmas." When she lifted the lid, lavender fragrance filled the room. She unfolded the ochre tissue paper and handed me the enclosed note, written on fine linen writing paper.

While I read the contents aloud, my mother pulled out the treasures hidden inside.

My dear Lucy,

Thank you for your marvelous quilt. It was an unexpected gift and now sits at the foot of my bed.

Mama removed five sets of beautiful kid gloves packed in tissue and placed them in front of my father. "I needed a new pair of gloves."

The gloves are French, one pair for your dear mother, another for you, the others for the girls in your quilting circle.

Papa inspected the gifts. "I don't know anything about ladies' gloves, but these look to be of the highest quality. Lucy, you must ask the girls to write a note of thanks."

Mama pulled out five embroidered handkerchiefs edged in lace and held one up to the light.

The handkerchiefs are the finest made. I am sure you will not find their like in Maidenhead.

Mama tucked a handkerchief into her sleeve. "Madame St. Pierre doesn't have anything so elegant in her shop."

An object wrapped in the ochre tissue glittered from inside the box. I hope the watch fob will please your father.

Mama held up a beautiful fob, the polished chain gleaming in the lamplight. "Braddock, look—it's sterling silver."

Papa laughed as he pulled his watch from his pocket and switched his old fob for the new one. "I know Ida comes from money, but her gifts are so extravagant that we must write her tonight."

I hope you and your family are in good health and that the blessings of our Lord are upon you. I look forward to the time that we meet in the flesh.

Boston is quite gay these days, and everyone is wearing narrow skirts. Small bustles are the mode for young ladies, but one still sees trains and large bustles on matrons. I've enclosed the latest Harper's Bazaar and hope you and your chums enjoy the fashion plates.

Mama looked deeper into the box. "What is this?" She retrieved another envelope of fine linen, with the words Reverend Hathorne written in a masculine scrawl, and handed it to Papa. Her face betrayed nothing, but I felt her unease.

Ida hadn't sealed the envelope, and Papa hesitated before removing the missive. He unfolded the letter and read in silence. I didn't know the contents, but his face darkened as he perused the document. After he finished scrutinizing the letter, he looked up at us. "I'm afraid the situation is direr than I thought."

Reverend Hathorne,

My named is Dr. Quinton Stoker. I reside in Boston with my daughter. As you know, Ida is engaged to your nephew, Sebastian. I have not told Ida, but there will be no marriage. I send this missive as a warning. The details are of a most shocking nature; unfortunately, everything I have written is true. After you have perused the pages, I beg you, burn them immediately. They are too dangerous to consign to the hands of others.

You are the only person on this earth to whom I can reveal this. Sebastian suffers from a horrible malady, and I fear he's quite mad. His father took him to Europe in the hope to find a cure for his illness but, alas, could not. No alienist had a cure for his mental state. He is a youth of noble character and generous to a fault, but when his illness is upon him, he is capable of monstrous acts. He is terrified I will place him in a lunatic asylum, although I have sworn I never will.

There are those who have used his condition to their benefit and have stoked his fear. Men of great power in Boston have ensnared Sebastian and flattered him into doing their bidding. They arranged for Sebastian to go to Montreal to acquire medical cadavers; unfortunately, I could not stop him. The poor boy is in the clutches of a secret anatomical society whose name I dare not utter or even write.

Warn your daughter's friends about Sebastian. He has a thirst for carnal pleasure. Despite his youth, women rush to him like moths to a flame. Although he tries to behave like a gentleman, he cannot stop himself when he sees a comely girl.

I will not allow him to marry my daughter. The boy is unbalanced. I must find a safe place for him before the scandal of his misdeeds makes him a pariah in Boston. My daughter is beautiful and will have other suitors. Please, keep Sebastian in Maidenhead until I can find a suitable sanatorium for him either in Massachusetts or on the Continent.

Continue walking in the path of the Lord.

Sincerely,

Dr. Stoker

My mother didn't utter a word when Papa tossed the letter into the fireplace. He watched it turn to ash, his face impassive. "I'll visit the inn tomorrow and try to reason with Sebastian."

Mama took him by the wrist. "Braddock, promise me you won't do anything out of anger."

He placed an arm around her shoulders. "I'd never use force with him, Madeleine. I'll be persuasive without violence, but Sebastian has to stay here in the rectory, where we can watch him."

****

That evening after supper, Velda, Pyrtle, and Cassie took their places in the parlor. I shared Ida's letter and elegant gifts with them. When I read Ida's missive aloud, Pyrtle and Cassie chortled at her jokes, but Velda didn't join them. Instead, she sewed away, a pout affixed to her lips.

Cassie held her gloved hands up to the light. "With these on, no one can see my calluses." She pressed a lavender-scented handkerchief to her nose before putting it in her pocket. "It's fit for a true lady."

Pyrtle looked at her as if she were a barbarian. "Cassie, a lady carries her handkerchief in her reticule."

My tomboyish friend appeared to be confused. "But I don't have a reticule and wouldn't know what to do with one anyway. I don't use a kerchief that often. I usually wipe my nose on my sleeve."

Pyrtle gave her look of resignation. "Cassie, a true lady would never wipe her nose on her sleeve, but I guess she could use her apron if she didn't have something better."

Velda had been in a prickly mood all evening and remained silent. She ignored her gifts and refused to touch Ida's letter. Her attitude took Pyrtle aback.

"Don't you want to read the letter, Velda?"

She turned her pretty nose up. "I'm not interested."

Cassie greeted Velda's words with a snort. She pointed to a fashion plate of a stylish young woman sheathed in a form-fitting toilette in Harper's Bazaar. "How can a girl row in such narrow skirts?"

Pyrtle chuckled at her naivety. "Ladies don't row in the city. They drive around in fancy carriages and sit in their parlors eating bonbons. Servants wait on them hand and foot. Must be a boring life, nothing I'd like. Probably don't have a brain in their pretty heads."

Velda had been stitching away in silence, but suddenly perked up. Although she spoke to Pyrtle, I knew her remarks were addressed to me. "Pyrtle, I been thinking. Your ceremony should take place on Hagatha's Leap. It's so picturesque."

All eyes turned to Velda.

Pyrtle's jaw nearly dropped to the floor. "Hagatha's Leap, the bluff where the lighthouse stands? It's a pretty place—beautiful, in fact—but no one would climb that steep path for a wedding. I'll be married in the arbor behind the rectory and take my vows beneath the pergola."

Velda pouted, her tone insistent. "But anyone can be married in an arbor. The Leap overlooks the whole cove, and besides, the story is so beautiful." She tilted her head in my direction. "Hagatha, a girl of unblemished reputation, leapt to her death rather than surrender her virtue to a drunken sailor. What a shining example of moral rectitude. I took Sebastian there and he declared it the most beautiful place on earth. Besides, didn't the Pilgrim Fathers name our town Maidenhead in honor of a virgin's most chaste secret? Imagine a girl so intent on keeping her purity that she killed herself. I think I'd rather die than be defiled."

In light of her behavior with my cousin, some would find her words hypocritical, but I didn't chastise her. "Well, Velda, weak creature that I am, I'd choose to live."

Pyrtle was so intent on finishing her part of the quilt, she spoke without looking up from her stitching. "Seems to me a lot of young ladies from old days preferred defilement to death. Just look at the church's baptism records, all those lasses who had their babies three or four months after getting hitched."

Cassie responded with a giggle. "Maybe whoever kept the records couldn't count to nine." Everyone laughed except Velda.

We worked until seven-thirty that evening. Barring the border that still needed to be added, we'd almost finished the Rose of Sharon quilt. We stepped back, admiring our handwork.

Pyrtle appeared delighted. "It will be grand, the best we've ever made."

Velda stroked it against her cheek. "I think it's

enchanted."

She inhaled the fabric. "We're all in this quilt and will be part of it forever."

As if guided by an unknown spirit, we touched the quilt at the same time. Pyrtle gave voice to what we all were thinking. "Yes, it is enchanted."

After we'd folded the quilt and put away the frame, my redheaded friend took my arm. "Lucy, my brother's working the teletype tomorrow. He still can't spell a lick, but Mama insisted he learn, so I'll finally have the morning free. Shall we make some of your wonderful chowder and bring it to Mrs. Tateshall, the chandler's wife? I hear she's been ailing."

"What a wonderful idea. Perhaps we can bring some to Modesty and take a bowl to Caleb Potter, too. No one has seen him in a while. He must be under the weather."

While many might think me guilty of the sin of pride, some in our village swore my chowder was the finest in Massachusetts. I've often wondered—if Our Lord Jesus Christ could feed the multitudes with loaves and fishes, what would He have done with a kettle of chowder? I nodded. "That's a capital idea, Pyrtle."

The grandfather clock chimed, letting us know that the sewing would end.

The girls and I were still tidying the parlor when Kimball stepped into the drawing room, lantern in one hand.

"The lamplighter's ailing, and some of the men are liquored up on whiskey, so I came to walk the girls to their homes." He held out a box carved from rosewood in his other hand. "Brought you something, Lucy."

Pyrtle tittered. "Perhaps we should wait in the

hallway, girls." My three friends left the chamber, giggling and whispering all the while. Kimball and I stood alone.

"For me?"

He nodded, an ear-to-ear grin on his face. "Of course, who else? It's called a ditty box, for earbobs and the like. See, I carved your initials inside the rose on top."

When I opened the box, I discovered another carving, a heart intertwined with the initials L.H and K. P. I'm sure my face flared red, but I hoped he couldn't see it in the dim light.

"Kimball, it's so beautiful, my second surprise of the day. A young lady sent gloves and handkerchiefs in thanks for one of our quilts. This is so much grander, only one would think we'd promised to each other, but of course, we're not." My lip quivered, and I felt my eyes dampen. "I'm afraid I can't be engaged to anyone."

He finished my sentence by putting his lips on mine, a chaste kiss, like fathers give their daughters, but I don't think he meant it chastely. Luckily, my friends were still in the parlor and no one saw it. He pulled away, smirking like the cat that ate the canary.

"Miss Lucy Hathorne, whether you believe it or not, we're betrothed."

I placed my lips to his right ear, scalding tears rolling down my cheeks.

"No, I can't be your intended, Kimball. I can never marry. I found out something horrible." I took a breath and spoke in a rush. "There's madness in my bloodlines, insanity among the Hathorne males. That's why Sebastian behaves in such a strange way. I might bear a bunch of lunatics."

Kimball took me by the shoulders and looked me directly in the eyes. "I've heard the story bandied about, but it doesn't matter a whit to me. Massachusetts is full of mad people. Our children would fit in perfectly."

Kimball winked at me, his eyes sparkling, and then strolled away without looking back. I'd once thought him the most annoying boy in all of New England. Now, I liked the kiss even more than the ditty box.

****

The next morning, I started my chowder for the unfortunates confined to their homes. Pyrtle arrived, carrying a small gunnysack into the kitchen. "Got the potatoes all ready, Lucy."

We prepared a cauldron's worth, a brew of quahogs, mussels, salt cod, potatoes, salt pork, cream, and bacon.

Pyrtle looked into the pot. "The villagers will devour this in no time. Before we cook up another batch, let's call on Caleb Potter. Nobody's seen hide or hair of him since the day we mourned the dead sailors."

We were off to the white woods and Mr. Potter's hut. The place appeared even more desolate than usual. Pyrtle glanced my way. "Goodness, why is it so quiet?"

Mr. Potter never locked his door, since the only unwelcome intruders in Maidenhead were cold and illness. Pyrtle knocked before entering.

"Caleb Potter, it's Pyrtle Brigham and Lucy Hathorne come to bring you breakfast."

When he didn't respond, she opened the door. The intense, eye-watering stench of decomposition hit us like a bucket of sewage. Our knees buckled, and Pyrtle clutched her stomach and vomited at the threshold. I wrapped my shawl around my nose and stepped inside.

The overwhelming stink of decay permeated the room. The buzzing of a thousand blowflies busily laying their eggs punctured the stillness. Caleb, or what was left of him, perched on a chair at his table, still dressed in his army uniform. His unruly mop of dark hair topped the remains of his skull. Caleb's face, however, had disappeared, replaced by a mass of writhing maggots. An empty rum bottle sat atop the table.

I turned, rushed out of the cottage, grabbed Pyrtle's hand, and we rushed away. "Rum took poor Caleb down, and he won't be eating chowder this day!"

Chapter Seventeen
Death Angel

Pyrtle and I raced to the Red Dog. Mr. Potter's drinking partners usually dawdled at the entrance, passing a bottle of rum back and forth, but not that day. I peeked into the tavern, a dank, malodorous place filled with soused sailors. Pyrtle and I steeled our shoulders before we strode inside. We must have been quite a sight, our dresses askew, hair rumpled, but most of the customers were too drunk to notice.

My words came out in breathy gasps. "Caleb Potter—dead as a doornail—in his hut."

Pyrtle found her voice. "From the smell of him, he's been gone for a while."

The men roused out of their stupors and rushed from the place.

Pyrtle dashed to the inn to find the constable, while I searched for Dr. Farnsworth. I reached his home and yanked on the bell pulley until Mrs. Farnsworth answered the door. "Whatever is the matter, Lucy?"

"It's Caleb Potter. Pyrtle and I found him dead in his hut. Such a horror, ma'am."

It took a moment for her to comprehend my words. "What dreadful news about that poor, tormented man. I'll go to the rectory and tell your father. You'll find my husband making his rounds in the old part of town."

Ten minutes later, I spied Dr. Farnsworth heading

toward an ancient stone shanty with a thatched roof. He walked at a rapid pace, his medical bag in hand, a determined look on his face. I called to him, breaking his concentration.

"Dr. Farnsworth, Dr. Farnsworth, Caleb Potter is dead."

He made an abrupt stop. "Caleb Potter? Dead, you say?"

My breaths came in heaves. "Yes, sir. I'm afraid he died a while ago. He looks horrible, stinks like the devil. He's still wearing his uniform, so he must have died the day we prayed for the sailors."

The doctor shook his head. "The poor fellow has found peace at last." Dr. Farnsworth's voice carried down street as he ran off in the direction of his house. "My patient will have to wait. Let me change."

A few minutes later, Dr. Farnsworth had donned his roughest clothes—patched trousers, threadbare shirt, and worn fishing boots. "If his body is as far gone as you said, my good shoes won't be worth a nickel if I get too near."

He followed me to the woods, where we met the burying men, who waited several yards away from the hut. They'd started a fire, heated the chowder, and devoured it on the spot. "Ain't right to waste good chowder."

Constable Heath stood in front of Caleb's hovel, his skin green with nausea, a kerchief over his nose. "Tried to go in there, but the stench drove me back."

Dr. Farnsworth pulled a cigar from his breast pocket and lit it. "This helps with the stink. I learned the trick during the war. Can't do a dissection in my house, with the smell, but I'll take a look at him."

The constable took his arm. "Be careful, sir. Pedro, his bear, is likely in the hut. I warned Caleb about keeping that beast as a pet."

The burial men grumbled among themselves. Finally, one spoke up. "Don't worry about Pedro. If he's there, I'll shoot him straight away, and blast him cold as a wagon tire. Once a beast has tasted human flesh, you can't do nothing with it."

Dr. Farnsworth shook his head. "I know the creature. He wouldn't have touched Caleb. If he's in there, he won't hurt me."

The doctor called out, "Pedro, Pedro," before pulling his kerchief over his nose. He entered the hut, staggered out a couple of minutes later holding a rum bottle, and vomited up his breakfast.

"Caleb's dead, all right, but not from rum. I think someone poisoned him. The beast must have stayed with the body but left when it started to rot." He pointed to a battered canvas sail rolled up against a wall. "Wrap Caleb in that, dig a hole nearby, and bury him right away. I can't embalm the poor fellow. He's too far gone. Be careful with him. You don't want to get the smell on you."

Dr. Farnsworth said a few quiet words to the constable. He turned from him and signaled to me. "We should be off to the parsonage, Lucy. I must talk to your father." He called out once again. "Pedro, come here, Pedro."

I heard neither a whimper nor growl. The doctor looked around the hut once more. "The only witness to Caleb's death can't name the culprit."

We marched under a canopy of pine toward town. Dr. Farnsworth's angry voice echoed throughout the woods. "I never thought we'd find a murderer in our midst. We've lived by the letter of the law for so long, but now what can I say? Devilish is the only word for it, dear girl. I'm afraid it will get worse. I've treated smallpox, cholera, and measles, but insanity is beyond my skill as a physician."

His words confused me. "What are you saying, sir?"

Dr. Farnsworth's face turned as red as an apoplectic, his mouth set in a grim line.

"I'd bet my soul Sebastian was involved. That empty bottle of rum had remnants of some substance in it, probably poison. Thank the Lord I don't have to go back to Caleb's cabin of horrors to retrieve it. Of course, I can't prove murder, but your parents can attest to the boy's insanity."

I stepped away from him. "Dr. Farnsworth, I admit it, my cousin is afflicted, but why would he kill Caleb Potter?"

His anger softened. "I don't know. Perhaps he saw Caleb's suffering and wanted to put him out of his misery as he would a sick animal. Come, we must talk to your parents."

He shook his head and marched off with me trailing at his heels, barely able to keep up.

****

The heavenly warmth of molasses and cinnamon greeted us when we entered the rectory. I turned to Dr. Farnsworth, my mouth watering despite having seen Caleb's body. "Mama must be baking molasses cookies."

My mother stood over the stove, her back to us, while Papa poured hot water into the teapot at the kitchen table. They turned in our direction when they heard our footsteps. Papa stood the moment he saw Dr. Farnsworth and offered him a chair. "Atticus, you must have tea with us." He took in the doctor's attire and grim expression. "Whatever is the matter?"

Dr. Farnsworth shook his head. "I'm afraid we have no time for tea. Lucy and Pyrtle found Caleb Potter in his hut. He was long expired." Mama gasped at the doctor's words.

My father stared at me, his mouth agape. "You came upon his body?"

I nodded, still unable to believe what I'd seen. "Yes, Papa. Pyrtle and I brought some chowder for Caleb, but we found him—"

The doctor placed a hand on my shoulder. "Caleb had been dead for some time. I'm alarmed that two innocents discovered such horror. I promise to look in on Pyrtle, but we have to visit the mayor first. We must tell him that Caleb's death might be murder. I'll test the dregs at the bottom of the bottle, but I fear they're poison." He held up the rum bottle. "I've shared my thoughts with Lucy. Could Sebastian have had a hand in Caleb's death?"

Mama shook her head as if pushing the thought from her mind. "Never, not my nephew." She removed her apron, and smoothed her hair. "Let me get my bonnet and cloak." She rushed off.

Papa stayed rooted to the spot, his gaze fixed on me. I thought he might break into tears. "Lucy, will you be all right?"

As a daughter of the church, I knew I had to be strong. "Yes, Papa, I think so."

Concern etched his face, but duty called. "I would

take you with us when we speak to the mayor, but I'm afraid you must stay in the rectory in the event of visitors. Everyone will soon hear about Caleb's death and will want guidance. Don't leave, my darling, and be vigilant."

He left me alone with my memories of Caleb Potter's body. I'd seen deer and wild boars rotting on the forest floor, but never a human body in that revolting condition before. Luckily, Pyrtle only smelled Mr. Potter and didn't see how horrible he looked. Still, I wondered how my friend was faring.

Could Sebastian have been involved in such an abomination? I remembered Dr. Farnsworth's words: Perhaps Sebastian saw Caleb's suffering and wanted to put him out of his misery as he would a sick animal. I stood alone, mired in confusion and uncertainty.

When the front door opened, I jumped up so quickly I hit my knee against the tabletop. I heard faint footsteps as someone crossed the threshold, followed by Velda's voice. Thankfully, the intruder wasn't my cousin. "Lucy, I must talk to you. Are your parents around?"

"No. They went to town with Dr. Farnsworth. I'm sure you've already heard the sad news. Caleb Potter is dead."

I made my way from the kitchen just as she hung her cloak on the rack. Velda appeared to be in a horrid state. Her face was puffy and weeping had painted her eyes and nose scarlet. "Yes, I heard, but that's not why I came to see you. Oh, Lucy, something dreadful happened."

"What could be more dreadful than Caleb's death?"

"There are worse things."

Without asking, I knew her pain must have involved my cousin. "Come to the kitchen and have some tea."

She didn't say a word, just watched as the aromatic leaves steeped in boiling water. I poured a cup for her before I dared to broach the subject. "You've been crying. What's wrong?"

She broke into another round of sobs. Tears tumbled from her eyes and rolled down her cheeks. "I'm so ashamed. I lied to you about Sebastian. We had an assignation soon after he arrived in Maidenhead, and we loved each other from that moment. Now he wants to return to Boston." She stopped speaking long enough to wipe her nose with her napkin. "Without me."

It took a moment for me to digest her words. "What?"

"You heard me, he wants to abandon me and return to the arms of his Boston doxy."

After another uncomfortable silence, I found the nerve to ask the question. "Is your monthly flow late, Velda?"

She glared at me. "No. Of course, Sebastian tried to get me with child. He said God told him to breed an army of Hathornes." Her mouth tightened, and her words rushed out of her mouth. "Dear Lord, it's so confusing. He even spoke of marrying you."

A blast of ice crawled up my back again, and my skin turned to gooseflesh. Velda ignored me and continued her sad rant.

"I told him marrying you would be like wedding his sister. He said the great Egyptian kings did it and so would he. Lucy, I know you have no interest in him that way, but he kept babbling on about making babies with you. He plans to return to Boston, without me. Oh, Lucy, what am I to do?"

I hesitated for a moment. "Perhaps I should ask my parents, or maybe Kimball—"

Velda jumped from her chair. "No, you can't tell him. I know my brother. He'll hunt Sebastian down, kill him, and they'll hang him. Oh, Lucy, I'm ruined!"

I pulled her close in a sisterly embrace. "I won't tell a soul, but perhaps you should speak to Bathsheba. She's a midwife and can help in case of, uh, she'll know what needs to be done in the event you don't have your monthly flow."

My words angered her, and she rose from her chair. Velda walked into the hallway and spoke over her shoulder without turning back. "I don't need Bathsheba. I'll deal with Sebastian in my own way." Her mouth curved into a grim smile. "I'll go to Boston and speak to Ida."

I followed her to the entryway. "Velda, I beg you, don't do that. It will be a horrible mistake. Ida is blameless in this situation." Velda turned back to me, her face flushed with rage. I had never seen my friend in such a state. "'Ida is blameless'? He still plans to marry her and live in comfort in her great house without telling her that he took my virtue. Why shouldn't I tell her? What do I care about Ida Stoker, anyway? That bitch had something that belongs to me, something I want, and I'll make sure she'll never possess it. I'll destroy Sebastian's name throughout Boston and make sure Ida is as miserable as I am."

Her dreadful words caused me more pain than if she'd reared back and struck my face with all her might. I looked deep into her eyes and saw the hatred coiled like a cobra ready to strike.

At that point, my frustration got the better of me. "Sebastian isn't a 'something.' He is a disturbed boy. Perhaps now you understand how different he is from the rest of us. Velda, how can you be so cruel toward a young woman who has never done a thing to you?"

Velda gave a shrug of her dainty shoulders. "She has everything I want—wealth, position, and Sebastian! I won't allow it." She turned and walked out the door. "Goodbye, my friend. I'll hold you to your promise."

I called after her retreating form as she raced down the cobbled path, "Velda, please come back. I'm not supposed to leave the rectory."

When I stepped onto the porch to follow her, the two codgers from the dry goods store were trudging up the steps. "We just heard the news about Caleb Potter. We came to speak to your father."

Velda raced down the street with such furious speed I knew I'd never catch her. I waved the two of them into the rectory. "Please, I made tea. My parents went to visit the mayor but should be back soon."

They followed me to the dining room table and regaled me with stories of Mr. Potter. "He was a good soul, just too fond of drink. Shame, him dying that way, but Caleb never did anything by half measure."

Thankfully, they didn't mention my cousin. The old men chatted away about times past. I feigned interest in their small talk, but my thoughts kept returning to Velda.

I'd speak to Mama upon her return. She'd be the soul of discretion and help Velda through her pain. At that point I realized that, if left to his own devises, my mad cousin would destroy everything I loved about my beautiful village.

****

The old fellows left after slurping down two pots of tea. "We'll be shoving off now, Miss Lucy. Got to tell folks about Caleb."

I set a chicken to boil and spent the remainder of the afternoon working on the quilt. Quilting took my mind away from Velda's words, but not from my cousin. Why had the Creator cursed my family with such a horrible malady? How could a young man who'd devoted himself to medicine take a life, especially of a harmless drunk like Caleb Potter?

Mama's voice carried from the foyer to the kitchen. "Thank you, Atticus. Have a good day."

She removed her bonnet and cloak. I searched her face but found it expressionless. "Mama, what did the mayor say about Mr. Potter?"

"He was cordial, but since he considered Caleb a vagrant, he thought Maidenhead all the better for his death. We found Sebastian working in the apothecary with Mr. Crackbone. When your father told them of Caleb's death, Sebastian smiled at the news. He said wasn't it a blessing from God the poor fellow's pain had ended."

Her words were like a punch to my stomach, and I couldn't stop an involuntary yelp.

My mother turned and gazed into my face. "Lucy, what's wrong?"

Before I could stop myself, I began blathering about Velda. "Everything. Velda came to the rectory after you left. She imagines herself in love with Sebastian." I spoke in a whisper. "Mama, she gave him her virtue."

My mother closed her eyes. "I feared she had."

"There is more. Velda swore she'd go to the city and tell poor Ida. It was horrible, Mama. She used the most vulgar language, words I've never heard her utter before. Please don't tell Papa that Sebastian had his way with her. Although she denies it, I fear she may be enceinte."

Mama sank into the chair. "I'll keep Velda's story to myself. I won't tell your father, but we must help her. Give her time to think. Bring her to me tomorrow. I promise to be gentle."

Velda would be furious when she discovered I'd revealed her secret, but I'd be prepared for her anger.

Chapter Eighteen
Hagatha's Leap

October 5, 1880
Dear Lucy Stone,

I hope this missive finds you in good health and fine spirits. My name is Lucy Stone Hathorne. We first met at my christening sixteen years ago, though I have no memory of it since I was an infant. My dear mother, Madeleine Hathorne, wrote to you of my imminent birth and declared her intention to make me your namesake should I be a girl. You were gracious enough to make the trip to my village, Maidenhead, and attend my baptism.

For a number of years, you have corresponded with my father, the Reverend Braddock Hathorne. He taught me to admire your valiant efforts in the fight for suffrage for all, and be patient; unfortunately, once again, there is to be a Presidential election and we women cannot participate. It pains me that any common seaman has the vote, yet our government continues to deny women this basic right.

I support your great work and have enclosed one dollar that I have saved to help your effort.

Sincerely,

Lucy Stone Hathorne

I folded my dollar into the letter before stamping and sealing the envelope. A groan breached the silence and wafted up the stairway. Another followed, and then one more.

I left my bedchamber, following the noise to the pantry where we did our canning and pickling.

Sunlight tinted the whitewashed walls pale yellow, and the air smelled of yeast and fresh flour. Mama stood at her worktable, hunched over in agony. She kneaded a blob of dough into tortured knots, her blue eyes brimming with tears.

I saw the agony in her face, placed a chair beneath her, and made her sit.

"Mama, is it your monthly visitor?"

She gave a nod, her distress obvious.

"Then you should lie down."

Mama rarely complained about her monthlies, but that day I heard the pain in her voice. Despite her personal agony, she waved my concerns away with a sweep of her hand.

"No, Lucy." She pointed to the change jar kept next to the pickled beets. "Take a quarter to the apothecary. Ask Mr. Crackbone for a bottle of Mrs. Pinkham's Vegetable Compound. I'm told it's a sovereign cure for ladies' ailments. I've saved some cornbread and a bit of cod for Pedro. Before you visit the apothecary, go to Caleb's shack first and leave something for the beast. Go to the inn. Bring Velda to me."

It would be like Mama to think of an animal despite her own agony. "Mama, I can go to the woods later."

"No, Lucy, go now. Dr. Farnsworth is sure Pedro is still alive. I hate to think of the poor runt alone."

I took twenty-five cents from the jar and grabbed

my basket, cloak, and bonnet. The weather had chilled again, but despite the cold, the forest came alive with the sound of honking geese. They would soon leave Maidenhead for warmer climes.

"Pedro. Pedro." I heard no eager growl.

The constable had padlocked the door, but I smelled the stench of decomposition wafting from inside the cottage. After I dropped the scraps near the hut, I turned back toward town and set off down the cobbled road toward the apothecary shop.

Once inside, the shrill jingle of the brass bell above the apothecary's door announced a patron had crossed the threshold. The lanterns smelled of camphene since the old druggist couldn't abide "Rockefeller's devil juice," as he called kerosene. He never forgot those halcyon days when whale oil lit the world.

Bottles and tins of every shape and size covered the wooden shelves—ointments, tinctures, and potions everywhere I looked. Mr. Crackbone spent his days grinding herbs and powders for his magical compounds. The old apothecary raised his head from the counter and peered at me through faded gray eyes.

"Well, if it isn't Lucy Hathorne. Pray tell, what do you need, my dear?"

I looked around the shop and saw Stone's Cascana Quine Bromade, Stickney and Poor's Paregoric, Lloyd's Toothache Drops, but no Mrs. Pinkham's.

"May I purchase some Mrs. Pinkham's?"

He retrieved the Pinkham's from under the counter and handed it to me. "I'm guessing your poor mother might need something stronger for the pain of uterine distress."

He added a glass vial containing a reddish-brown

liquid. "Laudanum should do the trick."

Although Mama kept a supply of laudanum at home, we could never keep enough, with Sebastian around. Mr. Crackbone shook his head when I tendered the coin. "No, my dear, take them as gifts from me. Please, give my regards to your mother and Reverend Hathorne. Tell your father I'll see him at Sunday service."

"Thank you, Mr. Crackbone." I looked around the shop. "Where is my cousin, sir?"

The old man appeared confused. "Don't know where he went. Zeke Newberry stopped by the shop, told the boy something about Velda, and they rushed off together."

The bell jingled once more, and he acknowledged two townswomen with a nod. "Good morning, ladies."

I deposited Mama's medicine into the bottom of my basket, took a step onto the sidewalk, and nearly collided with Pyrtle as she scurried down the wood planks. "Where are you rushing to, Pyrtle?"

Pyrtle's brows knotted in concern. "Thank the Lord I ran into you. Did you hear? Velda's gone missing. Kimball, Zeke, and Sebastian are out looking for her."

Her words floored me. "Velda? Missing? How could she be missing? She came by the rectory yesterday." In light of her condition, I prayed she hadn't done anything rash. "Pyrtle, this is dreadful."

"Yes, it is. What will I do about my quilt?"

"The fact that Velda has gone missing is more important than a quilt."

Pyrtle grabbed my arm. "But I'm to be wed. I'll need my quilt. Every married woman has to have a quilt."

I felt heat coming to my face and my upper lip curled involuntarily. Instead of saying something I'd regret, I handed her my missive. "This is an important letter addressed to Lucy Stone. I request you mail it right away, and please be careful. I've enclosed a whole dollar."

I turned and flounced off. Before I reached the door, I called out to her over my shoulder, "I'll find Kimball."

I'd failed Velda in her hour of need, and she'd fled to Boston. My hands shook at the pain she might cause there. In his lunacy, Sebastian had ruined Velda's life.

****

Except for an old woman snoring in front of the hearth, the inn appeared deserted. I looked about the lobby, saw nothing, and turned to leave. Before I could reach the door, I heard the faint but bitter sound of weeping. I journeyed down the corridor and found Mrs. Prince with Cassie. Cassie flung her arm around the poor woman's shoulder as she poured her heart into a drenched handkerchief. "Cassie, where is my Velda?"

When I approached Mrs. Prince, she flung herself into my arms. "What am I to do, Lucy? My little girl is gone."

I felt myself as culpable as Sebastian. His malady propelled his acts, but I had no excuse. Why hadn't I forced Velda to stay?

Cassie spoke to her in gentle tones. "Lucy and I will join the search, Mrs. Prince. We'll find her."

My friend's words seemed to bring the poor woman comfort, and she released me. The news of Velda's disappearance had taken over my thoughts and I'd forgotten about Mama. I handed over my hamper.

"Mrs. Prince, please ask Fatima to bring this to the rectory. Mama is ailing something terrible and needs the medicine in my basket."

Cassie and I rushed off to begin our fruitless search. My friend jabbered away, ignorant of the facts that only I knew. "Those romantic novels filled Velda's head with flapdoodle and made her sillier than ever."

The truth sat on the tip of my tongue, but I couldn't tell Cassie our friend had given her virginity to a lunatic she now followed to Boston.

She continued chattering. "Two days ago, Velda begged me to help her search for the last of the wild strawberries. She wanted to pick some for Sebastian. She claimed to have seen a strawberry bush on Hagatha's Leap. Well, I gave her a talking to. The girl's so lovesick she sees things that aren't there. I climb the bluffs every day and there are no strawberries anywhere, but she wouldn't listen."

I gave a nod of agreement. "What a preposterous idea. The wild strawberries were gone by August. Besides, Velda never went there."

Cassie stopped walking, turned, and faced me. "How do you know that she never went there?"

How I wish I'd held my tongue. I had an ailing mother at home and didn't want to climb the bluffs on a blustery day. "I meant Velda should know better, because we picked the last of the strawberries a month and a half ago."

My words seemed to appease her. She didn't notice my discomfort and chatted on as we continued our march toward Hagatha's Leap. "Velda's been so flighty of late. She walked off in a huff and said she'd look for them alone."

"But if Velda went to hunt strawberries yesterday, why would she still be there?"

Cassie kept up her brisk pace. "Perhaps she's injured herself. Miss Lucy Hathorne, if you're truly Velda's friend, you'll go with me."

We headed to the bluffs in silence. A fierce wind battled our capes but couldn't stop Cassie. She ascended the steep path with the speed of a mountain goat, and I could barely keep up. With each step, I knew how fruitless our trek would be. The wind whipped us at every step like Simon Legree in Uncle Tom's Cabin. It teased our skirts and nipped at our heels like a pet dog. I stumbled and almost lost my balance twice, but Cassie insisted we push on.

"Come, it's just a breeze."

"A breeze?" Our cloaks billowed around us, and it took every ounce of my strength to keep my balance. When the gust blew sand in our faces, my frustration finally got the best of me.

"Cassie, we won't find Velda here."

From the way her mouth tightened, I knew my friend was miffed. "This is the second time you've said we won't find her on the bluffs. Do you know something you're not telling?"

I had her full attention. "No." Although I averted my face, she saw through my falsehood. "What do you know?"

The truth bubbled out. "Velda has run away."

Cassie stopped her climb, her raven locks blowing in the breeze. "What?"

Once I'd begun blabbing, I couldn't stop myself. "Oh, Cassie, I swore I wouldn't breach her confidence, but I must. Velda came to the rectory yesterday in the most emotional state, all because of my cousin. She fancies herself in love with him and is on her way to Boston to confront poor Ida. Velda said such cruel things I couldn't believe my ears. She said Sebastian belonged to her. At this point, I don't think she cares who she hurts. You do understand why I couldn't tell anyone, don't you?"

Her shoulders sagged, and I feared she would burst into tears. "Yes, of course I do, and I won't say a word. Shouldn't someone go to the city to find her?"

The idea held danger. "If I tell Kimball, I'm afraid he'll kill Sebastian. To be honest, I wouldn't blame him if he did. If I tell my father, Velda will know I breached her confidence."

Cassie's face colored. "Did your cousin, well, you know…"

I couldn't tell another lie. "Yes."

She screamed into the wind. "The whoremonger!"

I'm sure I blanched at her strong language, but I agreed. "Please try to understand. It's part of his malady." I felt my eyes misting and wiped my tears with my sleeves.

Cassie placed an arm on my shoulder. "I never told anyone, but the varlet tried to kiss me…twice. I wouldn't let him. He's engaged to be married, and besides, I have feelings for another." Admitting she cared for Zeke must have been difficult, but my heart leapt for my friend. "Should we turn back?"

I shook my head. "Since we've made it this far, we might as well continue."

Cassie said nothing more, just trudged up the steep path with me at her heels. Although I knew Cassie would never tell anyone, I'd betrayed the secret and felt horrible.

When we reached the bluff, the heather looked like a massive pale pink and purple carpet. The sea loomed before us, the water painted gray by blustery clouds. We moved closer to the edge. Cassie pointed to a withered blackberry patch.

I looked beyond the wilted undergrowth and saw the flash of a red scrub as brilliant as the burning bush from the Old Testament. "Lucy, over here. Would you believe it? I found them, wild strawberries!"

Nestled among the shriveled berries, cosseted from the elements, a scrub full of succulent fruit had managed to survive. The berries were like globs of heavenly nectar rather than corporal fruit. We plucked the tiny berries from the vine, wiped the dirt away with our kerchiefs, and devoured them on the spot, the sweet essence dribbling down our faces.

Cassie placed her sticky, strawberry-covered hand in mine, and for one magical moment, everything was as it once was. The schooner had never arrived in Maidenhead, mad Caleb still talked to spirits in the white birch grove. Pyrtle and Velda donned muslin dresses and joined us to pick berries. Velda read to us from Jane Eyre as we stuffed ourselves with the last of the summer fruit. A beautiful reverie, but fate made it a short one.

A scream traveled up from the beach. The voice belonged to Sebastian. "Velda!"

Chapter Nineteen
Velda

Cassie and I made our way down the steep path from Hagatha's Leap to the shore. I felt a chilly wind to my face and ice to my back as we rushed to the beach. A woman's frock lay on the sand, one of Velda's gowns. Sebastian held up two dainty slippers I also recognized as belonging to my lost friend. He caressed them at his cheek and fell to his knees with a moan.

A crowd of people collected on the beach. Without warning, Kimball rushed toward us and tore the slippers from Sebastian's hands. My cousin jumped up from the beach, and the two boys circled each other like young lions from rival prides. Kimball hissed at him, "Bastard! If any harm has come to my sister, I'll kill you."

Sebastian lurched forward, and they would have come to blows if Dr. Farnsworth hadn't interceded. "Stop it, you fools! We must search for Velda. God forbid she's drowned. If she has, we must find her. Come, everyone."

When my cousin began keening like a madman, Mrs. Brigham took Sebastian's hand in hers. "Come with me, dear boy. You must lie down."

Off they went.

Half the town followed Dr. Farnsworth on what I feared would be a fruitless search.

I whispered to Cassie, "Kimball needs me. We'll search for Velda together."

She nodded and off she went. Kimball's usual cocksureness had abandoned him. For the first time I looked into the face of my beloved and saw a lost and vulnerable boy.

"Why, Lucy? Why did she do it? I know she wasn't looking for strawberries. She did away with herself, didn't she?"

"Please, Kimball, don't judge her."

Our lives had once been so simple, but now nothing would ever be the same.

I moved closer and our hands intertwined. "I think Velda is waiting for us to find her, Kimball. She hasn't washed onto the beach yet. Perhaps we should search the grotto where we played as children."

He sighed. "We?"

"Yes, we."

Kimball averted his face without saying a word, and I feared I'd have to seek her alone. "Do you remember all the things we discovered in our grotto, Kimball? Could the rocks have trapped her?"

He released my hand and I heard the anger in his words. "If they did, let someone else find her. You've never shared a boat with a corpse. I have. It was a horror, and it wasn't my sister's." When he turned to me, his eyes brimmed over with agony. "Why did she do it, why?"

"She and Sebastian imagined themselves in love, Kimball."

Enraged, he pulled his hand away. "And what does walking into the sea have to do with love?"

"I don't know. Perhaps she saw the depth of

Sebastian's lunacy and realized her folly." My voice broke. "I can't stop thinking about my friend lost in the sea, crying for her mother."

When Kimball spun me around, rage had deserted him. He cupped my face in his hands. "If we leave now, our search can begin."

We stood together, gazing into each other's faces, unable to move. What a strange and wonderful feeling.

****

Few trespassed into our place of solitude and reflection, our little grotto, for only the foolhardy or the very young chanced the strong riptides. Nature created an archway out of boulders and the Pokanokets and Pocassets had painted the rocks with tribal symbols.

As children, Kimball, Cassie, Zeke, and I called it our secret place. In the summer, we'd paddle the warm waters and search for the treasures hidden there. Besides a harpoon, we'd discovered a splendid ship's compass, a rusted musket, and empty rum and beer bottles.

I looked up at the placid sky—blue, cloudless, with no signs of the rancor around us. Kimball and I rowed into the limestone cathedral in Zeke's dinghy, the rippling of water the only sound.

We spoke in hushed tones, for our voices bounced from the ceiling and echoed throughout the grotto. "Let's go farther, Kimball."

He paddled on, his back facing me. "Your wish is my command."

Silence enveloped the vast chamber. Without warning, Kimball whispered a poem of lost love.

"It was many and many a year ago,
In a kingdom by the sea,

That a maiden there lived whom you may know
By the name of Annabel Lee;
And this maiden she lived with no other thought
Than to love and be loved by me.
I was a child and she was a child,
In this kingdom by the sea;
But we loved with a love that was more than love—
I and my Annabel Lee;
With a love that the winged seraphs of heaven
Coveted her and me."

The beauty of the bittersweet words so consumed me, I couldn't speak. Blood rushed to my head. I wondered if he heard the furious beating of my heart. Kimball's whisper breached the silence. "You must know that I'm your slave, Lucy Hathorne. I love you with all my heart and soul."

I couldn't answer. Then, in the dim light, I caught sight of a piece of ivory-colored fabric flapping against the rocks deep in the grotto. "Look."

Dread filled our little canoe. We paddled forward, the water lapping our boat, the stillness surrounding us. It seemed an eternity before we reached the rocks. They held a ripped petticoat and torn bodice in their stony grasp, ones that belonged to Velda. Kimball pulled the underwear into the dinghy without a word. A chill moved down my spine; my blood ran cold.

****

By the time we reached the beach, we were both sobbing. Kimball yelled out, his voice ragged from crying, "We didn't find Velda."

Cassie was the first on the shore, with Mrs. Prince at her side. He handed the sodden underwear to his mother. "Lucy and I found this in the cove."

Mrs. Prince placed her hand to her mouth and retched.

Dr. Farnsworth moved toward us. "There's nothing to be done except to keep searching. She'll wash up soon." He spoke in gentle tones. "The poor child must have done away with herself."

Mrs. Prince rested in Kimball's arms. It pained me to think the poor woman knew her daughter had died a suicide. If the townspeople suspected she'd taken her own life, many might object to her lying in consecrated ground.

I glanced at Cassie. We didn't exchange a word, but she barreled her way past the searchers, going nose to nose with Dr. Farnsworth. "Suicide? Velda would never do such a sinful thing." She threw her shoulders back. "The way I figure, she went looking for wild strawberries, got all sweaty, and took a swim."

Dr. Farnsworth spoke to Cassie in gentle but condescending tones. "My dear child, there were no strawberries, and Velda would never have gone for a swim."

Cassie stared at Mrs. Prince for a moment. She handed her fruit-filled kerchief to the good doctor, a look of defiance on her face. "Strawberries, wild strawberries. Lucy and me found these today when we went searching for Velda. The wind blew like the devil, the gale fierce enough to knock us both into the sea. Velda must've got dirty, and knowing how picky she was, uh, is about her looks, she wouldn't want anyone to see her covered in grime. Maybe she went swimming to wash off, and maybe the tide swept her away."

Dr. Farnsworth opened his mouth as if ready to

argue, but he didn't. Instead he looked from Cassie to Mrs. Prince, and finally, Kimball. "Yes, of course, Cassie, the poor girl had an accident. We'll continue our search until we find her."

Zeke walked onto the beach with a group of fishermen. His face turned as red as a raspberry when he spied Cassie. He pulled off his cap, giving her a polite nod. A group of village women surrounded a tearful Mrs. Prince and escorted her off the beach.

Hot tears rolled down my face. I'd never see my beautiful friend again. "Cassie, I failed her."

She gave her head a violent shake. "You didn't fail her. Romance bewitched her, and she refused to listen."

Cassie took me by the shoulders and turned me in Kimball's direction.

"I'll meet you at the inn. Go to him, Lucy. You're the only one who can comfort him now. Be strong, be strong." She marched off away toward town.

I kept my eyes fixed on Kimball. He turned as if feeling my presence. We gazed at each other, our faces red with tears. I wrapped my arms around him.

"These will be hard times for you, with you leaving for Cambridge soon. Mama and I will watch over your mother while you're away at Harvard."

His anger subsided, and his laughter was a sad trill. "Harvard? No, Mother will need me, without Velda. Harvard will have to wait."

We locked hands and trudged away from the shore. As we walked through the streets, men removed their caps and the ladies acknowledged us with curtsies.

Bathsheba waited at the apothecary door. She placed a gloved hand on Kimball's shoulder. "I brought Velda into the world."

His lips opened, "Bathsheba, I—" No more words tumbled from his lips.

Since Kimball couldn't answer, I spoke for him. "Thank you, Bathsheba. You are a true friend."

When Bathsheba walked away, Kimball's shoulders slumped like an old man's. "I saw Sebastian bawling like a baby. I know he loved her in his own way, but how can I forgive him?"

My hand encircled his. "You're a Christian, so you must, just as I must. It's the only way we can keep our sanity."

His fury returned. I knew he didn't hear my words. "Why didn't Velda confide in me instead of putting a knife through our mother's heart? She could be vain and flighty, but I can't say goodbye to my Velda."

In one brief instant, Kimball had changed. His eyes lost their mirth, and the set of his jaw became hard and unforgiving. He wore his new maturity with sadness, as if he had aged a decade in one day. The boy I'd grown up with was no more.

"Please, Kimball, your mother needs you. Velda needs you. I need you too."

He turned and took my face in his hands.

"Can it be true? The girl I love needs me. I think I must do whatever she commands because I'm her slave."

The blood rushed to my head so quickly I feared I'd swoon. Had Kimball uttered those words at another time, I might have laughed them off, but not now.

By the time we reached the inn, the townspeople had packed the lobby, but the silence was deafening. A few of the men passed a jug, but most were stone sober. I heard a few remarks as I passed.

"That dear girl, where could she be?"

"So young, so comely."

"How I'd hoped Velda would fancy my boy one day."

Townsmen surrounded Kimball. I walked down the hushed corridors to Velda's room. The thought of what faced me slowed my stride to a crawl. Through the quiet, I heard a low growl. The hair on my forearms stood on end. The growl metamorphosed into a fearsome scream.

When I reached her room, I expected to hear the wailing of despair. However, instead of keening, I heard Mrs. Prince's angry voice. "Dear God, how could she?"

I walked into the chamber and discovered the doors to Velda's wardrobe flung open. Except for a worn skirt and discarded bodice, her gowns had disappeared.

Cassie searched her bureau. "Velda loved Jane Eyre and Wuthering Heights and kept them here, but they're gone, along with her fans and handkerchiefs."

Kimball walked through the assembled mourners and made his way to the room.

Mrs. Prince, her face mottled with rage, held a letter up to her son. "This was waiting at the front desk. Read it."

He read aloud,

"Dearest Mother,

By now, I'm sure you're angry at my little joke, but I have wonderful news. Mr. Hiram Endicott, a gentleman known to you, has asked for my hand in marriage and I have accepted!

My darling Hiram has admired me for years and, as you know, is quite wealthy. We've rushed off to New

York, and he has promised me a carriage of my own and servants aplenty when we arrive there.

I am so sorry for the ruse, but I knew you never approved of him. Besides, I wanted to teach a certain young man a lesson. One should never trifle with another's heart. Please don't be vexed at my scheme. I thought the shoes on the beach and my old rag of a frock were a dramatic touch. In the event you have not seen it, Hiram even had a servant put one of my torn petticoats in the grotto, and we had a jolly laugh. Perhaps it was overdramatic, but I thought it had a certain flourish.

Do give Lucy and the girls my love. I hope my silly hijinks did not scare them. I know Kimball will be vexed, but so be it. Please let Pyrtle know that I shall be the first of us to marry. Perhaps the girls will make a quilt for me in the future.

I shall write again as soon as Hiram and I are settled.

Your devoted daughter.

Velda Rose Prince Endicott."

Mrs. Prince grabbed the letter from his hands, threw it to the floor, and trampled upon it. "That cruel, selfish girl. He'll never marry her, just trifle with her. He'll cast her out when he's done. She might as well have thrown herself into the sea. She's dead to me."

Kimball knelt to retrieve the missive. "Velda was always flighty and vain, but never vicious until she met Sebastian Hathorne."

Mrs. Prince suddenly went ramrod straight. "No, she might have hidden her wickedness from you, but it was always in her heart." She turned to her son. "Give the men rum punch for their efforts. Let them toast our beautiful, cruel Velda."

Cassie took me aside. "I must leave now. They'll need me at the lighthouse. Go to Kimball, Lucy. You're the only one who can help him through this now. Be strong, my friend. Be strong for Kimball." With that she rushed off.

****

I kept my eyes fixed on Kimball as he cleared up the empty glasses in the lobby. He turned as if feeling my presence. We gazed at each other, our faces red with tears. I wrapped my arms around him.

He turned and took my face in his hands. We gazed at each other for an eternity.

Chapter Twenty
The Autumn of Our Discontent

Velda's flight cast a pall over our village. My family and friends walked the streets of Maidenhead in a state of perpetual sadness. No matter how I tried, I couldn't bring a smile to Pyrtle's face. Kimball's good spirits seemed to return, but I knew they were part of the farce he played for his mother's sake. He burned with anger over Velda's affair with my cousin, and I feared the two might come to blows or even worse.

After Mrs. Prince discovered Velda's flight, Papa took Sebastian aside. "In light of what has happened with Velda, you must return to the rectory." My cousin acquiesced.

One afternoon I returned from town to find my father affixing a lock to my bedroom door. He handed me a key. "Lucy, I insist you lock yourself in your room every night. I don't want you ever to be alone with your cousin."

"But, Papa, I—"

His expression silenced me, and I nodded in agreement. For the next two weeks, Papa watched Sebastian's every movement, while Mama reacted to every titter or sob like a skittish cat.

Sebastian barely spoke, answering requests with polite grunts. He spent his days in silent reflection or with Mr. Crackbone at the apothecary. In the early mornings, he'd roam the forest or the cemetery, but in the still of the evening, I'd hear him sobbing.

I had no idea of what was going through Sebastian's twisted mind, and as my father ordered, I stayed away from him; however, the contents of his Saratoga trunk fascinated me, and I wondered what secrets it held.

One morning after Sebastian left for the apothecary, I crept into his bedchamber. The elegant trunk sat in a corner, the expensive leather gleaming persimmon red in the dim light. I examined every inch, from barrel staves to leather straps, before attempting to open it. I tried lifting it, but Sebastian had secured the trunk with its silver lock, and the domed lid wouldn't budge. I ferreted about the room, hunting for a key, but my search proved fruitless.

Even the weather mourned. It turned cruel as if infused with grief and fury. By October, fogbanks hung in the air like clumps of clotted cream. I worried most about Cassie. She'd buried herself under a perpetual cloud of gloom and taken to sitting in the town square at dusk. One morning I found her at the dock, alone and brooding.

"Zeke asked about you."

Her dark eyes flashed when I mentioned his name. "He can go to the devil along with your cousin, for all I care. If that's love, I'll have nothing to do with it. I'll die a spinster and spend my old age knitting before a fireplace. Velda's romantic notions destroyed her. It would have been better if someone had slit her throat."

The vitriol behind her words shocked me to the core. "Your hate won't bring Velda back. Besides, poor Zeke's been moping around town since the day you stopped talking to him. You know he loves you, yet you've devastated him with your coldness. He didn't do a thing, yet you blame him for Velda's transgressions. I didn't realize your capacity for cruelty."

Her face reddened, her anger palpable. She harrumphed like an old salt and spat out dark words as she stomped away. "I don't blame Zeke, but I'll never turn into a lovesick fool."

I gazed into her face, hoping to see a hint of my old friend. Even in her anguish, Cassie stood as straight as a ramrod, her tears unshed. Nothing could break her.

The smell of the sea beckoned, and we walked toward the ship with crimson sails, which had caused such misery. The chandlers had done their best by the exquisite craft and she looked even more beautiful than when she'd first sailed toward Maidenhead. The Bon Ami would soon be on another voyage and leave Maidenhead forever. Good riddance. How I wished she'd sunk to the bottom of the bay.

Cassie looked up at her red sails and spat. "Some city folks paid Mr. Tateshall a tidy sum for fixing the schooner. I wanted to open the seacock and scuttle her, but my pa said no."

I gazed upon the scarlet lady whose bold sails contrasted against the gray sky. How could something so beautiful have brought such evil?

****

The following morning, I searched the woods once again for Pedro. Caleb Potter's hut sat alone and desolate, with no hint of life, yet every time I neared it, I felt a prickle on my back, as if someone watched me. Was it foolish to think a wounded bear roamed the forest instead of slumbering in a cave? Who else devoured the scraps I put out every morning? I left half my breakfast along with a few scraps of fried bread in front of the cottage and prayed none of the varmints in the forest got to them before Pedro.

The thought of the poor stunted beast alone with no one to look after him saddened me, but I knew that, somewhere in the woods, Pedro waited for his master to come back to him. Could he have returned to the shack? I doubted it. My curiosity spurred me to take a step closer to the hut, but a lingering whiff of decomposition stopped me from going inside.

I traveled on to the forest. A mist shrouded the trees as if nature had draped a veil over the woods. When I arrived at the True Believers' Burial Ground, three laborers cut through the cold ground with spades. The earth hadn't frozen rock hard yet, and they could lay the dead in their earthly beds. Winter would arrive soon enough, and then those who'd passed would have to rest inside a stone vault until the spring thaw. The men threw their backs into their labors, slicing through the dirt, turning it over by the spadeful. They kept rhythm by chanting an old sea shanty.

"It's all for me grog, me jolly, jolly grog—

It's all gone for beer and tobacco.

Well, I spent all me loot in a house of ill repute,

And I think that I shall go back there tomorrow."

A tall, slender youth entered the cemetery—Sebastian. I watched him stroll among the graves, the gravediggers' off-key singing serenading him while he removed dead leaves and dried flowers from his mother's grave. The flowers had deserted the bower weeks ago, but he'd woven wreaths from bittersweet vines he must have found on the path leading to town.

Papa had requested that I stay away from him, but there were workers nearby, so we weren't alone. He knelt at the foot of his mother's grave. I crept into the cemetery and took my place next to him.

My beautiful cousin turned to me, his eyes filling with tears, and greeted me with a weak smile. "I loved my mother, you know." He took my chin in his hands and turned my face back to him. "Did you want to ask me why I came to Maidenhead?"

"Yes."

"For you, dear Lucy, for you."

Sebastian wiped away the tears with his sleeve and stared into my face. I pulled away, but he pulled me back. "Because you are so like my dear mother. You possess her grace and elegance. I wanted to see you one more time before I wed, but when I saw you in the flesh, I needed more. Marriage. I know how fruitless it is."

"Sebastian, we are as close by blood as brother and sister. Of course you love me, just as I love you—we're cousins after all—but marriage, never."

He didn't reply to my words. We rose and left the dead to rest. As we walked, Sebastian shared Caleb's sad tale in the most fitting place, the tranquil woods.

"I'd thought of him as a kindred spirit. Everyone misunderstood him, just as they do me. Caleb was a man of many talents, well read, but tormented by the death of the girl he loved, a young lady he met in Louisiana during the war, a dusky beauty like Cassie. They'd planned to marry and move to Canada, but she died and took his soul with her. I'm afraid he longed to join her. It's only fitting they're together."

He turned to me, an earnest look on his face. "I

didn't kill him. I swear it."

I had to believe him. "Yes, I know."

We reached Caleb's little hut, and he placed the last of the wreaths on the spot where the men from the Red Dog had buried Caleb that horrible day. When we arrived at the rectory, Sebastian gazed into my face with such sweetness and intensity, I feared he'd burst into tears. Instead, he put my hand to his lips and bowed.

"You must excuse me, dear cousin. I promised Mr. Crackbone I'd assist him today."

I said nothing, but my thoughts remained with poor, tormented Sebastian for the remainder of the day.

****

A fearsome brume enveloped Maidenhead, the ground clouds smothering her in a heavy murk. The fog nearly obscured the garish banners proclaiming this year's Presidential election, the candidates, Mr. Garfield and General Hancock. Although the town's men usually voted for the party of liberation, women couldn't cast a ballot, another slap in the face for my sex.

My mother handed me a stack of letters readied for posting. "My darling, I wouldn't ask you to venture out in this horrible weather, but they need posting, and I have to prepare food for those who are ailing. I've heard there's influenza in the old part of town, so perhaps you should drop by the apothecary for Dover's Powder."

I wrapped myself against the cold, a knitted beret covering my head, a shawl cocooning everything but my eyes. I plodded down the path to town, one foot in front of the other. When I entered Brigham's with

Papa's letters in hand, the heat from the potbelly stove enveloped me.

A familiar fragrance, tobacco, wafted through the store. The old men, smoke spewing from their pipes, squared off across the chessboard, their brows furrowed in concentration. Both men doffed their caps when I entered, and one turned back to his opponent, glaring at him. "You've been looking at the board for an hour. What in tarnation are you planning to do?"

The other fellow made his move and sat back in his chair, a smirk on his weathered face. His adversary stared at the chessboard in silence. Hours would tick by between moves, but time didn't matter to either of them.

I walked over to the telegraph machine and unpeeled my bindings.

"Goodness, Pyrtle, it may be mid-October, but I'm already wearing my winter frocks. I stopped by to post these letters."

She took the letters and placed them in a pile with others. "Can't say when they'll go out, with this blasted fog. Have you heard? There's winter fever in the old part of town."

While the world knew it as influenza, grippe, or sweating sickness, midwives and healers called the yearly scourge winter fever. "Winter fever, this early?"

Pyrtle answered with a disinterested nod. "Folks are saying a sailor brought it from Maine. Nothing a dose of Dover's Powder and a swig of whiskey couldn't take care of."

One of the old men sitting at the chessboard shook his head. "Nah. My mother swore on the old remedies, a bowl of sliced onion under the bed, garlic, and boneset tea work best. Camphor balls strung around the neck and a little kerosene with sugar is sovereign medicine, too."

My redheaded friend made a face. "Well, if garlic, raw onions, camphor balls, and kerosene don't cure you, I'll wager the smell will. It's best not to catch influenza in the first place. I've never had it and don't plan on getting it."

I remembered my own bout with winter fever. "I had the influenza once. It was so dreadful that I nearly died."

Pyrtle and the old men stared at me in silence. I hemmed and hawed for a moment, trying to think of a pleasantry that might erase my words, and remembered the quilt. "Pyrtle, I have news that might bring a bit of cheer. Mama and I bordered your quilt last night."

When she looked up, I saw agony in her eyes. "My quilt? Goodness, I'd forgotten about it since Velda—" Her words stopped short and she went back to perusing fashion plates of bridal veils. "Which one do you like best, Lucy? I'm thinking about having Madame St. Pierre order this one."

She pointed to a lace veil I found charming in its simplicity. "It's lovely, Pyrtle, but veils are all you've been talking about for the past weeks. Must I remind you once again you won't be wed until summer?"

Pyrtle scrutinized the engraving, ignoring me. "A wedding takes a lot of planning, and summer will be here before we know it."

"Oh yes. I'd better shove off before the fog gets thicker. Goodbye, Pyrtle."

My friend grunted a reply. I left the store and trod through streets blanketed in fog, moving at a crawl.

I had somehow found the road home in the heavy mist. Despite the brume, Dr. Farnsworth's buggy raced down the cobbled street. He appeared deep in thought, so preoccupied his carriage almost collided with a wagon. When I called out, "Dr. Farnsworth," he stopped his horses and looked down at me, disapproval etched on his face.

"It's freezing, child. What are you doing out?"

"It's Lucy Hathorne, sir. We had letters to post."

Doctor Farnsworth adjusted his spectacles and pulled at the reins. "Please excuse me, Lucy. A child in the old part of town has come down with influenza, and others are suffering. Bathsheba helped me for a time, but now Old Modesty, her great-grandmother, has pneumonia, and she can't be spared."

"What are Modesty's chances, sir?"

Dr. Farnsworth's mouth twisted, his expression grim. "I'm afraid she won't last much longer."

I couldn't remember my last encounter with the blind seer without shivering. Still, if the ancient woman was at death's door, I should visit her.

"Go home, Lucy. If someone becomes ill, wrap them up warmly, give them whiskey, quinine, and Dover's Powder, if old Crackbone has any left. Pray, my dear. I'm afraid there's little else one can do."

"Yes, sir."

By the time I arrived at the apothecary, tales of the illness were on everyone's lips. Villagers ignored the fearsome weather, and the queue stretched out from the shop onto the street. I took my place among them and heard the concern in their voices.

"The grippe is spreading among the Portuguese."

"Did you hear that Jason Bliss sent his wife and

children to Rachel's Pride? He's got family there. Wish I could've gone with them."

Mr. Crackbone's reedy voice carried from the shop to the sidewalk. "Mrs. Allgood, I know your husband thinks whiskey is the best medicine against influenza, but laudanum is cheaper and will keep him from drunken mischief. Give him beef broth, quinine, wine, and tincture of squill for a cough. Most importantly, make your man rest. Chain him to the bed if you must."

I finally reached the front of the queue, my patience rewarded. Sebastian worked away in the rear of the shop and appeared deep in concentration. Although I wanted to say a word to my cousin, he remained calm, and I thought it best not to disturb him.

Mr. Crackbone's gray hair was in disarray, his frustration obvious. "Don't tell me influenza has struck the rectory?"

"No, sir, but Doctor Farnsworth said to keep Dover's Powder on hand."

The old man shook his head. "Sorry, I'm out of Dover's and most every other influenza medication. I even went to the Red Dog to buy whiskey, but there is none. I've sold the last of the ammonia carbonate and wine of ipecacuanha, too. Boil some barley water in the event of a cough, and please take this medicine with my regards. I ordered it for Dr. Farnsworth, but they only sent two bottles, so I kept one for myself, just in case."

The old man winked. He looked about the shop before he handed me a small flagon of Dr. Hawke's Sovereign Cure for Grippe. The engraving on the label showed a fellow in an oversized top hat, scythe in hand, chasing a skeleton named "La Grippe." I shuddered at the garish image affixed to the bottle but took it anyway.

After I hid the medicine in my reticule, I made my way out of the shop, past the desperate townsfolk milling about.

****

When I returned to the rectory, Mama sat in the parlor, taking in her second-best gown, a green-and-black tartan plaid.

"You'll be a college girl soon, my darling, and must have proper frocks. I don't wear this gown much. It should be perfect for you."

"Thank you, Mama."

I'm sure she expected a smile, but no matter how I tried, I couldn't muster one. "What's wrong, Lucy?"

"Mr. Crackbone had already sold the last of the Dover's Powder and everything else except for this." I handed her the bottle of the grippe medicine. She shuddered at the lurid label just as I had.

"Whatever is it?"

I shrugged. "Mr. Crackbone says it's the last of the influenza medicine. I don't like the bottle either, but we might need it. I met Dr. Farnsworth as he made his rounds. Old Modesty is ill. May I visit their house later today? With all the death and dying, it's important to put on a brave face, isn't it?"

My mother spoke, the sound of her voice as musical as chimes tinkling in the wind. "Yes, it is, my love."

Chapter Twenty-One
Modesty Chaffee

I tried the latch but found the weathered portal bolted shut. No family in Maidenhead locked their doors. I pounded with the bronze knocker. The door creaked open, and a blast of hot air hit me square in the face. Bathsheba stood at the threshold, her eyes burning fierce in the candlelit room.

"There's pneumonia in here. Go away."

"Bathsheba, it's Lucy, Lucy Hathorne. Dr. Farnsworth said Modesty is ailing. I've come to read Scripture to her. You nursed me when I had a fearsome grippe three years ago and nearly died. Please let me repay you."

Her eyes softened. "Very well. Come inside, my dear."

The fire in the hearth roared like a blast furnace. The stifling room smelled of camphor, barley water, and candle wax. Faint gasps for air, Modesty's last attempts at breathing, emanated from a cot set up in a corner of the dimly lit room.

Bathsheba guided me to her great-grandmother, who lay in her tiny bed. She placed a fine upholstered parlor chair next to the ancient's cot. "Sit, my dear."

Bathsheba took a place across from me on a battered wicker stool. She'd dressed the shriveled old woman in an ivory-colored dressing gown smelling of cedar, with a lace cap covering her white hair. I whispered into her silver horn, "Modesty, it's Lucy, Reverend Hathorne's daughter. I've come to read to you from the Bible."

She turned her head at the sound of my voice. One look in her face and I pulled away. Modesty usually wore tinted spectacles to conceal her disfigurement, but no longer. Instead of eyes, she'd been born with two malformed slits, tiny, undeveloped, and unseeing. I recoiled at her deformity, thankful she couldn't see my repulsion.

The old woman spoke in a voice so small I strained to hear her. She smelled of lavender, old age, and pain-easing whiskey.

"You'll read to me from the Good Book? Thank you for your kindness, sweet child. This world is a cruel place for an old blind woman. They wanted to smother me at birth. My mother stopped them, but there were times I wished she hadn't. My life has been a hard one, and I'm glad to leave it."

I spoke into the silver horn once again. "Shall I read to you from the Psalms, Modesty?"

The old woman nodded. "Of course, my dear."

I opened my Bible. "I've selected one of my favorites, Psalm 139." I read,

"Lord, thou hast searched me, and known me.

"Thou knowest my downsitting and mine uprising, thou understandest my thought afar off.

"Thou compassest my path and my lying down, and art acquainted with all my ways.

"For there is not a word in my tongue, but, lo, O Lord, thou knowest it altogether.

"Thou hast beset me behind and before, and laid

thine hand upon me.

"Such knowledge is too wonderful for me; it is high, I cannot attain unto it.

"Whither shall I go from thy spirit? or whither shall I flee from thy presence?

"If I ascend up into heaven, thou art there: if I make my bed in hell, behold, thou art there.

If I take the wings of the morning, and dwell in the uttermost parts of the sea;

"Even there shall thy hand lead me, and thy right hand shall hold me.

"If I say, Surely the darkness shall cover me; even the night shall be light about me.

"Yea, the darkness hideth not from thee; but the night shineth as the day: the darkness and the light are both alike to thee."

Modesty went into a coughing spasm before I finished the verse. She licked the spittle from her dry lips and held fast to my hand. "You were kind to share the verse with me, Lucy Hathorne, and I shall reward your generosity. My time on this earth will be over soon. Let me read your palm in thanks."

There were many in Maidenhead who believed in her visions, while others cautioned against necromancy. Papa understood the power of the spirit and praised her gifts. "God might have deprived her of sight, but He gave her second sight, an even greater blessing."

Although I remained unsure of her skills, I clasped her hand tightly. "Yes, of course."

She nevertheless seemed to sense my reluctance. "Dear child, my gift comes from our Father in Heaven. He wishes me to share it with you. I see the past and future with great clarity."

The ancient woman touched my palms with the pads of her fingers, humming all the while in a monotone. In the next instant, she began to shake, and her blind eyes opened.

Old Modesty's breathing became heavier, her voice fainter. I strained to hear her words.

"My soul sees things these blind eyes can't."

Her eyes held no glimmer of life. She tilted her head slightly and droned on as she stroked my palm. "Four girls surrounded a field of silk roses. Ah, now there are three. One has abandoned Maidenhead for the life of a wastrel. Hold the others close."

I pulled my hand away. How could Modesty have known about the quilt or Velda's running away? Why should I hold Pyrtle or Cassie close?

Modesty took my hand back and massaged my fingers with increased vigor.

"Don't be afraid of my words, dear girl. All is not well with your friend, the golden beauty. Her beauty is an affliction. She will suffer and make others suffer along with her."

Despite the roaring fire in the overheated room, something cold walked across my spine. My skin turned to gooseflesh. I turned to Bathsheba. Had she told Old Modesty about Velda? Without me saying a word, Bathsheba shook her head. No.

"Your father is a man of the cloth, yet he taught you not to fear the mystic arts. They are part of you as much as the ash woods behind the rectory. Embrace them as you would Holy Writ. Death has come to Maidenhead on crimson sails, and nothing will stop it. Be strong, my dear." She went silent and trembled, as if receiving a message. "It is near. The Hathorne evil is near."

The augur squeezed my hand, perhaps to comfort me, and traced the lines on my palm with her forefinger. "My poor tyke, the truth can't hide from me. I am leaving this earthly plane soon and can't aid you."

She stopped talking, and the breathy rattle of death punctured the silence. Bathsheba bent over her. Without warning, the old woman's lips began to move. The midwife listened to the great-grandmother's faint whispers. She turned to me, her eyes wide, her face pallid. She took Old Modesty's hand from mine and placed it on the ancient seer's chest.

"What did she say to you, Bathsheba?"

"Nothing of importance, just ramblings. Go home to your mother, and may God bless you."

"Goodbye, Bathsheba."

Chapter Twenty-Two
Death on Crimson Sails

A blast of ice hailed me the moment I left
Bathsheba's cottage, as if I'd left an oven and walked
into the Arctic. I thought about the blind seer's words
as I made my way through the chilly gloom. Perhaps I
should have ignored what she said, but I knew she had
more to tell me. What could she have whispered to
Bathsheba? I trudged on with a shrug. The dead took
their secrets with them. Maybe I'd never find out. I
wrapped my cloak closer. Raucous laughter and dim
light spilled from the door of the Red Dog Tavern. The
off-tune singing of drunken sailors filled the frozen air.

The brume enveloped me. Soon, I wouldn't be able
to see my hand in front of my face. I trod down the
pavers, one foot in front of the other. A lantern glowed
from the piazza. The rectory beckoned.

The smell of pea soup drifted down the corridor, a
cheery hello the minute I stepped into the entryway. I
made my way to the kitchen and found Mama slicing
bread.

"The fog is coming in fierce, Mama. I visited
Bathsheba's cottage." I stripped off my heavy clothes
by the warmth of the stove, unwrapping myself, layer
by layer. "Dr. Farnsworth doubted Modesty would last
the afternoon."

Mama didn't look up from her task. "Perhaps it's a

comfort to her that she'll soon be in the bosom of the Lord."

Before I could reply, the rectory door opened. A pair of heavy boots clomped down the corridor. Cassie stood before us, out of breath, her body swamped under her heavy clothes. From her grave expression, I knew she carried dire news.

"Mr. Tateshall made his way to the lighthouse after hearing from Mr. Crackbone. Those city ruffians just shoved off in that big schooner, and they took Sebastian with them."

Mama gave a loud gasp. "No!"

"It's true, Mrs. Hathorne. Sebastian didn't want to go, but they forced him. I thought, Good riddance, get him out of Maidenhead. Then I got to pondering. Despite the evil he's done, the boy is daft and should be protected."

I looked at Mama, who wrung her hands. "It seems that we can't even break bread any more without another calamity. Reverend Hathorne is visiting with Dr. Farnsworth."

Mama and I exchanged a look. "Lucy, go tell your father, but there's nothing to be done in this foggy weather." I buttoned up my heavy boots and wrapped myself again as quickly as I could.

Cassie and I rushed from the rectory. The murk surrounded us, yet we managed to find our way to Dr. Farnsworth's practice. A frazzled Mrs. Farnsworth, her dress askew, her hair hanging in clumps about her shoulders, opened the door.

"Mrs. Farnsworth, can you please ask my father to come to the door?"

She twisted her errant locks into a bun and secured

it with a hairpin. "I'm afraid Reverend Hathorne has gone off with my husband. Grippe broke out hard in the old part of town, and they're tending to the sick." Her face had a greenish cast to it. "I've been under the weather myself."

She looked from me to Cassie. "Whatever is the matter, girls?"

Cassie shifted from one foot to the other. "Some fellows came to sail that schooner back to Boston. I'd say good riddance and hope the blasted thing would land on the rocks, only..." She glanced my way. "Only the villains kidnapped Lucy's cousin."

Mrs. Farnsworth stared at us as if in disbelief. "What? I wouldn't think anyone but a fool would chance sailing in this fog. I'll tell my husband and Reverend Hathorne the moment they return."

Somehow, despite the murk, Cassie and I managed to find our way to the chandlery. Unfortunately, Mr. Tateshall confirmed our fears, and things were much worse than I'd thought.

"The crew took off in the schooner half an hour ago. I told the drunken scoundrels they were mad to travel in this brume, but they laughed me off and said they knew what they were doing. Mr. Crackbone went to Constable Heath, saying they'd forced young Sebastian to go with them. Kimball heard and came by a few minutes later. When the constable refused to follow them in this fog, Kimball vowed to bring Sebastian back with him, come hell or high water. He asked to use my old sailboat moored at the dock. He's a sterling lad, so I said yes."

Cassie and I exchanged a look. "Kimball went out in this weather?"

Mr. Tateshall gave a nod. "Yeah, sure did."

Cassie took my hand. "Crazy Sebastian can go to blazes, but Kimball is as dear to me as a brother. We have to go after him."

We rushed from the chandlery and managed to find the dock through blankets of gray smoke. Through the dim light, I made out kerosene lanterns strung up on the dock as beacons. An ancient oysterman blew notes of caution through a rusted tuba. A fierce, louder blast rang through the murk.

Cassie looked into the distance toward the direction of the bluffs. "Pa must have lit the old cannon to warn ships away from the rocks."

Zeke sat in the bleakness, whittling away on a piece of basswood. He doffed his cap and beamed when he caught sight of Cassie.

"Well, hello, Cassie, and you too, Lucy. I'm stuck here on the dock until the fog lifts. What are you two doing out in this weather?"

Cassie took a step in front of me and smiled for the first time in days. "Zeke, we need your help. Kimball's in danger."

Even in the gloom, I saw his confusion. "What the devil are you talking about?"

She glanced my way and then turned back to Zeke. "It's evil bad. Some rowdies came from Boston to pick up the schooner. The villains forced Lucy's cousin to go with them. Kimball went chasing after them in this fog."

Zeke's brow furled in confusion. "Why would he do that? He hates Sebastian Hathorne."

She shrugged her shoulders. "We don't have time to explain now. Just know Kimball took off after him like a darned fool and might drown for his effort."

Zeke paused before pointing to his dinghy. "Can't let that happen. Get in." He handed Cassie a rusty lantern. "You sit at the bow, Cassie, and beam this light into the fog."

We scrambled into his little boat and shoved off. Zeke had fished the bay since childhood and somehow managed to maneuver the boat in murkiness as opaque as clotted cream. He rowed at a slow pace, keeping time with the low monotone of the tuba, ever mindful of what could be before us. When we moved into the murk, he handed me a heavy brass bell.

"Ring this like your life depends on it, Lucy. There've been some evil accidents in fog banks this heavy."

The bell had a loud, metallic clang, and I rang it with all my might. As we sailed, the fog devoured the shoreline, and the air tasted sharp and salty. Cassie pointed her lantern into the gloom while Zeke rowed on, his oars pushing us farther into the misty blanket that encased the bay. He tried to keep our spirits up, but the gray smoke enveloping the boat made good cheer impossible.

"No wind, dead calm, so the schooner couldn't get far. The fog is as heavy as chowder, but I've seen worse."

Cassie answered with a shake of her head. "I was born in Maidenhead, and in all my sixteen years, I've never seen anything like this." She called out into the gloom, "Kimball Prince, where the devil are you?"

If we lost Kimball in this void, he'd never know I loved him as deeply as he loved me. I wouldn't let him die without hearing it from my lips.

"Kimball, it's Lucy, your Lucy. I haven't told you, but you must know that I love you with all my heart. Please, come back to me."

My declaration must have amused Cassie no end. Her laughter filled the foggy air. "Lucy, you chucklehead, he already knows you love him. Everyone in Maidenhead knows you love him. You always have."

From the heat on my face, I knew it blazed as red as the flash of scarlet on the murky horizon.

Without warning Cassie spotted it through the mist. "Do you see it? In the distance—crimson sails. It's the schooner. It didn't get far. Kimball must be near."

We called out in unison. "Kimball, Kimball, Kimball!"

Silence answered our calls. The three of us sat in stillness, until, out of nowhere, we heard a ferocious boom, followed by another. A scream penetrated the haze. "Help me! The schooner rammed me!"

A loud clonk followed the roar of a bullet, and a splash loud enough to be a body flopping into the water. "Help me, help me!"

Fear showed on Zeke's face. "It's Kimball. Lord, I think they shot at him."

Zeke's boat held nets, a knife, lanterns, and some threadbare blankets. Cassie picked through the supplies with her free hand. "We'll need something to throw out to Kimball when we find him. Do you have a life ring?"

He handed her a length of frayed rope. "No, just this rotten cord. I bought some hemp, but my pa took it."

Cassie scrutinized the cord before she handed it to me. "It's in bad shape, but it'll have to do. Tie it to the center thwart, Lucy."

Part of the rope fell to pieces in my hands. "Rats must have gotten to it, Cassie. It can't hold Kimball."

Cassie tested a length in hands. "It's all we have. Pray that it holds the two of us. Kimball is out there, and he'll drown if we don't get to him."

She yelled again. "Kimball, how are you?"

His voice yelled out from the black water, "I'm bleeding bad."

Cassie gazed into Zeke's face and screamed into the brume. "I'm coming in after you."

Kimball cried out from the dark water. "It's too dangerous. After the schooner rammed the sailboat and overturned it, someone shot at me. Lucky for me he couldn't shoot straight in this gloom. I'm holding on to the hull."

Cassie handed me the lantern and stripped off her cloak and scarf, but I stopped her from going further. "No, Cassie!"

I removed my boots and stood. The craft swayed back and forth, but I soon found my sea legs.

Zeke looked up at me, shocked. "What do you think you're doing?"

"Kimball's hurt. I'm going after him, that's what I'm doing. Cassie, help me out of my skirt."

She stared at me, incredulous. "Girl, are you daft? You can't go after him in this fog."

I unwrapped my scarf. "You may be the strongest rower, but of the three of us, I'm the best swimmer. Besides, wouldn't you do the same if it were Zeke out there?"

Cassie and Zeke exchanged a shy look before averting their faces. She inched over and unfastened my skirt from the bodice.

I stood up in my petticoat. "Blast these petticoats, but I can't go after him in split-drawers. It's as Lucy Stone wrote, 'Women are in bondage; their clothes are a great hindrance to their engaging in any business which will make them pecuniarily independent—'"

Cassie yelled at me, "Now is not the time for a lecture on suffrage, Lucy Hathorne." She ripped my petticoat with the knife. "Hope you weren't fond of that petticoat. Now it's in shreds." Cassie wrapped the fabric around my legs like trousers.

Kimball gave a cry, and I called out to him, "Kimball, keep yelling and I'll find you."

We heard the blast of the cannon followed by the low moan of the tuba. I secured the rope around my waist and slipped over the side. The lantern beamed through the gray fog and shone on an overturned sail. A blond head jerked up from the water.

"Zeke, he's over there." My voice pierced through the murk. "Kimball, my darling, I'm coming for you. Hold on!"

The light followed me as I swam to Kimball's boat. I glanced back. Cassie and Zeke paddled closer. Despite the freezing water, I felt sweat roll down my face and my stomach knot. Could I survive more death? Zeke's voice stirred me from my thoughts. "Lucy, you've reached the sailboat. Keep your eyes on the light."

I found Kimball paddling in the water. The nasty gash on his forehead blinded him with gore. "I'm here with you, my love."

I held him by the neck and trod water, pushing through the sea with one arm. Cassie kept the lantern's light shining on us, and I swam toward Zeke's dinghy without breaking stride, one stroke, two strokes, three.

In spite of the fog, the encumbrance of my petticoat, and the fact Kimball outweighed me by at least forty pounds, I moved with the speed of a champion.

Zeke called out, laughing in spite of our predicament, "Before I lose my courage, I must say it to the world—I love you, Cassie Silva. I love you with all my heart."

I heard Cassie's voice whisper, "Well, if I have to love somebody, I guess it would be you, Zeke."

At that moment, I must have been the happiest girl in the world. My nightmare had ended. I'd saved the boy I loved, and my close-mouthed friend had declared her devotion to Zeke. How we would celebrate!

Fate, however, had other ideas.

Another craft tore through the waves and sliced its way toward us. Zeke yelled out, "Stop, you fool!"

The world went black in an instant.

Chapter Twenty-Three
Vá com Deus

My eyes slowly adjusted to the dim light. A candle flamed in the void. Brightly colored paisley paper covered the walls, and heavy oak furnishings filled the chamber. A vase covered with hand-painted flowers sat on a nightstand. The place smelled of vinegar and carbolic soap. Alien hands had wrapped me in a crazy quilt smelling of lavender and cedar chips. I sat up, but my aching head forced me back onto a goose-down pillow. I tried once more, but fell back again.

I hoped my friends weren't suffering. Perhaps they waited for me at the inn. We had so much to discuss, including Cassie's confession of love for Zeke. Despite my aching ribs, I giggled at the thought of the two most taciturn people in Massachusetts pledging their affection for each other.

I had no memory of how I found myself in this strange room, but I recognized the quilt as one that the girls and I had stitched for Mrs. Farnsworth long ago. Someone had brought me to the doctor's practice. "Hello, is anyone here?"

Silence. No one shared the chamber with me. It occurred to me I must have been the only injured one in our motley crew. Praise the Lord. The realization my friends were unharmed soothed my pain.

When I attempted to sit up once more, my aching

body forced me down on the bed again. I closed my eyes and hoped sleep would take me away, but I heard keening, voices speaking alien tongues, and whispers from other rooms. My sense of foreboding grew.

I propped myself up once again, placed my feet on the floor, and stood. Wooziness suddenly overcame me, and I grabbed the bedpost. For the first time I noticed my clothing. Someone, most probably Cassie, had removed my ripped petticoats and drenched gown and dressed me in one of my old frocks, a frock of faded gingham. I had a faint recollection of a boat colliding with us but couldn't remember the particulars. Zeke, Cassie, or Kimball would have to tell me about all that had occurred. We'd lost Sebastian, but we had each other.

I took a tentative step forward and then another. My pain returned, but I pressed forward. A hand mirror sat on a circular table. I picked it up and examined my face. Despite a bruise on my forehead, I looked much the same.

Somehow, despite the throbbing pain in my head, I managed to find my way to the door. Muffled voices carried through the corridor, and I moved toward them like someone in a somnambulistic state. Like a bolt out of the blue, another sound from the opposite direction stopped me in my tracks. Wailing permeated the stillness. One foot in front of the other, I followed the sound of grieving to the rear of the house, away from the voices.

Lamentations bitter, dark, and masculine, flooded the corridor. I stopped when I recognized the voice, my dread increasing, icy needles pricking my spine. The grieving turned into fierce howling. I dragged myself down a corridor papered in the same gaudy covering as the bedroom, and crept toward a room in the rear.

The sobbing grew, the intensity so bitter it sounded as if someone's heart had been ripped from their body. When I stopped at the door, the hairs on the back of my neck must have stood on end. I knew the room by reputation. I'd heard of it since my childhood. Dr. Farnsworth embalmed the dead there. The doctor kept it locked to protect it from prying eyes, yet I heard sobs coming from inside.

I stood at the death portal for a long while, unable to turn the knob, paralyzed by a fear that had plagued me all my life. Perhaps I could face down a storm or a dead calm, but opening closed doors had frightened me since childhood. I'd always feared what lurked behind them, but never as much as what might lie behind this one. Perhaps my friends hadn't survived. Would I find three bodies behind the portal? No, it couldn't be.

I mustered every ounce of my strength to turn the knob. Once inside, my eyes adjusted to the gloom. Zeke sat alone in a dark chamber, sobbing with every fiber of his being. My knees began to buckle when I looked further. Old Modesty lay on a marble-topped table, her shriveled body clothed in black, her hands crossed over her chest. Cassie reclined on the adjoining table, her head resting on a wooden block. Dr. Farnsworth had draped a sheet across her body, shielding everything except her face. A large bruise covered her forehead, but she seemed tranquil in death.

Zeke looked up when I entered and wiped his face with his sleeve. "If you're wondering about Kimball, he's alive and resting at the inn."

He rose from the chair and moved toward our

friend's body. His fingers caressed her ebony curls. "Why couldn't they have killed me instead of my Cassie?"

Zeke gave her a final look and walked out of the room without a word. Perhaps I should have left him alone in his grief, but I followed him, trailing him when he headed toward the woods.

The early light barely shone through the thick forest pergola of scarlet and rust.

Anyone seeking serenity in the woods that day wouldn't have found it. Foragers combed the forest floor, and I heard shots in the distance, most likely hunters tracking white-tailed deer. I followed Zeke past Caleb Potter's shack in the white grove. The hut had sat forlorn when he was alive. After his death, everyone avoided his place. The wind set the glass chimes to tinkling. Some thought Mr. Potter's spirit haunted the woods. Perhaps it did.

Mist shrouded the forest. I wanted to turn and head back to the rectory, but Zeke traveled through the haze, marching on until we reached a place of solitude townsfolk rarely visited. A breeze rustled the maple leaves, and I swore I heard the fairies singing their strange tune—Go away. The forest belongs to us.

Zeke stopped in front of the massive tree stump cloaked in emerald-green moss and ringed by a circle of pines. The settlers called the hallowed spot the "round table."

My hands touched the ancient wood. "Two hundred years ago, my ancestors felled that ancient oak to build our church."

Zeke chortled. "And my ancestors swore the forest would never forgive them."

I circled the old stump. "As children, the girls and I played here in the summer. We'd pick blackberries, weave flowers into our braids, and wreath the trees with vines. One day a fog bank, almost as heavy as the one yesterday, rolled in and trapped us. We couldn't find our way out through the brume, so we pretended we were wood nymphs. We heard the woodland elves singing to us, and we danced around that stump until the sun showed her face."

Zeke averted his eyes and looked into the woods. He stood ramrod straight.

"Please, Zeke, don't blame Kimball for what happened. He felt he had to chase down the schooner to bring my cousin back."

He relaxed his shoulders, and more tears rolled down his face. "Kimball and Cassie were raging against your cousin, but I didn't know why. I kept after Kimball until he told me what happened with Velda. Sebastian is as mad as a hatter, but daft as he is, he shouldn't have touched her. I don't blame Kimball. You can't have a lunatic like him on the loose."

Zeke slumped down on the edge of the trunk. "Pa told me that if I traveled, if I saw the world, I'd learn the ways of women. I told him I loved Cassie and other girls didn't mean nothing to me. She'll always be the only one for me."

He spun around and made his way toward the town. I followed.

****

Maidenhead said a polite goodbye to Old Modesty. Papa officiated over her final farewell, and she took her place among the ancients in the True Believers' Burial Ground.

Cassie's death, however, brought our village to its knees.

Dr. and Mrs. Farnsworth embalmed my friend, pumping her body with poison before holding a wake for her for three days. Once word of her death got out to the Portuguese and Cape Verdeans, folks from as far as New Bedford braved the cold to grieve with us.

Mourners of every color and faith packed St. John the Baptist Catholic Church to the rafters. The pungent smell of the incense and burning candles filled Maidenhead's tiniest place of worship. My brave friend's corpse lay before the altar in a coffin with a glass top. They'd laid her out in her Confirmation dress, filled the casket with lavender and fresh pine, and covered her bruised face with a flowered veil. Someone had placed a rosary in her hands.

When the priest began his eulogy in English with the words, "Our daughter Cacilda gave her life to save another," the wailing began anew.

Zeke sobbed on my shoulder. Kimball sat on my other side, his face devoid of expression. I put up a brave front for him, but my heart had broken once again.

After the ceremony, we moved to the little Catholic cemetery behind the church. I knew Cassie would have wanted to lie in the True Believers' Burial Ground, but her faith made it impossible.

Kimball stood next to me, watching as six fishermen lowered her coffin into the earth of the Catholic graveyard. He stood as rigid as a piece of granite. "I killed her. If it hadn't been for me, Cassie would be alive."

I knew there was no comforting him, yet I tried.

"No, you're wrong. She died saving a beloved friend from evil men."

He didn't reply, but I sensed bitterness and quiet rage.

Within a week of Cassie's death, Zeke left Maidenhead without a word, and I mourned the loss of another friend.

My sadness worsened when Papa took off for Boston in search of Sebastian. "I'll find the boy if I have to tear the town apart."

I wondered how fruitful his search would be.

****

That night after we'd said our final goodbye to Cassie, I curled up in my narrow bed, warmed by a flannel blanket Mama had unpacked earlier. I cried myself to sleep, drifting into an earlier time, a wondrous Fourth of July before life had taken a bitter turn. I could almost hear the brass band as it marched to Pocasset Square, playing "Rally Round the Flag, Boys."

The Independence Day celebration had begun with a parade led by veterans of the war. Papa and Caleb Potter marched in their uniforms, joined by some of the sailors who'd fought in the Boston 54th and 55th All Colored Regiment. Pedro moved in lockstep with his master.

All of Maidenhead strolled to the beach beneath a stunning azure sky that day, the men in summer whites, the ladies in cotton gowns with bonnets festooned with red, white, and blue ribbons. Cassie and I dashed into the water with the tide lapping at our ankles, and then Pyrtle and Kimball joined us. Velda, mindful of her white lace frock, watched from the dock.

What a jolly day—that is, until I looked into the

horizon.

In my dream, a schooner headed toward the beach, a beautiful craft, bigger than any I'd ever seen. Her brass fixtures gleamed in the hot sun, a hull of polished mahogany, her crimson sails billowing as she cut through the water. We stood on the beach, transfixed, unable to move as she sailed forward, her pace glacial.

She wasn't heading toward the dock but to the beach, yet no one moved. We all stood stock still and smiling, entranced as she floated closer and closer. Finally, the craft came within inches of the beach. I knew she'd crush us beneath her, but no one moved. She was so close I could see into the wheelhouse. Sebastian Hathorne stood at the helm, a placid smile on his beautiful face as he headed toward the citizens of Maidenhead.

Chapter Twenty-Four
Boston

Papa arrived home in the evening, fatigued from his Boston travels. We sat together for dinner, and I heard frustration in his voice as he recounted his adventures.

"I have no firm proof, yet I know those Harvard fellows lied about Sebastian's abduction. I couldn't find the owner of the schooner. Dr. Stoker seems to be a virtuous fellow. He swore he knew nothing of the kidnapping or the whereabouts of the crew. Yet with his every word, I had a nagging feeling he was lying, and I couldn't prove it."

He fiddled with his napkin before he tossed it on the table in frustration. "Ida had questioned everyone who knew Sebastian. The poor girl was crestfallen and has no idea of his whereabouts and neither do his chums at the Harvard Medical School, or so they say. I searched for Sebastian in every corner of Boston, without success. The place is a city of liars and duplicitous characters."

Those words were the only full sentence he uttered for the rest of the evening. Throughout dinner, Papa responded to our questions with polite grunts.

When he finished eating, he kissed our foreheads, bid us goodnight, and retired.

****

Winter hadn't arrived to dress Maidenhead in a robe of snow, but though the calendar read October, a bone-chilling cold remained in the air. People dragged out their heaviest winter clothing and prepared for the worst. The frigid weather, together with the influenza, made life harder. I missed the laughter of children running though the square and farmers hawking their crops. Disquiet possessed our beautiful village.

Though he was mindful of the winter fever, Papa visited every home in the village, even the abodes of those who weren't of our faith. Mama and I cooked chowder and pepper pot soup and took turns braving the icy weather to bring them to those most in need. Our respite came in the evenings when we set up the quilting frame and sat in the warm glow of the drawing room fireplace. We chatted in Quebecois, delighting in our time together.

Mama left her chair and clasped her hands together as she marveled at our enchanted quilt. The roses burst forth from the snowy background.

"Oh Lucy, it's splendid. Pyrtle must see it too." Eight cloth rosebuds were laid on a white background in the midst of circled squares of red roses with pink centers. We'd bordered each square in red and edged the quilt with the scarlet from an old silk banner abandoned during a regatta. The roses burst from the snowy earth.

"Oh Mama, how I wish Velda and Cassie could see it."

She embraced me. "They do, they do. Their spirit is in the quilt, Lucy."

If only I believed her.

****

The next morning I bounded out of bed and dressed for the day. Papa had written his usual pile of correspondence that needed posting. I bundled myself against the chill—a knitted beret covering my head and a shawl cocooning everything but my eyes.

As I passed Madame St. Pierre's, I noticed Pyrtle standing at the counter. When I crossed the dress shop's threshold, the heat from a small potbelly stove enveloped me. I heard a voice speaking in a heavy Quebec accent.

"This is the perfect veil for you, Mademoiselle Pyrtle."

Madame St. Pierre was a wisp of a woman who wore her chestnut hair in the fashionable Titus cut with a fringe of dark curls framing her tiny face. She'd furnished her shop with elegant wrought iron furniture and covered the white walls with fashion plates. Stunning bonnets from Worth's of Paris sat on plaster heads placed on the wooden counter. The place smelled of fine perfume, vanilla-scented candles, and eau de toilette imported from France.

Pyrtle turned toward me, giggling at my appearance. "Goodness, Lucy, you look like an Egyptian mummy. I hardly recognized you."

"Well, Pyrtle, it may only be mid-October, but I'm already wearing my winter clothing. I was on my way to the store to post letters as usual. By the way, Mama and I bordered your quilt last night."

Since we'd lost our friends, Pyrtle had ignored her quilt. She continued perusing the bridal fashion plates. "Madame St. Pierre has ordered this veil."

Pyrtle had chosen a veil charming in its simplicity. "It's lovely, Pyrtle. You've chosen well. But may I remind you once again that you won't be wed until summer?"

When she looked up at me, the tears shimmering in her eyes took me aback. In all the years I'd known her, I'd only seen Pyrtle cry on the day we buried her father and, for a brief moment, when Velda abandoned us. And then she'd sobbed most for Cassie, although she remembered herself enough to sit quietly at the funeral.

"Oh, Lucy, with all this sadness around me, planning my wedding is the only thing that gives me joy. Ephraim Strong lost his baby boy last night, and two more of his children are down with the grippe. Then there's poor Mr. Crackbone. He's sick with it too."

"Oh, I hadn't heard the news."

"It appears to be a problem with his digestion. The old fellow is ancient. They've closed the apothecary until he's better. Don't know what we'll do without him."

A tear plopped onto one of the engravings. "How I'd hoped Velda and Cassie would walk with us on my wedding day."

No words could assuage her pain. "Look at the veils all you want, Pyrtle. Can you stop by the rectory after supper to see your beautiful quilt?"

She gave a nod of her red mane. "I will, Lucy."

"Dress warm, though. It's freezing outside."

Pyrtle's grief for our lost friends consumed me on the walk home after I'd posted the letters. In fact, my thoughts so consumed me, I almost bumped into another mummy rushing in my direction.

"Lucy."

We could only see each other's eyes, since we'd

masked our faces against the freezing weather. Kimball had kept his distance for the past couple of days. Why, I didn't know. Still, after gazing into the green depths of his eyes, my body heated, and I wanted to throw myself into his arms. Instead, I addressed him as a friend rather than a lover.

"Where are you going, Kimball?"

He flopped his arms around in a futile attempt to get warm. "It's evil cold, isn't it? I'd say it's more than a little nippy. I'm on my way to the chandlery."

"Mama cooked up a huge pot of pea soup and a batch of shortbread. Please come to lunch."

I could only make out his eyes but was elated to see his old twinkle. "That's an invitation I can't refuse. I'll stop by the rectory later. Tell your mother she shouldn't be out in this weather. Maybe I can bring some of that soup to the villagers. Did you hear about Mr. Crackbone being sick?"

"Yes, the poor man. Soup would probably cheer him up, too."

We stared at each other, not daring to express our love.

Although he couldn't see my face behind my bundled clothing, I managed a grin. "Aren't you afraid of the influenza?"

"Not me. I'm healthy as a horse." His eyes wrinkled in the corners, and I glimpsed my mischievous friend of old. "Remember, miss, you got me sick with grippe three years ago."

"No, I didn't. You had it first. It was you who gave it to me, Kimball Prince. Anyway, Mama finished Pyrtle's quilt last night. It's beautiful, the last thing Velda and Cassie worked on. You'll see it when you come by."

I finally got the gumption to broach the subject. I took his hand in mine. "Perhaps we'll make another for our wedding day."

He said nothing as he pulled his hand from mine. I tried to catch his eyes, but he averted his head, looking around the square. "There's another fog bank rolling in fast, Lucy. Perhaps you should get back to the rectory."

He'd erected a wall, and I didn't have the strength to breach it.

Although it was early in the day, the brume enveloped us. Soon, we wouldn't be able to see a hand in front of our faces. I heeded his words. "Goodbye, I'll see you later."

We didn't move, trapped in the mist as we were. We stood like statues for an eternity.

"I love you, Kimball."

He stopped me with his hand on my arm. "Lucy, I—"

With that, he marched off into the cold, leaving me alone and confused.

****

I stripped off my heavy clothes by the warmth of the stove, unwrapping myself layer by layer. Caldrons of soup bubbled on the burners, and the rectory smelled of good cheer.

"The fog is coming in, Mama. I saw Kimball in the square. He and I can deliver the soup for you. Pyrtle is coming for a visit, too. Please to be extra kind to her when she arrives."

"I thought we were always kind, Lucy."

"Yes, but we must be even kinder than usual. Pyrtle only pretends to be strong, but it's a ruse. She's still mourning Velda and Cassie, and probably cries between telegraph messages. I know she is trying to be brave, but she can't fool me. I wanted to take her in my arms, but with Pyrtle, a sisterly embrace just wouldn't do. Please, Mama, be solicitous about the wedding veil plates too. They've taken her mind off our friend's death."

Someone pulled the pulley, the door opened, and a girlish voice punctured the quiet. "It's me, Pyrtle, come to visit."

Mama straightened her hair and apron, and then scurried down the hall to take Pyrtle's cloak.

"My dear girl, I've made a lovely soup, and shortbread as a treat. Lucy told me about the fashion plates of your stunning wedding veils."

Pyrtle had covered herself top to bottom against the cold, but with her flame-colored hair, no one could mistake her for another.

For once, a huge smile covered my friend's face. "I have wonderful news. Lucy, Mrs. Hathorne, I just received a message from dear Mr. Goodbody. He's not afraid of the influenza and is coming to Maidenhead."

Mama took her in her arms. "Oh, dear Pyrtle, what a brave fellow your fiancé is."

Pyrtle appeared quite gay and, miracle of miracles, she even returned Mama's embrace.

"With Mr. Crackbone's illness, and the apothecary closed, Mother says we'll have to sell laudanum and quinine. Don't like the thought of it, but what can I do?"

She suddenly broke into a radiant smile. "I've other news. Mrs. Prince had planned a gown for Velda's birthday. She bought the fabric and already paid the dressmaker. The color isn't quite white, but it's fitting for a bride. Mrs. Prince asked me to wear it on my wedding day and I said I would. Can't waste a nice frock, can we? It will be as if Velda has returned to us."

My mother brushed a tear from the corner of her eye. "Of course we can't, dear girl. We must be practical. Shall we go to the kitchen and have our soup?"

Pyrtle and Mama left the room, chattering about the upcoming nuptials. I fought away my own tears. Images of those we'd lost crowded my mind: Caleb Potter in his uniform, Velda twirling her parasol while she giggled over her latest conquest. She would have loved the quilt. How I missed my foolish friend. I thought of Cassie's bravery, the ache so palpable I almost screamed from the pain. I'd never know anyone like her again.

Pyrtle's voice drifted from the kitchen, bringing me back to reality.

"This soup is delicious. Since I'll soon be a bride, I must have the recipe."

Her gaiety disappeared. "I came to tell you that since we've had nothing but death and sickness, Mr. Goodbody and I are pushing up the date of the nuptials. A wedding would bring smiles. I can't announce the banns because we'll marry next week."

She looked from Mama to me, perhaps expecting one of us would voice an objection, but Mama opened her arms to her once more. "Yes, a wedding will be wonderful."

Pyrtle gasped a sigh. "Don't know if I can round up another bridesmaid besides Lucy. Five of the girls from school are down with the influenza."

The perfect candidate came to mind. "Pyrtle, would you consider Fatima from the inn? She's thirteen, and is Cassie's cousin. I wager she'd be pleased if you asked her."

She broke into a glorious smile. "Of course, Fatima. Hadn't thought of her. I'll ask right away and tell the dressmaker too. She has some burgundy-colored taffeta she could sew up for the two of you. Since Mother doesn't have to pay for my wedding gown, she will for the bridesmaids' dresses."

We sat huddled together, warmed by the heat of the stove, and perused engravings of wedding veils that Pyrtle had brought with her. After admiring an elaborate affair that trailed behind the bride, she pointed to the one she'd selected. "It's simple, not the most beautiful, but right for me."

Mama gave her hand a pat. "Indeed it is. You will be a beautiful bride, dear Pyrtle. Now, shall we go upstairs and have a look at your lovely quilt?"

We led her up the staircase to my parents' bedchamber, a large, spare room dominated by the four-poster bed brought from England. Two chests sat atop a hooked rug. It smelled of lavender. Pyrtle gave a gasp of, "Lucy!" when I pulled her quilt from the cedar chest, the red roses on a field of snow illuminated by the hearth's light.

Pyrtle stroked the fabric, her face radiant. "It's beautiful. I think Mr. Goodbody will be pleased."

She put her nose to the fabric and inhaled deeply.

"Velda once called it our enchanted quilt. I know you'll think I'm mad, but I smell Velda's perfume and the sea Cassie loved so much. They're with us, Lucy—our friends are with us."

She sobbed, and Mama and I joined her, and then, without warning, the old Pyrtle emerged. "Well, I've taken too much of your time already. I must be off."

With that, she bundled up again and walked away.

Chapter Twenty-Five
The Bower

The fog lifted the day after Pyrtle visited us. Although the cold still cloaked the streets of Maidenhead, the brume had disappeared, a good omen, in my estimation. Perhaps we'd be able to move on despite our losses, yet I couldn't. My heart continued to ache, the pain permeating every moment of my day. I mourned two girls I'd loved since childhood, and knew life would never be the same. Although he wouldn't speak of it, Kimball's grief consumed him and had created a barrier between the two of us.

I awoke the next morning to ashen skies. Perhaps the deadly mist deserted Maidenhead, but a gloom remained. I vowed to be strong, but the thought of facing another dreary day almost pushed me back into my bed. Still, something called to me, an invisible lure to Sebastian's room.

His trunk remained perched in the corner, huge, still securely locked against intruders. I'd thought about forcibly prying it open in the hopes of releasing its secrets, but Papa had stopped me. "No, Lucy, the trunk belongs to Sebastian. Please, leave it."

I did as told, although the trunk continued to beckon me.

After I'd washed myself, dressed, and finished breakfast, Papa called me into his study.

Envelopes covered every inch of his desk. "Lucy, take these to Brigham's and ask Pyrtle to post them to the mail packet as soon as possible."

From the sheer number of missives, it appeared Papa was querying half of Boston. He'd written to every hospital, and though he didn't mention them, asylums too.

"Whoever abducted your cousin did so for a reason, but I can't imagine what. When I arrived in the city, I brought the matter up to Dr. Stoker. He changed the subject right away, and eluded my every question. It pains me to think of my nephew somewhere in that great city, mad as a hatter, and alone."

We hadn't spoken about Sebastian since Papa's return, but discovering Sebastian's whereabouts remained his obsession. "I'll find my nephew if takes the rest of my life. I owe as much to my dead brother and your aunt. They worshipped the boy."

I departed the rectory weighed down with a packet of letters. When I entered the store, I found Lincoln clocking away at the telegraph machine. His eyes widened the moment I placed the mound of correspondence on the counter.

"Goodness, Lucy, has Reverend Hathorne written to everyone in Massachusetts?"

I found two more letters at the bottom of my basket and handed them to him.

"Yes, I think he did." I looked around Brigham's. Although it buzzed with customers, and Mrs. Brigham appeared at her wits' end to serve them, I didn't see Pyrtle.

"Lincoln, where's your sister?"

He jumped up from his chair and threw the letters

into a burlap bag embossed with the words Domestic, U.S. Mail.

"Pyrtle's gone daft. She's getting fitted for her dress once again. How many times can a girl get poked and prodded? All she talks about is her wedding. Hope she comes back soon."

After all the tragedy, the news seemed like a godsend. "Well, tell her I'll stop by tomorrow."

With that, I shoved off and stepped into the icy air. For once, the bitter weather that held Maidenhead in its grasp appeared to have loosened its grip. The sun peeked from behind a cloud. I heard the clamor of masculine voices as fishermen brought their daily catches to the dock. Life in Maidenhead continued despite the fact that the winter fever continued its way through the village. I passed the Maidenhead Boot and Slipper Factory and heard the giggling of two girls. I turned, thinking I'd glimpse Velda sharing a silly jest with Cassie. Instead, two factory girls jostled each other against the cold. I walked away.

When I returned to the rectory, muted voices floated down from the second floor. I bounded up the stairwell and found the door to Sebastian's room open. My parents stood over my cousin's trunk. Somehow, someway, they'd managed to open it.

Papa clutched a cache of letters to his bosom, his lips a grim line. "Your mother and I thought we'd clean out this room, since Sebastian no longer uses it. Look what I found." He opened his hand. A silver skeleton key gleamed in his palm.

"I know I told you not to search, Lucy, because I feared what you might find. I'd foraged the chamber before and never found the key to the trunk." He pointed to a leather-bound journal. "He'd hidden it there, on the last page. I discovered these letters from Harvard. I beg you, my Lucy, please bring Dr. Farnsworth to us right away. We know now why Sebastian was kidnapped."

The hair on the nape of my neck rose.

Off I went.

****

Thirty minutes later, Dr. Farnsworth sat in our dining room perusing Sebastian's papers. "You were right to bring these letters to my attention, Braddock. Let me read from one of them so Lucy will understand."

Sebastian,

It is of the utmost importance that you never bring up the name of our group, the S......s Club either in conversation or correspondence. Thankfully, an editor at The Boston Globe purloined your letter before the newspaper published it. In it, you named both the group and its members. My son, you are closer to me than my own son, but you cannot betray our trust. The knowledge will ruin lives and end careers. You will pull down the medical school. I understand your pride in our work, but you cannot, you must not share our name with the world. If you persist, I cannot promise our members will be as generous as I am.

Your other father

Dr. Farnsworth looked at my father before folding the letter. "They call themselves the Spunkers."

Mama appeared confused. "That's a silly name."

"Yes, indeed it is, but I assure you, they aren't silly. The Spunkers have been robbing graves throughout Boston since the early days of Harvard. It's a dark business, and Sebastian shouldn't have trifled with it. Those villains kidnapped that poor, mad boy. Knowing them as I do, I'd be surprised if Sebastian hasn't ended up as a dissection specimen himself."

Mama broke down into sobs and threw herself into my father's arms.

****

At twilight, I busied myself with sweeping the kitchen floor. I stood up in the craft as I heard a stirring in the bower, followed by a gentle rap at the rear door.

The voice I loved most on earth murmured my name. "Lucy."

I grabbed a candle and moved through the dark scullery toward the glow of a lamp.

"Lucy, it's me, Kimball."

My pulse quickened, my breath shortened, and emotions flooded my body—joy, elation, and a bit of anger. Kimball had avoided me after Cassie's death, refusing to speak or share his grief. I'd wondered if he'd forgotten he loved me. My heart throbbed with such a wild pulsing I feared it would leap from my chest. I caught my breath and moved through the dim light.

I found him standing in the bower, his lantern casting a soft glow on his unsmiling face.

"Kimball, come in. I can put a pot of tea on. We have rhubarb pie—you love rhubarb pie."

His shook his head. "No, I can't stay. Mother needs me in the inn. I must ask you a question."

He took a step toward me, then stopped abruptly.

"On the day we lost Cassie, you called out to me when I was in the water. You said you loved me, that you'd always loved me, and you would marry me.

215

Please tell me. Were you trying to comfort a drowning friend, or did you mean it?"

I couldn't stop a sigh of frustration. "Of course I meant it. How could you doubt it? I fought my love for you, swearing I'd live as a spinster, but a large part of me knew that God wanted us together. You know you mean everything to me. I love you, Kimball."

He stood in silence, unable to speak.

I opened the door. "You must visit for at least a moment. My parents have missed you almost as much as I have."

For the first time since I'd know him, Kimball Prince appeared at a loss for words. "I…I don't deserve their affection. I don't deserve your love. Perhaps you wondered why I followed Sebastian, since I despised him." He paused as if gathering his thoughts, but when he spoke, his voice had filled with fury. "I planned to kill him."

I took a step back from the sheer vehemence of his utterance and the force with which he spoke.

"I followed Sebastian because I didn't want him to leave Maidenhead before I did away with him. If I'd caught him, I would have killed him."

Speaking the thought he'd held on to for so long seemed to release Kimball from the weight of the world. Tears rolled down his cheeks, salty bits of regret.

"My hatred for your cousin brought about Cassie's death, something I'll regret for the rest of my life."

We stood in the stillness, the only sound a muted gunshot followed by the distant honking of geese. He moved toward me, his eyes like green comets blazing in the darkness. He fixed me in his gaze, and I couldn't move.

"Come to me, Kimball. I love you no matter what."

I hoped my embrace could erase some of his pain. I prayed he'd take me in his arms and smother me with kisses. Instead, we stood in the stillness like marble statues before he turned and walked off into the dim light of dusk.

Chapter Twenty-Six
Nuptials

Kimball's words flayed my soul like a well-honed knife, yet I couldn't blame him for his hatred of Sebastian. Perhaps I could lay much of our suffering at my cousin's feet, but not all of it. Velda played a part in her own downfall. I'd make Kimball realize our love could overcome any obstacle and eradicate his guilt.

The next morning I marched to the inn, hoping we could speak. The air smelled of sweat and whiskey. I found Kimball bustling through the lobby as he served the town fathers, all of them already too drunk to stand. His customary smile had deserted him, and I found no trace of the brash youngster who loved to torment me with his jests. Instead, I found a taciturn young fellow with eyes full of torment.

When I took his arm, he pulled away.

"Please, talk to me, Kimball. You can't keep pushing me from you."

He gazed down at me, pulled his arm away, and averted his face. "Not now, Lucy. The fellows have drunk up our whiskey to ward off the influenza, and now they want rum. I have to serve them. Please, dear girl, leave me."

"All right, I'll leave, but promise you'll stop by the rectory, please. You are my love."

He didn't utter a word.

Although my heart ached, I left him and trudged on to the dry goods store, past wheezing people, their noses raw with frozen snot. Life went on despite the threat of influenza dangling overhead like the sword of Damocles.

I moved past Brigham's permanent guests. The two codgers who spent their lives playing a never-ending game of chess had returned to their perch next to the potbelly stove.

A redheaded demon with feverish eyes raced from behind the telegraph counter and tackled me. "I've been waiting all morning, Lucy. Where have you been?"

I considered confiding in her but thought the better of it. Why dilute her joy with my pain? "I had chores, Pyrtle. Besides, you didn't say to come in the morning. Do you still want me to play the harp at your reception? I know some angelic pieces by Schubert, Bach, and—"

Pyrtle snorted. "I don't want old-fogey music at my wedding, Lucy. Let's have some lively and gay tunes."

I couldn't stop a snort of my own. "Well, then, have the fiddler at the Red Dog play for your wedding."

Fire blazed in her hazel eyes. "Pooh, I'd never let that souse ruin a wedding of mine. I want you to play some popular tunes, ones that aren't part of your usual repertoire, 'Funiculi, Funicula,' 'Polly Wolly Doodle,' and maybe something bouncy like 'Oh, Dem Golden Slippers.' I found an old German fellow to play several polkas on his squeezebox, so your selections must be jolly too."

"Very well, Pyrtle."

Her color seemed high, and no wonder. Between her duties at the telegraphy machine and preparations for her wedding, I feared she'd taken on too much.

"Pyrtle, you look feverish. You need to rest."

She tittered at the suggestion. "Rest? Lucy, how can I rest when I have a wedding to plan? Everything has to be in place before Mr. Goodbody arrives. I've invited all the townsfolk. Wait until you see the wedding cake. The baker is loading it with cherries and plums. The frosting will be the same ivory color as my dress, and he'll festoon it with all manner of twirls and scrolls. Everyone knows I'm getting married, and everyone will be there. At last my dream has come true!"

Mrs. Brigham tried to intercede. "Pyrtle, my love, let your brother handle the telegrams. Go upstairs, have some tea, and take a nap."

Pyrtle scoffed at the suggestion. "Mother, I'm not a baby. I don't need a nap. I can work and plan my wedding at the same time."

Mrs. Brigham and I exchanged a look. Nothing we could say would dissuade her, but I couldn't put my concerns aside.

"Half of Maidenhead has sneezed on you, Pyrtle, including some who've died since."

My friend bristled at my suggestion. "Half of Maidenhead has done more than sneeze on you, Lucy Hathorne, and you're as strong as a mule."

I pounded the counter, though I'd have rather pounded my obstinate friend on the noggin. "But I've had influenza, Pyrtle. You haven't. Dr. Farnsworth says folks who've had it are less likely to get it again."

She sighed in frustration. "Stop. There'll be no more talk about influenza. I still have the matter of a cake, a bouquet, and decorating the inn for the festivities afterward. I always dreamed of a summer wedding in the church's arbor, but in this weather, the Inn will have to do."

"Let Kimball and his mother take care of it."

When she rolled her eyes, I knew the conversation had ended. "No. Father always said if you want something done right, you've got to do it yourself."

Arguing with her exhausted me. "Very well, smarty, work yourself into the sick bed, for all I care."

Two days later, Fatima and I met at the dress shop for our fitting. Madame St. Pierre had cut wine-colored taffeta into princess-style gowns with a lovely flounce at the hem. Neither of us had ever worn such elegant frocks before, and we pranced through the place imitating the elegant gaits of the fashionable belles who summered in Maidenhead. Fatima twirled a lace parasol and kicked up her heels in a gay dance.

She caught her reflection in the mirror and giggled. Velda's beautiful gown of taffeta and lace clothed the dressmaker's dummy. The fabric looked as if a magical weaver had spun it from the palest wheat. As luck would have it, the gown's lace was a perfect match for Pyrtle's veil. With her flowing red hair, she'd make a lovely bride indeed.

I heard the tinkle of the shop's bell as the door opened. Pyrtle and her mother crossed the threshold. The moment I saw my friend I knew the worst. Her eyes glistened like pale amber, and she seemed so woozy her mother had to assist her. When she stumbled, we ran to her, but in typical Pyrtle fashion, she pushed us away. "Thank you, I can walk. Goodness, Mother, I think we laced my corset too tight."

Madame St. Pierre looked from Pyrtle to her

mother, quiet alarm etched on her pinched face. When she clutched her handkerchief to her nose, I knew she'd guessed the problem.

"Perhaps Mademoiselle Brigham should have her fitting later."

Pyrtle, defiant as ever, gave a toss of her head. "Later? I'll be married in four days. There is no 'later.'"

Mrs. Brigham placed a supporting arm around her daughter's waist. "Don't waste your time. I'm afraid Pyrtle won't listen, Madame St. Pierre."

Pyrtle spied the bridal gown and took another uncertain step toward it. Her face shone with perspiration. She broke out into a coughing fit and collapsed. Madame St. Pierre didn't fit her that day.

Chapter Twenty-Seven
Till Death

Dr. Farnsworth confirmed it. "The girl had influenza and it's turned into something worse, pneumonia."

The news spread through the town and carried gloom with it. Maidenhead's heart broke once again.

Two days before the hoped-for wedding, Mrs. Brigham informed Papa of Joshua Goodbody's imminent arrival by mail packet. "The lad is coming, and I couldn't tell him the truth over the wire. Please, Reverend Hathorne, what should I do?"

Papa, Dr. Farnsworth, and I walked up to the dock, the greeting party awaiting the expectant groom. Joshua leapt from the small craft, a huge smile on his freckled face, the same earnest boy who'd visited in the summer. His grin disappeared the moment he saw us.

"Lucy, where's Pyrtle?"

Dr. Farnsworth turned to my father before he could utter a word. Papa gave him a nod, and the doctor took his hand in greeting. "Hello, my boy, I'm Dr. Farnsworth. I hate being the bearer of bad news, but Pyrtle contracted the grippe. Unfortunately, it's worsened. I'm afraid there won't be a wedding."

Joshua appeared dazed by the news. "Pyrtle? She's ill?"

Papa clasped the young fellow's arm. "Yes, son,

quite ill. In fact, Dr. Farnsworth doesn't think the dear child is long for this world."

It took Joshua a minute to digest the information. "Can Pyrtle speak?'

Dr. Farnsworth studied Joshua's face. "Barely. Why do you ask?"

The young man suddenly beamed as if illuminated by an inner lantern. "If she can speak, sir, we'll wed. I came to Maidenhead to marry Pyrtle, and marry her I will. I'm not afraid of influenza. I've had it before and survived. For whatever time she has left, it will be as my wife."

Papa digested Mr. Goodbody's words. He glanced at Dr. Farnsworth. "You're a determined young man, Mr. Goodbody, but I'd expect nothing less from Pyrtle's beau. I'll marry the two of you. Dr. Farnsworth, will you stand up for him?"

The good doctor took Mr. Goodbody's hand and gave it a hearty shake. "Yes, of course."

My father smiled and relaxed his shoulders. "We'll go to her right away. Lucy, come with us."

I shook my head. "Shouldn't we get word to Kimball? He'd want to see Pyrtle wed."

Dr. Farnsworth placed his arm around Mr. Goodbody's shoulder. "Kimball Prince is like a brother to your fiancée." The doctor turned to Papa.

"Braddock, why don't you rustle up Zeke, and I'll search for Kimball. My wife's attending to Pyrtle. Lucy, will you help prepare the bride for her wedding? Perhaps Mrs. Prince will wish to help, too. We'll join you in one hour."

****

I entered the warmth of the dry goods store and

found Lincoln laboring behind the telegraphy desk while Mrs. Brigham folded blankets. She rushed to me, anxiety scrawled across her face. "Lucy, how did Joshua take the news? I couldn't bear to tell him."

"He's a sterling fellow. He still wants to marry Pyrtle and won't be put off. We only have an hour to ready her."

Mrs. Brigham's eyes widened, and she shook her head in disbelief. "He wishes to marry her despite the fact she's dying?" It took a moment for her to digest the information. "Very well." She turned to her son. "Lincoln, we'll have a wedding in an hour. Send the gentlemen upstairs when they arrive, and then secure the store."

Both of the old geezers jumped up from the chessboard. One gave a whoop of joy. "A wedding? We're having a wedding! We'll let folks know."

The men scurried off to spread the news throughout the village.

Mrs. Brigham and I mounted the rear stairwell that led to their lodging above the store. Mrs. Farnsworth's gentle voice greeted us. "A nice bath will remove all the sweat, dear girl."

We walked into Pyrtle's bedchamber and found Mrs. Farnsworth and Bathsheba bathing her with lilac soap. The influenza and its cousin, pneumonia, had taken a sad toll on my lovely friend. Pyrtle looked as fragile as a butterfly, her skin so transparent the blue veins stood out in her face. She coughed up blood and sputum into a handkerchief. Her strength abandoned her, and she slumped onto her pillow.

She had covered the walls of her bedchamber with fashion plates of bridal gowns and veils. Her own veil sat propped on a parlor chair. The incessant hacking had exhausted my friend, but she perked up when we entered. "Lucy, my dear friend."

Her mother rushed to the side of her bed. "Pyrtle, I have news. Mr. Goodbody is here in Maidenhead and wants to marry you today."

She appeared confused. "Me? He wants to marry me?" Pyrtle attempted to sit up but didn't have the strength. "Then I must hurry to meet him."

Her mother placed a comforting hand on her daughter's cheek. "He'll come to you, my love. Mr. Goodbody refuses to let the grippe stop the nuptials."

Mrs. Brigham looked about the room and straightened her shoulders. She pinned up her sleeves in preparation for work. "Well, if they're going to wed, we'll do it in my bedroom. Pyrtle can lie on my bed. The lovely chemise I bought from Madame St. Pierre for her wedding night is in the cedar chest. Mrs. Farnsworth, will you help me dress her?"

Pyrtle's speech came in halting breaths, but her eyes glistened with tears. "Oh, Lucy, I'm so happy... I'm going to be a bride after all... Please, comb my hair and...put on my veil."

Pyrtle managed to hack out a few more words. "Mother, please put my quilt on the bed...Mr. Goodbody hasn't seen it. It's the loveliest...in all of Massachusetts."

Mrs. Brigham took her daughter's hand. "Of course, of course it is, my darling. Don't speak. You must save your strength for the ceremony."

Pyrtle watched in silence as her mother walked away before signaling me closer. I placed my ear next to her lips. "Lucy, I have a secret... I've never shared it with another soul... Old Modesty once told me...I wouldn't live to see my eighteenth birthday." She coughed up once more, and I wiped away the spittle. "That's why I wanted to marry so badly."

I stepped away from my last friend, barely able to contain my tears.

An hour later, Pyrtle sat atop the quilt on Mrs. Brigham's four-poster bed. Mama walked into the chamber, a child's tiny hand in hers. We had found a little girl to carry a basket filled with dried rose petals. The child disengaged herself from her mother and sprinkled the dried flowers around the chamber. Mrs. Prince followed. They'd festooned each of the bed's columns with white ribbons and paper flowers and had strung paper lanterns around the room.

Fatima and I had donned our bridesmaids' gowns and stood near to the bed, paper nosegays in our hands.

Bathsheba had garbed Pyrtle in the lace nightgown. Despite her lack of strength, Pyrtle managed to grasp a bouquet of dried flowers. The veil partially covered her hair that fell in red waves about her shoulders. The beautiful quilt covered her legs.

Mr. Goodbody walked through the crowd that milled in the drawing room and spilled downstairs to the store. He took his place next to Pyrtle's bedside. "Please, everyone, my name is Joshua."

A pall enveloped everyone, miring us all in grief. There would be no joy with this wedding.

Although the bride couldn't walk, the old fiddler from the Red Dog managed to pick out a rusty version of "Dulciana's Wedding March" on his violin. It had all the joy of a funeral dirge.

Papa had deleted all references to Paul in the

solemnization, along with the "obeys" since he felt women shouldn't bow to mortal men. He spoke at a clipped pace, his eyes fixed on Pyrtle, her every gasp for air sounding like her last. I prayed she'd last through the ceremony.

"Dearly beloved, we are gathered together here in the sight of God to join together this man and this woman in holy matrimony, into which holy estate these two persons present come now to be joined. Therefore if any man can show any just cause why they may not lawfully be joined together, let him now speak, or else hereafter forever hold his peace."

Silence shrouded the chamber except for Pyrtle's heavy breaths and Papa's voice.

"Joshua Goodbody, wilt thou have this woman to thy wedded wife, to live together after God's ordinance in the holy estate of matrimony? Wilt thou love her, comfort her, honor and keep her, in sickness and in health; and, forsaking all others, keep thee only unto her, so long as ye both shall live?"

"I will."

Pyrtle, her eyes feverish, grasped at her bouquet.

"Pyrtle Mae Brigham, wilt thou have this man to thy wedded husband, to live together after God's ordinance in the holy estate of matrimony? Wilt thou love him, comfort him, honor and keep him, in sickness and in health, and, forsaking all others, keep thee only unto him, so long as ye both shall live?"

She barely uttered the words before closing her eyes: "I will."

"Who has the ring?"

Kimball handed Joshua a golden band. Joshua slipped it onto the ring finger of Pyrtle's left hand with blinding speed. "With this ring I thee wed, with my body I thee worship, and with all my worldly goods I thee endow."

Pyrtle's wheezing became a rattle. Papa hurried the ceremony.

"For as much as Joshua and Pyrtle have consented together in holy wedlock, and have witnessed the same before God and this company, and have given and pledged their troth either to other and have declared the same by giving and receiving of a ring and by joining of hands, I pronounce that they be man and wife together."

Pyrtle smiled radiantly before she took a final breath.

The sound of sobbing wafted from the stairwell. The fiddler ended his tune. We all stood like statues, trapped in time, mired by stillness, unable to speak.

I rushed over to my friend's prone body and screamed with all the passion I could muster. "Pyrtle, don't leave us, we need you. Don't leave us!"

Silence crept through the room with sadness following. No one uttered a word. Sobbing permeated the stillness. I pulled the quilt up around her shoulders and Kimball took me by the shoulders and led me from the bed. Joshua fell against a poster, his grief finally come to the surface.

Then, a gasp and Papa's voice cut through the grief. He pointed to the bed. "Look at her hand."

The hair at the nape of my neck stood on end. I saw an imperceptible twitch of her finger. A whimper, as soft as a spider making its way across a web, made its way through the chamber followed by a breathy sigh.

Pyrtle coughed, her eyes fluttered open, and she

gasped a reply. "What did you say, Lucy?"

A collective exhale of relief filled the room. I rushed to her side and took her hand. "I said, 'Don't leave us.'"

My friend seemed confused by my words, and she managed a weak, "But why would I leave on my wedding day?"

A scream rang out from the crowd. A huge clap of applause followed it. "She's alive! Pyrtle is alive!" Mrs. Brigham rushed to her daughter's side. "Pyrtle, my darling little girl, you are a bride, you are a bride." She called out to the crowd, "Everyone, there's cake, punch, and rum downstairs."

A roar went up through the crowd. Instead of a funeral repast, we would make merry.

"She's alive! Our Pyrtle is alive!"

The fiddler began a gay tune, and one by one, jubilant people left the bedchamber.

Joshua knelt next to her bed and stroked Pyrtle's cheek. "My love, my darling girl."

Joyful tears rolled down Bathsheba's cheeks. I whispered to her, "What did Modesty tell you on that final day?"

She stared at me for a long moment. "She said a dark girl would die valiantly, and Pyrtle would visit death's door, but decide not to enter. She saw an evil hovering over Maidenhead."

I averted my head. Kimball took my hand and led me downstairs.

Chapter Twenty-Eight
Farewell, Sebastian

The festivities lasted throughout the afternoon, with the citizens of Maidenhead intoxicated with joy and rum punch. For a while, it felt like old times before the dying had started. Dr. Farnsworth gave Pyrtle a sleeping draught, and she slumbered through the festivities. I heard him whisper to my father, "I can't explain it, but I swear, the girl died."

Papa answered my question with a quizzical smile. "The Lord sent her back to us, and that's all that matters."

In the late afternoon, my parents decided to return to the rectory for dinner and invited Joshua to join us. All of Maidenhead reveled over Pyrtle's marriage. Men passed bottles of rum, and women tittered between sips of sherry.

Kimball and I slogged down the wooden sidewalks at a slow pace behind my parents and Joshua. When they moved out of sight of the square, Kimball took my hand in his. After the rancor of our last meeting, my heart leapt.

He stopped in his tracks. "That evening when I came to you, I told you the truth. I'd done a horrible thing. I followed the schooner to kill your cousin. Yet you said you still loved me. Is that true?"

I took his face in my hands. "Of course it's true. I

spoke of college and following Lucy Stone's path, but you knew I loved you all along. If you wish it, I'll ask Papa to marry us right away."

He broke into the most glorious smile I'd seen in weeks. "No, we'll wait until we finish our education. Knowing you're my betrothed will make the delay sweeter."

Kimball dug into his coat pocket and pulled out an old kerchief. "I've been carrying this around, waiting for the perfect time to give it to you."

A large diamond flashed from an aureate circle.

"Mother planned to give it to Velda. When I told her your words that day in the boat, she said you must have it."

I'd never seen anything so beautiful. "Kimball, I can't take such an extravagant gift."

"But you must, Lucy." He fished around in his pocket once again before pulling out a gold chain I'd seen many times before.

"This was Velda's. I'm sure she'd laugh at its simplicity now, but she once loved it. You can wear the ring around your neck until we announce the banns. I'll ask your parents for your hand tonight."

"But I want everyone to know."

"And they will, they will, but please, let me ask your parents first."

"Very well, Mr. Prince." I looked around the empty streets. The festivities were continuing at Brigham's. "Now that you're my fiancé, you have my permission to kiss me."

Kimball seemed momentarily unsettled, but only momentarily. "Yes, of course, we should kiss."

He moved closer. Our lips met, and we exchanged

a brief yet sweet kiss. "Thank you, Kimball."

I took a step forward. His mouth touched my eyes, my cheeks, and my nose. He opened his sweet lips and pressed them on mine. The intensity left us both breathless. Kimball took me in his arms, and I felt his warmth against the freezing cold.

The rectory blazed with radiance. We walked into the corridor and found every lantern and candle alight.

By the time we walked into the dining room, Mama placed a tourtière, a French Canadian meat pie, peas with potatoes, and a bottle of elderberry wine on the table. I hesitated about revealing our plans so soon after Pyrtle's marriage, but I couldn't stop Kimball. "Reverend Hathorne, Mrs. Hathorne, Lucy and I, well, we…"

Papa pointed to two empty chairs before Kimball finished his announcement. "Children, take your seats. A packet arrived from Boston today with important news. Sebastian Hathorne is dead."

Sebastian lived no more.

Despite the evil he'd done, it took every bit of my self-control not to burst into tears. A wave of relief rolled over me when I realized his death released me from being the object of his obsession. My father gripped the dinner table. Kimball's face was expressionless. Tears rolled down Mama's cheeks, and she braced herself against the dinner table.

A confused Joshua looked around the table. "Who is Sebastian Hathorne?"

Papa stumbled over the words. "He…uh, oh…Sebastian is…was our nephew, a boy of eighteen. He'd suffered much, and now it's over."

Our guest shook his head in disbelief. "I'm so

sorry, Reverend Hathorne. After our great joy, we still have to deal with death. Was it winter sickness?"

Mama clasped hands with my father, and he continued the sad story. "I'm afraid our poor nephew suffered from a horrible affliction, neurasthenia. He might have ended up in a lunatic asylum, but unsavory types abducted him. I couldn't find him no matter how hard I searched."

He read the missive aloud:

"Dear Reverend Hathorne,

I send distressing news. Sebastian must have escaped from the blackhearts who kidnapped him, only to fall victim to violence on the docks. The authorities found his remains after he had been beaten and robbed of his possessions. I have identified his battered corpse. He is now at peace.

Dr. Stoker."

Papa folded the telegram. "I pity his poor fiancée, a mere child. This has been a trying day, especially for you, Joshua. Please, let's all hold hands."

My mad cousin lived no more. How I wanted to regale my family about my glorious future with the most wonderful, handsomest young fellow in all of Massachusetts, but I couldn't. I reached for my beloved's hand under the table while Papa said grace.

"We bless you, Father, and thank You for your gifts, your bounty, and for all. Your mercies fill our hearts with gratitude, Father, in the name of Jesus Christ our Lord. Amen."

I glanced at Kimball sideways and read his thoughts. Our announcement would have to wait.

Despite the evil he'd done, Sebastian's death dimmed our joy. Kimball wasn't his usual ebullient self. Still, although my parents mourned my cousin, they must have felt the same relief I did with his passing. Small talk wasn't my strong suit, but I took it upon myself to enliven the conversation.

"Well, the celebration for Pyrtle certainly was gay. She came back from the brink. Still, she'll be living away from Maidenhead."

Joshua nodded. "I plan to take her away as soon as she's strong enough to travel. My aunt will look out for her and fatten her up with her cooking."

We mumbled in agreement and continued eating, with occasional conversation regarding the day's nuptial event.

After our somber meal ended, Kimball and Joshua gave a hasty thanks to my parents and left for the inn. Our announcement would wait, but in all honesty, the news of Sebastian's death trumped everything else. Papa cleared the table and joined Mama and me in the kitchen. Death surrounded us. He placed the letter on the kitchen table.

"A day of such sadness could end on this note. Sebastian is dead. I'll grieve for the boy for the rest of my life, but the Lord has freed him, and for that I'm thankful."

He wrapped his arms around Mama's waist. "Sebastian is free, my darling girl, liberated from suffering, released from torment. He can't hurt another soul with his lunacy. It breaks my heart to say it, but except for the end to this plague and having dear Pyrtle with us, I couldn't think of better news."

****

That night, I sat alone in my bedchamber, sobbing for dear life. I couldn't stop my tears, first one, and then another, and finally a downpour. In the quiet of my bedchamber, my kerchief had become my close companion. I cried for my friends, poor Sebastian, and my lost childhood.

Finally, I couldn't cry another tear. I held my ring up to my lantern, marveling at its beauty. The facets glinted in the light as they carved multicolored prisms on the walls of my room. Without warning, Mama walked into my room.

"Lucy, where on earth did you get that?"

"Kimball."

I snatched the ring from the lamplight, but Mama was quicker and took it from me. "It's quite beautiful, but how could a boy like Kimball afford something of such value?"

"Mrs. Prince intended it for Velda, but after what happened, she wanted me to have it. The chain is Velda's, too."

Mama gazed into my face. "Did Kimball ask for your hand?"

I couldn't lie to my mother. "We'll wait until after college, but yes, he wants to marry me. He was going to ask you and Papa for permission this evening, but the news about Sebastian made him wait for another day."

My mother returned the ring before kissing my cheek. "Goodnight, my Lucy."

My ring glimmered in the lantern light. I placed it under my pillow and then fell into a deep slumber. What a sad, happy day.

Chapter Twenty-Nine
Farewell

Water for washing boiled on the stove, and the kitchen came alive with the smell of bacon and johnnycake. My engagement ring nestled in my bosom, concealed by the lace handkerchief I'd tucked into my bodice. How I wanted to blurt out my good fortune, but I'd resolved to wait for Kimball. I heard the tinkle of the door pulley, and my heart raced faster than a team of stallions. "I'll see who our visitor is."

I raced down the corridor and opened the portal. Kimball stood at the entryway, a bottle resting in his hands. We stood in silence, ignoring the frigid air around us, both of us longing to fly into each other's arms. Instead, we spoke in polite tones like casual acquaintances meeting on the street.

"Kimball, you must come in from the cold. I'm going to visit Pyrtle later, but you must breakfast with us."

He gave me a shy smile. "I brought a gift for your parents."

"Well, you must give it to them."

I turned and felt his hand on my arm, as electric as if lightning had struck, yet I remained calm. He moved closer, and I felt his hot breath against my cheek. "Lucy, please, I'm burning with passion. I love you, my darling."

"As I love you."

We strolled into the dining room, our hearts pounding like twin drums. I thanked the Lord no one could hear the violent pulsations.

Mama jumped up from her chair. "Kimball, how lovely. Come join us for breakfast. Lucy, set another plate."

I dashed into the kitchen, grabbed a plate, a cup, and cutlery. When I darted back into the dining room, Kimball had already placed his gift on the table. "It's port, not whiskey, but Mother thinks it might be useful against the influenza."

After breakfast, Papa sat back in his chair.

"I have an idea. Let's take a walk in the woods before Lucy visits Pyrtle. Kimball, please join us. We have so many reasons to give thanks. Perhaps we can visit the cemetery today."

An hour later, the four of us made our way to the forest. Someone had burned pine chips, and the woods smelled of spice and smoke. Mama took a deep breath, inhaling the scented air.

"Ah, it's wonderful to walk in the woods. All Hallows' Eve will be on us soon enough. I'm afraid there won't be any celebrating, but I'll carve a face on a pumpkin and place it on the piazza, as I usually do."

Kimball's laugh warmed the forest air. "I'm afraid it will be a sad All Hallows'. No bonfires or doughnuts, though I did tell a child that old chestnut, the same one Bathsheba told me as a child. Of course, I'm not the storyteller she is, but I've heard the tale often enough. Stingy Jack was a mean, ugly man and a horrid drunk, but the Lord blessed him with a silver tongue. His fame from his drunken deeds was so great even Satan himself went after his black soul. He said, 'Stingy Jack, I'm taking you to the fires of hell to burn for all eternity to pay for your evil deeds.' However, Satan didn't reckon on Jack's gift of gab and was hoodwinked by him."

Kimball arched an eyebrow and grinned, his teeth flashing as they used to. My heart leapt because my Kimball had returned. "The old drunk made the devil promise he would never drag his soul to hell. That's not the end to the tale. When Stingy Jack finally died of drink, he faced a dilemma. He was too much a sinner to enter Heaven, but the devil had promised not to drag him into hell. Stingy Jack roams the netherworld, that strange place between good and evil, between life and death, to this day. An ember from the darkest pit of hell inside a hollowed-out pumpkin lights his way."

Mama applauded, and Kimball took a deep bow. "You are a gifted storyteller, my boy."

We continued our trekking until Papa stopped in front of Caleb Potter's forlorn hut.

"Let's pay our respects to Caleb and spare a kind thought for poor Pedro, too. I do so hope Caleb is happier in his heavenly abode than he was in Maidenhead."

His words chilled me more than the weather. We held hands, bowed our heads, and prayed in silence for another lost friend. Before we pushed on in our trek, Mama glanced in my direction. "Lucy, did you bring something for Pedro?"

I placed a fat piece of bacon and the remains of the tourtière on the steps.

"Yes, of course. Kimball leaves food for Pedro, too. Between the two of us, he's surely the best fed bear in all of Massachusetts."

Papa looked about the shack. "Pedro will have his winter sleep soon—that is, if he's not slumbering already." He looked up to the sky. "The weather seems to be holding. Let's go on to the Burial Ground."

Except for gravediggers cutting into the earth, no one walked in the desolate place. The scattering of oak trees stood naked and black, their branches outstretched like the skeletal arms of an ancient corpse. We made our way among the graves. Mama pointed to a small dirt mound wreathed with tansy, amaranth, statice, and yarrow. "Modesty lies there."

We trudged past rows of weathered Pilgrim tombs in the oldest part of the cemetery. Two children, a girl of about twelve and a tyke no more than four, roamed among the graves in the rear of the cemetery, then made their way toward the exit.

Suddenly, a tiny voice cried out from the cemetery gate, "Reverend Hathorne!"

Mama's head whipped around at the sound. The little boy with the cherubic face, who so loved Papa, gave a shriek of joy and rushed toward him.

As he grabbed at Papa's jacket, he hacked away, his eyes feverish, his cough so violent I feared the boy would collapse.

Mama screamed out to the girl, "The child has winter fever! We must take him home."

The little boy looked as if he might expire at any moment. His eyes burned bright in his face as if heated by an inner fire. The other child, a girl of about twelve, looked almost as sick, but she managed to sweep him up in her arms.

Papa's face turned scarlet with anger. "How could you go out in this cold knowing you're both ill?"

The boy's sister dismissed his words with a shrug of her shoulders and a cough. "There's nothing wrong with us, Reverend Hathorne, just a slight fever. Our home has imprisoned us for so long I couldn't stand being there for another minute." She repeated her lie once again. "We're not ill, I tell you, just a bit lightheaded."

With that, she swooned against my father. Luckily, he caught her before she keeled over and fell to the ground.

Papa took the girl's prone body in his arms. "Kimball, help us. Lucy, Pyrtle is on the mend. Go visit her, darling girl. We'll take care of the children."

Kimball gave me a push. I rushed from the graveyard to the feverish cries of a lonely girl.

****

Although it pained me to leave my parents and Kimball, I walked to Brigham's for a visit with my Pyrtle. Two muscular fellows were loading a lovely mahogany casket onto a wagon. I knew Dr. Farnsworth had ordered it for Pyrtle and thanked the Lord that she had no use for it.

I climbed up the back steps toward the apartments and entered. Mrs. Brigham gave a joyful yelp, her happiness tempered by her nerves. "My girl made a rousing recovery, but her strength hasn't fully returned. I'm afraid your visit will have to be brief, since she's had a stream of callers and is exhausted."

When I walked into the overheated parlor, I found well-wishers had packed the room with wedding gifts and cheer. Pyrtle was ensconced on a plump chaise lounge, the quilt wrapped around her shoulders. She'd garbed herself in a simple brown dress and had twisted her girlish braid into the upswept coiffure of a married woman. The roses had returned to her cheeks as if to spite the pneumonia. She greeted me with an impish grin, and I knew her feisty spirit had also come back. Mrs. Brigham returned carrying a tea tray with two cups, placed it in front of us, and left the room. I pulled the ring from under my bodice.

"Pyrtle, Kimball and I are engaged."

She stared at the ring. "Goodness, Lucy. It's so beautiful!"

I nodded in agreement and held the golden band up to the light. "We won't say our vows until after we finish college and the banns are posted, so please keep it a secret."

She sat back against an overstuffed pillow. "Just who would I tell, the town busybodies? They won't show their faces here because they're afraid of influenza. Besides, your wedding isn't happening until you and Kimball have your schooling finished. That's four years, by my reckoning. And remember, I'll be your matron of honor."

I patted her knee. "Of course you will." I took a sip of tea. "I know you believed in Modesty's prophecy, Pyrtle, but thank the Lord, you proved her wrong."

All of a sudden, the mood changed, and her face darkened. She looked about the parlor and spoke in a murmur as light as the fluttering of a butterfly's wings.

"Modesty wasn't wrong. I did die. I swear I did."

I felt the hairs on my arm stand up and the now-familiar chill travel down my spine. I'd seen her pass on with my own eyes and heard Bathsheba's words. I knew she told the truth.

"I felt myself moving toward a beautiful light. I

saw Cassie."

"Uh…Cassie?"

Pyrtle gave a weak nod. "You think I'm mad, don't you? Well, I know what I saw. Then, I heard your voice begging me to stay, and you placed the quilt around me. I felt its warmth surround me, so I awoke. Lucy, it brought me back—you brought me back."

Pyrtle closed her eyes, her voice barely perceptible. "Yes, the enchanted quilt brought me back, Lucy, but I'll never tell another soul, even Joshua. It's our secret."

We sat in stillness for eons, sipping tea, while I digested her words. I didn't doubt them. She had died, but I too would never tell a soul, people would think me mad. Finally, I stood.

"Pyrtle, I'll keep our secret until the day I die, but I must go now. I know you're leaving Maidenhead tomorrow, and I'll see you off."

I walked across the square, pondering the sweet mysteries of life and death.

****

When I returned to the rectory, our parlor fireplace roared with the same ferocity as the one in Modesty's hut. Papa knelt beside my mother and stroked her forehead.

"Those children we met today live in the part of town that the influenza ravaged first. Some children have died there."

"Do you think the boy has the grippe?"

"Of course he does. He looked feverish and coughed the entire time. I still can't imagine why his sister would risk taking him out, especially when their little brother died of the grippe."

Papa nodded. "Poor boy was a lonely tyke who

only wanted to play."

I relaxed, but my father hadn't finished. He bore into me with a fixed stare. "What's this about Kimball giving you a ring?"

His intense scrutiny forced me to avert my face. "Well, you see, Kimball and I realized we love each other very much. After what happened with Pyrtle and Joshua, perhaps—" My giggling gave way to tears. "We thought we shouldn't wait to be betrothed because we might die like everyone else. Kimball was going to ask you for my hand at dinner but he couldn't. Oh dear, he'll be so upset that you know. We planned to marry after college, but now perhaps…"

Papa stopped pacing and stared into my face.

"Kimball wants you to go to college?"

"Yes, Papa, and he knows about the madness in our family and it doesn't matter to him one whit. I'll go to Radcliffe. I'll be close to Maidenhead since Kimball and I will be in Cambridge."

My parents exchanged a look. "I met Kimball in the street today. He asked permission to call on your mother and me after dinner. Now I know what he wants. I'll keep your confidence, my Lucy. I couldn't think of a better husband, as long as you both finish your schooling before you wed."

Papa looked over to the cooking. "Some of your soup would be welcome, my darling wife." He pulled out a chair for Mama. "Sit down, Madeleine. Let me serve you."

****

I arrived at the dock the next morning just as Joshua assisted Pyrtle onto a sailing packet bound for Provincetown. Boxes cluttered the dock, wedding gifts from well wishers along with Pyrtle's bridal trousseau. Mrs. Brigham cried into a handkerchief while Lincoln and Kimball loaded Pyrtle's luggage onto the small craft.

Dr. Farnsworth glared at the couple, his arms folded. "Joshua Goodbody, I've told you a hundred times, Pyrtle isn't strong enough to leave Maidenhead yet. Give her a week under my care and you can move her afterward if you wish."

Joshua turned his back to him. "Don't cluck over my wife like a mother hen. Rachel's Pride is not some frontier town loaded with hostile Indians. We've a doctor there who'll attend to her, and my aunt's cooking will have her up on her feet in no time. I won't stay in this death town for a moment longer."

I didn't speak, but my friend appeared too frail to travel even the short distance to Rachel's Pride. Her eyes looked like giant hazel lamps beaming from her wan face.

Pyrtle bestowed a weak smile upon me. "I knew you'd come to see me off, my Lucy. Don't worry about me, dear friend. I'll have my quilt to keep me warm."

The last of the boxes finally loaded, Joshua placed an arm around my shoulders. "You and Pyrtle will be together again one day, Lucy."

"Yes, I know."

I watched as Pyrtle sailed off to Rachel's Pride and took a piece of my heart with her.

****

It appeared as if all of Maidenhead had packed our church that Sabbath. Papa give a mighty sermon, his best.

"We have much to celebrate, my friends. Although

she has now left Maidenhead, the Lord in His infinite wisdom spared our dear Pyrtle Brigham."

The congregation broke out into applause and "Hallelujahs."

"My dear people, you have suffered greatly from this hateful catarrh, but know your trials are shared by our neighbors. From King's Harbor to Ezekiel's Cove, an evil contagion remains in the air like a gluttonous guest who refuses to leave the supper table. Remember, Our Lord in Heaven has a plan and will not desert us. We will prevail, and all will be right once again."

All did not become right again. Divine Providence didn't reward Papa's faith. The wicked autumn turned even more wintry, and bodies of the very young and the very old filled the True Believers' Burial Ground. Many called the influenza "sweating sickness," while midwives and healers knew the scourge as "winter fever." Before Mr. Crackbone contracted influenza and the apothecary closed, he had reminded us that this plague, "la grippe," had struck Maidenhead before. "It plagued the Pilgrims. Some called it 'the jolly rant,' others, 'the new acquaintance,' one that no one wanted to meet."

The influenza worsened and spread with lethal speed. When Papa spoke that Sunday, he knew the deaths in Maidenhead hadn't sated the grim reaper's appetite. The disease raced from village to village, wielding its scythe with blinding speed.

****

That evening I waited for Kimball to join us for Sunday dinner. I'd practiced on Mama's harp for most of the afternoon, selections from Oberthur and Alvars. As I plucked the harp strings, I imagined my friends quilting away and felt the warmth of their smiles, and despite the joy and misery of the past days, I felt strangely comforted.

Someone warm and smelling of cloves and Florida water stood behind me. My visitor covered my eyes with his calloused palms. "I have a fever, dear girl, a burning passion for you."

I pulled his hands away, turned to him, and lifted my chin. We feasted on each other's mouths and tongues, our passion unbridled. The kissing would have continued forever if Papa hadn't intruded.

"Hmmm, I see Kimball enjoyed your harp recital, Lucy. Perhaps you can tear yourselves away from one another and join the family for dinner."

We walked into the dining room, both of us careful not to further enrage my father.

Although Kimball visited daily, we'd never found a proper time to discuss our nuptials. Papa ignored my betrothal and spoke of other things. "I met Dr. Farnsworth today. More of the elderly have come down with influenza, and he sees no end to it and thinks it may be worsening."

Kimball took a deep breath before addressing Papa. "Mother wanted to close the inn, but I talked her out of it. I reminded her of my father's bravery during the war and how he gave his life for the Union cause." He took my hand in his. "I'm so glad to be joining your family, sir."

My father stared at him without uttering a word.

When the grandfather clock rang out seven o'clock, Kimball rose to leave. "It's late and I should be on my way. Thank you, uh, Mrs. Hathorne, for the wonderful dinner." He glanced my way, but quickly averted his head. "I'll see you all tomorrow."

My father sat back in his chair, satiated. A wide grin on his face, he gave me a sideways glance. "Lucy, don't be rude. Walk your fiancé to the door."

"Yes, Papa."

Kimball and I sighed simultaneously as we strolled to the door, savoring every short moment. He took me in his arms and gave me a sweet, delicious kiss. I savored the heat of his body and listened to the wild beat of his heart. "Kimball, I love you."

I felt his breath against my neck. "Not more than I love you."

When he left, I almost followed him from the rectory, but thought the better of it.

I heard Mama stirring upstairs. I returned to the dining room and set about clearing the dinner dishes. Papa joined me and carried several plates into the kitchen.

"Lucy, about you and Kimball." I braced myself for a sound talking-to. "I understand being madly in love—I was a boy once—but I ask you both to take care. Remember poor Velda. Passion can be quite dangerous."

He kissed my forehead.

"Now you must excuse me, dear girl. I'm exhausted and should take to my bed."

Papa walked up the stairs, a smile on his face.

Chapter Thirty
Farewell Again

The next morning I opened my eyes and lowered my blanket to my chin. The chilling cold attacked my nose. I covered my face once again and snuggled back into the warmth of my covers. All of a sudden, the lack of sound startled me from my lethargy. Nothing stirred in the house—no rustle from the kitchen, no laughter, no hum of life. A hush enveloped the rectory in the muteness of the tomb. The too-familiar ice traveled my spine as I climbed from bed.

When I opened my bedroom door, the silence assaulted my ears. "Mama? Are you there?" No one responded. I descended the stairwell, one foot in front of another, the only sound my bare feet on the wooden stairs. I reached the landing and heard nothing.

"Papa, where are you?"

The hall clock suddenly chimed seven in the morning, startling me completely awake. I took a step into the drawing room and found it empty. My father had closed the door to his study. I followed a tentative knock with urgent pounding. "Papa, Papa, where are you?"

After a furtive minute, I opened the portal. The disarrayed chamber sat empty.

I wandered around the silent rectory from there to the stillness of the dining room, the kitchen, into the summer kitchen and the scullery, and found nothing. Bullet gave a plaintive neigh from the barn. I knew he wanted a morning canter, and I'd attend to him later.

The arbor sat hushed and deserted except for a nest of tuneful chickadees that ignored the frozen weather to chirp their sweet song.

A dark and unspoken force pulled me back to the rectory. My head pounded, and something akin to poison sat in the pit of my stomach. I pushed myself into the stillness, my bare feet moving at a funereal pace until I stopped at the base of the stairs. No matter how much I tried, I couldn't take that first step.

Finally, by sheer will, I managed to climb the steps and found myself in front of my parents' bedroom door.

I placed my ear against the cold oak and heard nothing. Finally, frustration got the better of me, and I pounded like a madwoman. My knuckles turned red from the violence of my blows. Dread overcame me, but I flung the door open despite the apprehension that threatened to overwhelm me.

I found an empty room—at just the same time I heard someone pummeling at the rectory door with the same ferocity as the pounding in my head. A male voice bellowed from the other side of the door, "It's me, Kimball, and I've brought Dr. Farnsworth."

Papa never locked the rectory; he insisted it be open to all. Kimball pushed the door open and walked to the foot of the stairs. I was clad in my nightgown and froze on the steps. We faced each other for a long moment before I clutched my bosom. My nightgown reached my throat, but I felt naked under the warmth of my beloved's gaze.

"Kimball, I'm afraid I'm not dressed for visitors.

You must excuse me, Dr. Farnsworth."

The good doctor greeted my words with a loud harrumph. "Don't be ridiculous, girl. This is no time for false modesty. I pulled you out of your mother's womb. I have horrible news. The influenza remedy, Dr. Hawke's Sovereign Cure for Grippe, the bottle Crackbone gave you, was poisoned."

Propriety be hanged! I raced downstairs, yelling at the top of my lungs, "Mama, Papa, where are you?"

I heard the tread of boots from the scullery. Papa moved toward us, one of Mama's old tablecloths wrapped about his waist like an apron. I stood in the kitchen door, Kimball's gaze fixed on me.

"What is the hubbub, Lucy? Prudence, the laundress is down with the influenza, so I helped your mother hang the wash in the barn."

Crimson tinged his eyes, and he appeared a bit woozy. "Your mother and I drank Kimball's brandy last night. Powerful stuff. I'm afraid I had to have the hair of the dog this morning."

He looked from me to Dr. Farnsworth, confusion written across his face. "Atticus, why are you here?"

Dr. Farnsworth pulled an emptied bottle of Dr. Hawke's from his bag. "Crackbone died because of this adulterated drug. Whoever poisoned them knew I'd bought the bottles for my practice. Before he died, the old fellow said he'd given a bottle to Lucy. Imagine if I'd used them on my patients."

"And I gave it to Mama."

Mama bustled in from the scullery, her apron festooned with the wooden clothespins she used to hang the wash. "What is it, Atticus?" She looked at me. "Lucy, why are standing there in your nightgown?"

I took a step back. "Dr. Farnsworth said that Mr. Crackbone is dead, but not from winter fever or influenza. He was poisoned by the patent medicine the same as he gave us."

My mother broke down, but her tears lacked the bitterness of the past weeks. "Poor Mr. Crackbone, but we must praise the Lord. I found some Dover's Powder in the pantry and Kimball brought us the liquor, so I…emptied the bottle of Dr. Hawke's down the privy."

Dr. Farnsworth's laughter filled the house. "Thank the Lord! Sebastian poisoned those two bottles of Dr. Hawke's. I'd ordered the medicine, but Crackbone gave a bottle to your family and kept the other for himself. If he hadn't, I would have killed a patient and been ruined, and Sebastian would have been elated."

He paused, his anger mounting. "Whoever sent Sebastian on his hunt for cadavers should be damned to hell. I don't know his name, but he brought this horror to Maidenhead. Who would think that mad boy could reach out from the grave. Our poor, dear Lucy."

I felt a chill run down my back as if someone had walked on my grave. No one said a word until Mama piped up, "Lucy, please dress for our visitors. We'll have tea."

As I went upstairs, I heard Dr. Farnsworth's words. "I'll stay for tea, but not for long. I'm afraid the worst of the scourge is upon us."

****

None us knew how prophetic Dr. Farnsworth's words were. Influenza continued to ravage Maidenhead. Mama and I joined in the deathwatch throughout our village. Seeking respite in sleep was fruitless.

I'll take my memories of one horrible dawn to the

grave. The sea cried out to me before daybreak, and I answered her. What a pitiful sight I must have been, boots unbuttoned, hair coiling down to my waist, and eyes ringed with circles. Since so many had died or were sick, no one could remark upon my disheveled state.

I stood alone on the beach and watched the wind paint the sky in violet smoke before it blew across the bay. A beam flashed from Virgin's Light, and I heard a warning blast from the rusted cannon perched next to the lighthouse. Another treacherous fog enshrouded the reef and waited for ships to crash upon the rocks. The light flashed, followed by another flash and still another, signaling to a clipper ship navigating the hostile waters. Another craft, a schooner trawling the depths of Chastity Cove, seemed headed toward Maidenhead. It reversed course and turned back to whence it came. I said goodbye to the sea before joining Mama to help bury the dead of Maidenhead.

A devilish cold had enveloped Maidenhead that afternoon, and the villagers deserted Pocasset Square. Silence had replaced the cacophony of fishwives and greengrocers hawking their wares. No sea ditties spilled onto the street from the Red Dog Tavern; the only music was the swish of the wind. The living affixed black funeral wreaths to the tightly shuttered doors of every shanty. The influenza insured some doors had two or three.

Mama and I walked toward the old part of town, past the ancient huts built by the English. A cottage door opened. A young woman, weeping with every fiber of her body, placed a package wrapped in a muslin sheet on the threshold. I looked down at the bundle and knew from its size that it shrouded a baby. The gravediggers would soon retrieve the tiny body and the infant would sleep forever in the True Believers' Burial Ground with the generations who had passed before her.

The tread of my boots clacked across the puddle stones, shattering the silence. A frigid gust propelled a crudely printed handbill through the square. It unfurled at my feet. Mama picked it up. The lettering read Dr. Hawke's Sovereign Cure for Grippe, the same dreadful image as on the bottle poor Mr. Crackbone had given me weeks before.

She released it, and the macabre flyer danced in the wind. "We must be off, Lucy."

We'd prepared the children from the cemetery for waking and had dressed them for burial. When Mama and I reached their cottage, a dark-haired wraith flew out the door. The whiteness of the woman's skin gave her the appearance of a specter from beyond the grave. Her hair flowed down to her waist, her eyes were feverish and ringed with darkness, and joyous tears ran down her face. "He's alive! My girl is dead, but Alfred is alive!"

Mama looked at her, unable to comprehend her words. "No, I put the little boy in your daughter's dead arms myself. The child is dead."

I exchanged a look with my mother. "Mama, I fear grief has made the poor creature mad."

The woman laughed into the wind, cackling like a lunatic. "No! No, no, you're wrong, you're wrong! I'm not mad. My little boy is breathing, he's breathing! Go inside and you'll see! He's alive!"

We entered the little home. Without warning, the

wind shut the oaken portal. The sickeningly sweet smell of early decomposition hovered in the air. Lavender and evergreen mingled with incense, and almost, but not completely, masked a more disquieting scent.

A pine casket sat in the middle of the room. The coffin housed the corpse of a fair-haired girl dressed in a woman's gown of wine-colored faille, her jaw tied shut with a silk scarf, a little boy resting in her lifeless arms. The Lord had graced the lad with an angelic countenance, his tiny face ringed with golden curls, his body clothed in a suit of black velvet. Bathsheba had lined the coffin with branches of freshly cut lavender, and the burning candles sat at the coffin's foot and head.

I heard a gentle wheezing as if from a cat or even a badger, but I saw no critters in the home. When I swiveled around, I realized to my horror that the sound emanated from the coffin. I wanted Kimball at that moment. My skin turned to gooseflesh, yet my feet remained rooted in place as if my boots were encased in cement. I took one more step and faced the pine box, buoyed by faith in God. The Lord would wish me to be brave. Another step forward. I heard a gurgle, two steps, an audible sigh, three steps, until I stood at the foot of the coffin and stared down at the two children inside.

Mama and Bathsheba had prepared the bodies for burial the previous morning. The girl lay silent, her face pale and waxen, the scarf tied around her chin closing her lips for eternity, her eyes glued shut with candle wax. Bathsheba hadn't thought to do the same to the boy. His eyes had opened slightly and his rosebud mouth emitted a gurgling sound as if he breathed. I screamed as I backed away from the breathing corpse.

Mama hobbled toward the coffin, looked down at Alfred's tiny body, and jumped back, her eyes wide. "Almighty God in heaven, she isn't mad. The child lives!"

Someone pounded on the door. The portal opened. Dr. Farnsworth crossed the threshold. "I've never seen such a fierce gale."

He strode to the casket and scrutinized the corpse. "The lad is dead, but the wind is making mischief inside his tiny lungs."

Dr. Farnsworth shut the child's eyes before he closed the tiny lips. The rasping stopped.

The woman collapsed into a dead faint.

A crash punctured the quiet. The wind had forced the door open, and a swirling zephyr confronted me. I rushed to the threshold to fasten it shut, but a sight in the distance stopped me. A rim of fire revealed itself from behind a cloud and tinted the morning sky in shades of rose, while the Maidenhead funeral cortège greeted me.

A small boy with eyes as pale as water marched in front of a farm wagon the villagers had transformed into a hearse. The little boy wore a silk top hat festooned with a scarlet cockade, but he was otherwise dressed in black from head to toe. With each step, the child beat a mummer's drum to warn the living the dead were coming. Instead of cords of wood, the vehicle was loaded with bodies bundled in shrouds of linen, muslin, and sailcloth. Papa led the cortege. He'd dressed in his best frock coat and walked in lockstep with Kimball and Bathsheba. The old woman wore her usual black bombazine. Most of Maidenhead walked behind them.

Four great dray horses transported the gruesome cargo. The driver's flame-colored hair peeked from a black poke bonnet, her skin as white as chalk and her eyes as colorless as the child's. She'd covered her nose and mouth with a large kerchief and looked like a desperado. Six gravediggers carried shovels across their shoulders and kept in step behind the wagon.

Bathsheba and Papa joined hands and entered the hut. She walked over to the coffin and looked down at the child corpses. "Look at them, Dr. Farnsworth, laid out in lavender. Such placid expressions grace their faces, sweet smiles as they slumber through eternity."

Dr. Farnsworth replied, "Now it's time to get them into the ground."

Chapter Thirty-One
All Hallows

Four days had passed since the horrible morning of the mass burial. Thanks be to God, the Lord had provided a respite from the death and the freezing weather. The calendar read October 31, All Hallows' Eve, the last day of October, when the Irish celebrated the spirits of the dead walking the earth. Some in Maidenhead thought it pagan and found the celebration odious, but in years past, we had made merry, lit bonfires, fried doughnuts in hot lard, and carried carved gourds and pumpkins with lit candles to light our way. We'd had candlelight teas and decorated the drawing room with fruits, ears of corn, and jack-o-lanterns. Cassie, Pyrtle, Velda, and I used to toss apple parings over our right shoulders in the hope they'd reveal the initials of our true loves. Some of the more mischievous in town threw handfuls of flour or ashes on the unsuspecting. Others frightened their children with the story of Stingy Jack.

In the past days, escalating passion had ensnared Kimball and me. Perhaps our loss made us turn to each other for comfort, but we could barely keep our hands to ourselves. One night we'd climbed up to the widow's walk. After some ardent kissing, I felt something press against my thigh. Kimball shuddered and moaned before moving away.

"Lucy, we should remain apart to avoid the temptation of the flesh."

I took a step toward him and placed my head on his chest. "But I don't want to. I live for your touch."

"As I do for yours, but I promised your father we'd refrain until we married."

"But we love each other, Kimball, and love isn't evil. You're all I think about, day and night." I dissolved into a puddle of tears. "I have nothing but you. Please, Kimball."

He gazed into my face for a long moment and stroked my cheek. "No. I'm sure Mother's looking for me. Let's go downstairs."

Kimball had taken my hand and led me away. At that point, I would have given myself to him body and soul, I would have suffered my parents' wrath to be his lover, yet he refused.

****

On the afternoon of All Hallows' Eve, I trudged through town. Partisans of both sides had pasted posters announcing the upcoming Presidential election. I ignored them since no women could vote in the upcoming election.

I passed Crackbone's Apothecary and Stowe's Tonsorial Emporium, both boarded up as tight as Dick's hatband, and crossed the doorstep of Brigham's Dry Goods. The tapping of the telegraph register nearly obscured the singing of the wind. The two old men sat at the chessboard as they had in better times. Lincoln sat at the telegraph machine with Pyrtle's eyeshade covering his red hair as he deciphered each click of the machine.

Mrs. Brigham occupied herself with taking

inventory. "We're running low on kerosene and lanterns. We need to order more." She looked up from her labors and gazed at me.

"I'm here as usual with Papa's correspondence. He's in good spirits despite the cold. There's been an end to the dying."

One of the old chess players gave his head a shake. "Nah, there's been another case in the old part of town, a mother who has three babes. Heard your parents are going to nurse them."

The thought of another wave of winter fever made me tremble. Luckily, Mrs. Brigham handed me a letter. The address on the missive set my heart to racing. Lucy Stone had replied to me:

Dear Lucy,

I received your generous gift and thank you for it. Be assured the fight for suffrage will continue and our sex will prevail. Please continue helping us in our fight. Be ever valiant and live on.

Lucy Stone

I returned to the rectory, my heart singing, and searched every vine in the pumpkin patch in the arbor. The early frost had caused most of the pumpkins and squash to rot and stripped the scarlet foliage from the sumacs and dogwoods that ringed the island. We'd mourned the loss of Indian summer, and everyone had hunkered down to harvest what was left of the potatoes, parsnips, and rutabagas. The cold had plundered the patch of most of its bounty, but I foraged anyway, rooting about vine by vine. Nothing.

I felt warm breath against my cheek. Kimball opened his cloak to reveal an orange treasure, a fat pumpkin, the skin sculpted into a fearsome face. "Since it's All Hallows' Eve, I brought a pumpkin for the piazza. Hopefully it'll scare away all evil doers."

I caressed the giant gourd. The rectory sat deserted, and I feared what mischief the two of us could get into. Kimball must have read my mind.

"I won't stay, Lucy. Are you brave enough to join me in the graveyard tonight? I wanted to light lanterns for all the souls lost during the scourge. Shall we meet at seven?"

"Of course, my love."

Night came early. A few drunken revelers from the Red Dog had doused themselves in rum punch and stumbled through the streets. They found no torches or bonfires in celebration, no children carrying their jack-o'-lanterns, no cinnamon-and-spiced-cider perfuming the air. The fear of influenza had banished the usual pranksters, and the town's streets lay empty. I placed a lit candle inside the carved pumpkin before placing it on the piazza.

I moved to the kitchen, pumped a basin full of warm water, and heated it on the wooden stove. As I washed myself, my pulse raced and the hair at the nape of my neck rose, but I didn't know why. No one besides me had crossed the portal. I dried myself on an old towel and donned a crimson dress that had once belonging to Mama.

When I fastened my bodice, I imagined an intake of breath. I swiveled around in the darkness of the kitchen, but nothing stirred in the rectory. My heart rushed like a driverless carriage, and I couldn't rid myself of the unsettling feeling someone watched me.

Could I be going mad? I buttoned heavy boots and warmed my hands by the kitchen fire.

A rap at the door intruded. It began gently enough, yet it escalated into hard pounding. There were pranksters about, but this time they'd gone too far. I grabbed my lantern and raced to the front of the house. I took a deep breath and opened the door, half expecting a jester to fling a handful of flour into my face. No one stood at the threshold. I turned and walked down the corridor, but stopped when I heard another rap. I turned and opened the portal once more. No pranksters lay in wait, but it might have been prudent to secure the place.

I locked every door as I passed, mounted the stairwell, and searched each chamber. When I reached the door to my parents' room, ghosts of my imagination flooded my brain. By the time, I reached my room, my tears had nearly blinded me. I sat alone in the stillness on my tiny bed. Without warning, something penetrated the quiet. I heard a sound as delicate as the beatings of a wasp's wing. In an instant, all was quiet again. Perhaps I'd imagined it—no. I heard a faint tread, the sound almost imperceptible, as gentle as the murmurs of old women. Something moved downstairs.

Who intruded? I stood up, picked up the lantern, and walked down the curved stairwell. The lamp gave off a faint glow that barely illuminated the stairway. The darkness forced me to move slowly so the blackness wouldn't envelop me. One step, two steps, three, four, five, and a frozen blast caressed my face.

I'd fastened the door. Papa had changed the bolt, but the wind had nevertheless blown it ajar. Six steps, seven, eight, nine to the threshold, and I shut the oak portal once again. I stood against the entry wall, gasping for breath, alone with the quiet. I gasped in relief until I heard more steps. Someone besides me walked inside the rectory. I wanted to dash up the stairs and hide under my bed, and I almost turned back to the stairwell but stopped when I heard a footstep.

Someone plucked the strings to my harp.

Silence.

A sad refrain on a pennywhistle floated in the air. To my horror, the sound came from the parlor.

My heart pounded with such violence I feared it would explode. Still, I mustered as much courage as I could and shouted into the darkness, "Show yourself!"

No one answered, but I knew the silence was temporary. I walked toward the dreaded room. When I reached the parlor door, I heard the footfall once again, footsteps coming toward me.

A single step and I was at the threshold. My lantern barely illuminated the black chamber. I yelled out, "In the name of the Father, Son, and Holy Ghost, make yourself known."

I looked into the void and saw no one walking around. Perhaps my lack of sleep had caused me to imagine it. I took a breath and prayed. "Protect me, Father."

Unfortunately, the steps started all over again, louder than ever. Something or someone was near.

My skin turned to gooseflesh.

When I tried to flee, my feet were rooted in place as if cemented to the floor. I heard a rustle from behind the draperies, a sigh, and then familiar laughter. The Lord would want me to be brave. The candle inside the pumpkin bathed the room in an orange glow. I wailed like a banshee.

"Why are you screaming, Lucy?"

The louder my cries, the more the intruder begged, "Please, be quiet, my darling. I won't hurt you."

"It can't be. Sebastian, you're dead."

Chapter Thirty-Two
The Smiling Ghost

Sebastian moved toward me, a mad smirk spread across his beautiful countenance. I stepped back, but he kept walking toward me. The broad, orange-tinged shadows from the jack-o'-lantern he held distorted his features. In the eerie radiance of pumpkin glow, one would mistake him for Stingy Jack.

"My darling, it's me, your Sebastian. I know you thought I died. You see, I'd gotten into a dustup with those who captured me, a trivial matter concerning the Spunkers and a letter I sent to the Boston Globe. I wanted to tell the world about the Spunkers, but those cowards insisted on keeping their society a secret. Young men I once considered friends kidnapped me, the ignorant dunces. They would have placed me in chains had it not been for my protector."

He laughed once again. "My savior purloined a corpse of my height and coloring. A few blows to the face took care of the rest. When he brought dear Ida to identify me, she couldn't make herself look, so her father did instead. It's a shame he didn't examine the body closely. Unfortunately, my protector wanted to shut me away, as they all did. I had to escape."

His mad laughter echoed through the house. "What difference does anything make now? We'll be embarking on a wonderful adventure together. I'm a dead man and you have a husband."

"I have Kimball."

My words struck their mark, and he appeared genuinely taken aback. "I told you once that you were the reason I came to Maidenhead. You are my mother's very image. I knew I had to have you."

I took another step back. "But what of those poor sailors you killed?"

His smile widened. "Why do you bring up those sailors? They were trash and not worth a penny. I'd planned to delay their deaths until we reached Boston. Unfortunately, I made a mistake with the dosage. Oh, well, they are better off now."

Finally, it all made sense. "Did you poison Caleb Potter?"

Sebastian gave a sigh of exasperation. "Don't you understand that I brought him peace? I hated seeing the poor souse in so much pain. I even hated seeing those sailors die so painfully. Still, God meant me to survive or I wouldn't have been rescued."

Without warning, Sebastian shrieked with such ferocity it shocked me to my soul. "I have no one." He extended his hand. "Please, Lucy, join me. We'll leave Massachusetts together and travel the world."

Perhaps I could find a way to the tiny bit of reason he still had. "What of Ida?"

He grew pensive. "Ida doesn't matter a whit, she never did. I have my Lucy to love me and bear many children. They'll be real Hathornes, not half-Hathornes. Our offspring will conquer the world."

When I took a step to move past him, he barred my way. "No, you won't run from me, my Lucy. You're all I have, all I want."

I couldn't race into town. My only escape would be Kimball.

I turned, sped down the corridor through the kitchen, the pantry, and the summer kitchen, into the arbor.

Though darkness wrapped the forest in an ebony blanket, the woods beckoned, and I ran like a demon from the underworld. I raced on, the dim glow from a distant light my only illumination, running with such ferocity I feared my breath would give out. When I looked over my shoulder, I saw Sebastian behind me, racing after me like a wraith. If he caught up with me, I swore to use my lantern as a weapon against him. I sped away, screaming all the while, "Help me!"

The woods were empty, my screams unheard. I ran through the forest by lantern glow. Someone had arranged kerosene lamps on the path to the True Believers' Burial Ground, and I managed to find my footing despite the darkness. On and on I sped, praying my strength would hold.

I rushed toward a light in the distance, the cemetery. When I glanced over my shoulder, I saw Sebastian had gained on me. He might be taller and stronger, but I knew the woods. The heavy winter gown hampered my legs, but I didn't stop. My light sputtered and went dark. "Help, help me! Murder! Murder!"

Sebastian overtook me and grabbed at my arms, and I felt his hot breath against my neck.

"Leave me, Sebastian."

"Never. We were destined to be together."

I swung the lantern at his head and missed. The lantern dropped on the forest floor, and I scurried off into the blackness. I raced toward the cemetery, screaming my beloved's name all the while. "Please, Kimball, help me!"

Pale lights, ghostly in the freezing night, lanterns and candles set on the graves, illuminated the graveyard.

"Kimball! Kimball, where are you?"

Where was my love? Could he have abandoned the place? Would this night be my last on earth?

Then I heard a voice from the oldest part of the graveyard.

"Lucy, dear, I've been waiting for you. Look who came back to us."

Light flared in the distance. Kimball emerged from the darkness, holding a torch, Pedro at his side.

"Kimball, we have to run! Sebastian is alive!"

At that moment, Sebastian raced out of the darkness. He fell upon Kimball like a demonic wraith. Kimball swung his torch at his head but missed, swung once again but again the blow didn't connect. Pedro pulled at Sebastian's leg, but my cousin managed to kick him off. Without warning, Sebastian pulled a small caliber gun from his pocket and shot the tiny bear. Pedro lay on his side, whimpering like a whipped dog.

Kimball yelled out, "You bastard, look what you've done! Leave my Lucy alone, you bastard!"

"Your Lucy? She's my Lucy, you fool, my Lucy!"

The two fell to the ground with a huge thud. Kimball sat astride Sebastian, pummeling him with his fists. "This is for Velda, and this is for Cassie, and this is for my Lucy!"

The pistol fell out of Sebastian's hand and hit the ground. The two jumped for it, and suddenly a shot rang out. Time stopped. Kimball fell, and Sebastian jumped up and stood over him.

We faced each other in the night's silence. My spirit left my body, and my tears blinded me. I screamed like a madwoman, grabbed Sebastian's hand, and pointed the gun to my heart. "You've destroyed everything that's dear to me—Velda, Cassie, Caleb Potter, and now my love."

He stared at me as if I spoke a foreign language. "What are you saying about Cassie?"

"She's dead because of you. She chased down your kidnapper and the boat capsized. Why do you always bring death with you? Finish what you started. Kill me. I'd rather die than let you touch me."

His face turned into a mask of despair. "Cassie, dead? Oh, dear Lord."

Sebastian stared down at the pistol in my hand for a long minute before turning his gaze to me. I saw a flash of sanity in his eyes, but it disappeared, and he turned the pistol on me. "We were destined for each other, my Lucy. I'll soon join you in death."

Before he could shoot, a black form emerged from the darkness. Pedro had risen and was ready for revenge. The little beast sprang on him, ripping my cousin's throat with his claws. The gun went off into the air, narrowly missing me, as Sebastian's body slammed to the black earth of the cemetery. Sebastian's body landed next to Kimball, blood spurting from his throat.

Pedro crawled next to Kimball's prone form. I stood in the silence, tears running down my face. At the moment, I wished Sebastian had killed me too. Without warning, I heard a whimper followed by a groan. Kimball lived! I released the pistol and dropped to my knees next to my beloved's limp body.

Pedro placed his head on Kimball's chest, and Kimball's eyes fluttered open.

"My love, it's me, Lucy."

He smiled and looked up at me. "For such a brilliant young man, Sebastian's aim was bad, my love. He only winged me."

I sobbed in relief. "Thank God, my love. Promise you won't leave me."

"I promise. I'm afraid you'll never be free of me."

I cradled his head and stroked his hair while Pedro howled into the night sky like a hound.

I'll never forget that eventful Halloween even if I live to be a hundred years old.

Epilogue

Sebastian's death brought miracles to our village. Somehow, it exorcised the cold and banished the influenza.

Despite his grievous deeds, the diggers buried Sebastian in the cemetery. His final punishment was an unmarked grave in a deserted corner. He would never rest next to his dear mother. Perhaps I should have hated him for all he had done, but I remembered Papa's admonition and forgave him.

Kimball's wounds healed quickly, as did Pedro's. The little bear soon abandoned Maidenhead for the comfort of the caves and slumbered through the winter with his cousins. He returned to the forest after every spring thaw and roamed around Mr. Potter's lonely hut looking for his lost friend. Sometimes I visited with the stunted creature who traipsed the woods each year in search of his master.

Although Kimball and I looked high and low for Velda, we never found her. She didn't marry Mr. Endicott. He led the life of a wastrel and died in a boating accident. However, throughout the years, we heard tales of a golden beauty who seduced men with her comeliness and musical laugh. She used them ruthlessly, took every penny, and then discarded the poor fellows as soon as she'd spent their wealth.

Kimball never quite forgave himself for Cassie's

death and made weekly visits to her tiny grave in the Catholic cemetery. Zeke returned to Maidenhead after five years at sea. Although he never forgot his Cassie, he married Fatima and took over managing the inn.

Pyrtle Mae soon regained her title as the fastest tapper in Massachusetts. Years later, she became Postmistress of Pilgrim's Point after Joshua Goodbody became mayor.

After the influenza abated, Kimball left Maidenhead for Harvard. I joined him, at Radcliffe, a year later.

Dr. Farnsworth and Papa searched the whole of Boston and Cambridge for the culprit who owned the crimson-sailed schooner, but alas, never found him. They suspected Dr. Stoker knew the villain's identity, but he refused their every request to name him.

After he passed the Massachusetts bar, Kimball and I wed in the beautiful arbor behind the rectory. Mama and I stitched together my own Rose of Sharon quilt that I cherish to this day. Two years after our marriage, Papa christened the first of our three beautiful girls. We named her Cassie. Though her eyes were the same green as her father's, she had my Cassie's raven locks and love of the sea. Velda Rose and Pyrtle followed.

When Mama took my daughters in hand and taught them to quilt, I had my circle around me again. For that, I thanked the Lord.

A word about the author…

Lee René has worked as a lifestyle writer for magazines in Los Angeles, San Francisco, London, New York and Vancouver as well as entertainment journalist and movie reviewer in print, on-line and on the radio in the Los Angeles area. She has written for *The Lancet* and *History Today*.

She is a student of American history and her Young Adult works are usually set in the past. She writes Young Adult Gothic thrillers.

Visit her at:

https://leerene.com/

Thank you for purchasing
this publication of The Wild Rose Press, Inc.

For questions or more information
contact us at
info@thewildrosepress.com.

The Wild Rose Press, Inc.
www.thewildrosepress.com